'CAUSE DEAD'S NOT REALLY DEAD

THE WAYSTATION

By Laurie Jameson

McCRARY
PUBLISHING

McCrary Publishing
Norco, CA

Contact Info: lauriejameson@sbcglobal.net
Website: www.lauriejameson.com

ISBN (paperback): 978-0-9980596-0-0

Cover art by Anna Marie Abell
Edited by Bryon Quertermous
Interior design by Anna-Marie Abell

Printed in the United States of America
10 9 8 7 6 5 4 3 2 1

For my husband, who encouraged me to turn a dream into reality. Without you I never would have ventured down this road; it's scary out there in the dark. Thank goodness you always have a flashlight and a gun, though you might want to put on pants.

And for Anna, so much of this endeavor would have been a disaster without your help. Your enthusiasm kept me going and your wealth of knowledge kept me sane. Would you like some more toffee peanuts? More wine!

THE WAYSTATION

The Waystation is a timeworn structure that lies in the sunshine as if it were an old dog enjoying a well-deserved rest. Two ancient mimosa trees guard the front of the building and wave their fragrant lacy blooms, reaching out with dappled fingers of shade and dusting the bare ground below with their spent blossoms of pale pink. The weathered wood may have been the color of toasted wheat at one time, but over the years has faded to a soft silvery blonde. The two floors have many rooms and an attic that runs the length of the house. Numerous double-hung windows peer from its face and several curtains waft in and out on the sweet-scented breeze.

The deep porch extends from corner to corner with four over-sized rocking chairs and a large bench adorned with pillows, inviting you to make yourself comfortable. Five wide steps grace the front of the veranda where an orange tabby cat naps peacefully in a patch of sunshine on the top step, occasionally flicking the tip of his tail at the passing breeze. Scattered about the porch and steps are old wooden tubs and buckets that overflow with flowers, drawing in the beauty of the surrounding countryside.

Footsteps can be heard as a woman rounds the corner of the Waystation. She is pale and of medium height, in her mid-thirties with light brown hair pulled up and arranged in a bun on her head in a haphazard fashion. Wearing a long, full skirt of faded blue calico with a matching blouse and tan apron, her sleeves are rolled up above her elbows and she is drying her hands as she hurries toward a barn kicking up dust in her wake.

"Samuel" she calls. "Sam, are you out here?"

"Yes, Miss Sarah, I'm here," a rumbling bass answers from within.

She pauses briefly on the threshold to give her eyes time to adjust from the bright sunshine to the cool dimness of the barn. Her gaze sweeps the interior until coming to rest upon a tall, muscular man with skin the color of molasses. Samuel appears to be in his late teens or early twenties, with hands that seem capable of crushing a watermelon. He is dressed in the manner of a man who is used to hard work and understands which end of a horse needs feeding. He and a little girl are scrutinizing something on his workbench and don't look up as Sarah enters the barn.

"Well Miss Wren," Samuel rumbles in tones reminiscent of the Deep South, "I think if you give him some love and the right kinda food he needs, you could take the place of his momma just fine."

Wren, a child of five or six years, sits on the workbench next to a baby bird cradled in a faded piece of flannel. Gazing up at Sam with shining eyes she exclaims, "Oh, Sam, do you really think I can be his momma forever and ever?"

Chuckling, he strokes her cheek with abundant tenderness. "Yes, you can be his momma until he grows up, then you have'ta let him fly off and be with his own kind."

"That's okay," Wren answers smiling with pride, "Even when he leaves I know he'll love me forever. Maybe he'll even visit."

Sarah approaches Samuel and Wren, beaming in obvious excitement, "I have news." Both look up, expectant smiles appearing on their faces. "It's time; she's on her way."

Wren jumps off the bench and dashes to Sarah hugging her tightly, wrapping her little arms around Sarah's legs and pressing the side of her face against her skirt. "She's coming." Releasing Sarah, she turns and hugs Sam just as hard, though she is only able to get her arms around one of his big legs. She gazes up at his face towering above her and grins. "Rachel's coming Sam, she's finally coming."

CARA

She can see, but can't move a muscle; can't even blink. She can make out the underside of the bed where the dust bunnies clump together in furry forgotten piles, but that's it. She tries to lift her head, but her body won't cooperate.

Well, that's a problem, but at least I'm alive. Thank you for that small favor God.

There is a strong smell of urine with an underlying odor of shit. This is bad; really bad. Apparently, she's lost control of her bladder and bowels. She hasn't wet herself since she was five years old, and that loss of control scares her as much as anything.

What did you do to me Tony?

The violent memory comes crashing down in a flood; Tony pinning her against the bed and squeezing her throat. She couldn't breathe and her vision kept fading in and out with little pricks of light shooting through the blackness. The pain was intense. That's when her bladder let go and she realized she was lying in a puddle of warm pee.

God help me. Oh please, please help me.

Feelings of panic wash over her. She knows she's got to get out of here.

What am I going to do? I've got to figure something out before he comes back to finish the job.

She can hear him in the living room. It sounds like he's on the telephone and pretty freaked out too. She doesn't feel any pain, however, she does feel incredibly tired and can't seem to get enough air.

Think, Cara. You've got to do something.

3

But it's too hard to try and think. She feels drained and the air seems to have gained weight, almost as if it were too heavy to pull into her lungs. She slips into oblivion, taking her worries with her.

CARA
(30 MINUTES EARLIER)

Cara shifts restlessly for what feels like the hundredth time. She is incredibly uncomfortable. There is no such thing as a good position when you've been wedged between the bed and the wall for an hour, but at this moment, it's more important to be as small and inconspicuous as possible. She eyes the bedroom window, wishing the drop to the ground was a little bit shorter and the landing a little softer. Her bladder throbs every time she moves, and reminds her that peeing is getting to be a real priority; one she better deal with soon. She's afraid to risk making any unnecessary noise, and using the bathroom would draw attention to the fact that she's still in the house. If her boyfriend, Tony, has temporarily forgotten she's here, that's fine with her. She can hold it a little longer.

"Fucking piece of shit," Tony yells from the other room, causing her to jump. It sounds like he's starting to reach the point of no return. She's been there before, and is afraid, knowing this will probably end badly.

Her hand trembles as she pushes an oily strand of hair out of her face and tucks it behind her ear. She knows she smells. She feels nasty and wishes she could take a shower and wash her hair, but that will have to wait.

She lifts the edge of the comforter and peers at the dust under the bed, fighting the urge to sneeze. She lets it drop back in place and sighs, leaning her head against the mattress. She wonders if her best friend, Rachel, has talked to her boyfriend, Marco, yet. Marco is Tony's boss and the only one Tony respects enough and possibly fears enough to listen to. He might be able to talk some sense into Tony; calm him down and maybe even force him to get off the juice. He could make Tony

5

think that it's about the business, and that Marco can't risk having him high all the time. It might work. Then maybe she could get out of this alive.

Oh God, I hope so. I need Rachel's help.

In desperation, she'd finally broken down and called Rachel the day before, hoping there was some way she could help. Cara felt like crap for dragging her into this mess, but she didn't have any other options. Coming clean about how Tony had been acting was one of the hardest things she'd ever had to do. It made her feel like such a failure, like maybe it was partially her fault.

"I'm so sorry Rachel. Thank you for understanding. I've really missed you, you know."

"I've missed you too. It felt like you were never going to call me again. I've been worried. What the hell is going on?"

"It's Tony," Cara admitted. "He started shooting up with steroids again because he wants to 'seriously bulk up.' It scares me to death when he does it, because it makes his temper even worse than normal, and you know his temper is already bad enough as it is. And now, ever since we picked up that new delivery, he's been using non-stop; smoking and snorting it. Steroids and meth are a seriously scary combination. He hasn't slept in three days. It's a freaking nightmare. Every time I try and say something, he claims he needs to check it out and make sure the stuff is good quality. He says he's got a reputation to maintain, and that he can't risk putting shitty product on the street because it would affect sales." She stopped suddenly, drawing in a short, hard breath. "Oh, my God, Rach, don't tell Marco that Tony's using so much. He'll kill him."

"Cara, you're so full of shit. Why are you worried about him? He's the one being an asshole."

"Yeah, I know, but that doesn't mean I want Marco to beat the crap out of him or anything. Please, just promise you won't tell him that part."

"Alright, alright, I promise, but you're the one who's the victim here."

"I know it's stupid, but I don't want to risk doing anything to make him mad. He'll lose it if he finds out I told you. He's been getting worse for the last month. The steroids make him seriously aggressive all the time. He's so volatile I feel like this house is sitting on a case of dynamite. Anything can set him off at any time. I mean, holy crap, we have holes in the ceiling."

"What? Why? What did he do?"

"Okay, so you know this is a decent neighborhood, right? I mean, this area of Corona is nice. But mice keep getting in the house, probably because of the open hills behind us. They've been hanging out in the attic, and when they're running around up there squeaking and chattering away, it sounds like they're having a party, and that totally freaks him out. He hates rodents of any kind. He can't even stand hamsters. Every time it happens, he starts cussing and screaming at them, and then grabs the broom and starts pounding on the ceiling. He's a big guy, and a big, angry man with a broom handle and a popcorn ceiling doesn't end well. The ceilings in our living room and bedroom are starting to look like the surface of the moon."

"Cara! Oh, my God, that's awful."

"Last week was really bad. He was raging so much that he started chasing me through the house. I locked myself in the bathroom because it seemed like the safest thing to do, you know? I was pretty sure he wanted to kill me. But then he put his fist right through the door and looked through the hole telling me to come out. I finally caved, and of course, I regretted it. I've got the black eye to prove it. I can't even go in to the restaurant until it fades. I had to call in sick today and tell them I needed the rest of the week off too. I put a poster over the hole. It was the best solution I could come up with. At least now I can use the toilet without an audience."

"That's it. Cara, you need to get out of there before he really hurts you. Just the fact that he's been slapping you around makes me crazy."

"I know, I know, but, how can I? He said he'd kill me if I left and I believe him. You haven't seen him lately; he's different. Besides, I don't want to leave him. I love him. I mean, I love the guy he used to be without all the anger. We used to be so good together. I want my old Tony back."

"That's such bullshit! How can you want to stay with someone who says he'll kill you? Are you crazy? Oh, my God, I want to kick his ass."

"I know you're pissed Rachel, and I'm sorry for dumping this on you, but I need your help. You've always been there for me; like sisters, remember?"

"Of course, I remember. Sisters of the heart. We came up with that name when we were five."

"Right, so as my sister, I trust you more than anyone, but we need to be careful. Please, just talk to Marco and see if he can do something. I'll be okay until then, but don't wait. Do it right away, okay?"

"Okay, I promise. I love you."

"I love you too."

CARA

That was yesterday, and now here she sits, jammed up against the wall, shifting around in an attempt to find a more comfortable position and alleviate some of the pressure on her bladder, hoping for the best. Fingering the side of her jaw, she winces. It's sore.

You, asshole. I know you think I'm fat, and I get that you don't like fat chicks. You make sure everyone knows it too with that stupid "No Fat Chicks" bumper sticker on your truck.

She knew he'd be even more pissed off if he knew why she was filling out. Yeah, things would go from bad to worse instantly if he knew.

In truth, she is more beautiful than ever. Though still a very petite woman at only 5' 2", her naturally slim figure is now that of a vital, mature young woman instead of a busty twenty-one-year-old. Her skin glows, and taking the prenatal vitamins the doctor prescribed is making her hair shiny and her nails healthier than she remembers them ever being.

She delicately touches her eye and listens to make sure Tony is still occupied. It sounds like he's busy taking the stupid toaster apart again. He's torn it apart and put it back together four times so far. Amazingly, it still worked for a while, at least it did after the first three times. But, because it hasn't worked worth a damn recently, he's obsessing about it and tearing it to pieces over and over again.

That's what happens when you're a house tweaker, you tear crap apart and put it back together again.

It's cool with her though, because it has the added bonus of helping him to forget she's here. But it wouldn't do to let her guard down. He might be occupied now, but you never knew when he might decide to target her again.

LAURIE JAMESON

The lack of sleep is killing her. It's impossible to get any decent rest with Tony flying high all night, blasting music and banging on ceilings. All this time hiding beside the bed is getting to be more than she can take. She is exhausted and the baby is taking too much out of her. Finally, she can't fight it anymore. She closes her eyes, places her arms across her stomach, and shifts around until her head is in a more comfortable position.

God, please keep me safe. I'm too tired to do this anymore.

She tries not to cry as she reflects on the hell her life has become. She sniffles a little and attempts to pray, but she doesn't believe God is listening today. It's all up to Rachel and Marco now. She drifts off to sleep.

TONY
(30 MINUTES EARLIER)

He's focused…seriously focused and positive the toaster is going to work this time. He can feel it. He has cleaned and tightened everything he can think of at least twice, and believes this is going to be the one that does it. He never even considers the idea that he has been spinning out of control for so many days he doesn't have the ability for rational thought anymore. In his mind, he is the one who has it together; everyone else is totally fucked up and messing with him. Maybe when he finishes, he'll find Cara and bang her brains out. He runs that scenario over in his mind as he continues to tweak the toaster.

When his cell begins to ring, he considers ignoring it, but glancing at the screen notices the caller ID says Marco.

Shit, I'm gonna have to talk to him.

He mutters, "Be cool man, just be cool," and picks up the phone. "Hey, Marco, dude what's up?"

"Tony, what's happening, everything going okay man?"

"Yeah, yeah, it's cool. I'm just sitting here fixing this damn toaster again. Cara got something stuck down inside trying to get a Pop Tart out yesterday and it's been a real bitch getting it working again."

"Nasty, those things will kill you man, they're solid sugar. Why do you even keep that kind of crap in the house?"

"Yeah, I hear ya. I keep telling her that, but she loves 'em, you know, especially the chocolate ones." It was amazing how easily lying came to him these days.

"Whatever. Hey, listen man, what's up with the shit? Are you moving the stuff or what? You haven't exactly been keeping me in the loop lately and that's starting to worry me. I don't like not knowing what's going on."

"Yeah, Marco, no problem man. Me and Cara got deliveries lined up for later tonight. It's gonna be a good week. Chill bro, I got it under control. No worries."

"That's good dude, glad to hear it. That's the kind of shit I don't need to be dealing with today." He pauses for a moment before continuing, "Listen, I need to talk to you for a minute about something else."

Tony can hear stuff rustling around on Marco's end and he feels his gut tightening up like he's preparing himself for a punch.

"What's up with you and Cara man? Rachel is freaking out and saying you're hurting her girl, and if my woman's upset, I'm upset. You get what I'm saying?"

Tony can feel sweat starting to slide down his neck. What the hell had that bitch said to Rachel? He knew she'd talked to her on the phone yesterday, but damn.

"Dude, don't worry, it's fine. We were just having another fight yesterday. It's no big deal. You know how Cara is; she's a fucking drama queen sometimes. She probably said a lot of shit to Rachel 'cause she's still pissed off at me. She's not hurt man. Everything's cool, no worries. We're good." He can hear Marco lighting up a cigarette and wishes he knew where he left his; he could really use one right now.

Marco hesitates long enough to exhale and speaks with deadly earnestness, "All right, but remember man, I don't want trouble of *any* kind. I'm not gonna like it if the cops have to show up at your house over some domestic violence shit. It's bad for business and we don't want to be on their radar for any reason. You get my drift?"

"Yeah Marco, I got it."

"I'm not joking Tony. I know we're friends man, but you need to take this shit seriously, understand? There are people other than me you need to be worried about. People who aren't nearly as understanding as me."

"No problem. I told you, you don't need to worry about it."

"Alright, I'm gonna trust you, so be cool man. Get your shit together. Don't make me have to have this conversation again. I don't like getting involved in your personal crap. I've got enough hassle dealing with my own life."

"Sure, sure, whatever you say. I get it."

"Let me know when you've sold all the shit. I'll catch you later."

"Sure, you got it; later Marco."

Tony ends the call and throws his phone at the couch. He's incredibly pissed and feels like his head is getting ready to explode. He can feel his pulse pounding out the rhythm of a heavy beat in his temples.

That's all I need, for Marco to start sticking his nose in my business thinking I'm a problem, and just where the fuck are my cigarettes anyway?

"Fucking bitch!" he yells, picking up the toaster and throwing it against the kitchen wall where it leaves a dent. Bits and pieces of plastic and metal fly everywhere.

This chick is getting to be way more trouble than she's worth and now the damn toaster is actually broken. Fuck. Oh, she's seriously gonna pay for this one.

He charges out of the kitchen, through the living room and to the bedroom where he throws the door open so hard it bounces off the wall and slams back into him before he can catch it. This pisses him off even more and makes him want to rip the fucking thing off the hinges.

At first, he can't see her, but he knows she's in the house somewhere; he can feel it. Dashing into the bathroom, he yanks the shower curtain down thinking she might be hiding in the tub. The rod and curtain come down on his head and he angrily flails about until he manages to extricate himself from the plastic. Finally working free, he throws it all to the floor and realizes she isn't cowering in the bottom of the tub like he expected. He runs back into the bedroom convinced she must be trying to escape.

Then he hears it, whimpering, like a little puppy. He tracks the sound and sees the top of her head peeking up between the bed and the wall. With a roar, Tony launches himself across the bed and seizes Cara by her hair and arm. He yanks her up and over the edge, throwing her on the bed with such force she bounces. He jumps on her, sitting on her hips, and presses her shoulders deeply into the mattress.

Cara begins to cry, "Tony, please, please, stop."

He punches her in the mouth, screaming, "Shut up you fucking bitch! Who the hell do you think you are huh? Calling your girlfriend and whining about me? Are you trying to get Marco all up in my shit? What's your fucking problem anyway? You are way out of your league here Cara." He shoves her across the bed far enough to leave her head hanging off the edge.

It's about time this bullshit comes to an end.

Snot and blood are running down Cara's throat causing her to choke. Coughing and weeping, she begs through rapidly swelling lips, "Please, Tony, please, I'm sorry. I didn't mean to get you in trouble. I'll fix it. I promise. God, please stop, you're hurting me."

She slaps ineffectively at Tony's arms and tries to move him off her. She struggles to push up with her legs and shift his weight off her hips, but her feet keep slipping. He is simply too big, too heavy, and too angry.

It doesn't matter what she says, Tony can't hear her anyway. He doesn't feel her hands slapping at him and doesn't see the panic in her eyes. He can't see he has finally crossed a line there is no coming back from. All he can do is feed the rage boiling inside of him. A rage so intense it creates a red fog which surrounds him, burning a hole in his gut and pounding in his veins, and *she* is the reason why.

"Shut up! Shut up! Shut up!" he screams.

He clutches her throat and begins to squeeze. When that doesn't satisfy the furious surge of anger, he leans forward and puts all his weight on her neck, bending it farther and farther back.

This bitch is going to shut the fuck up. I'm done with this bullshit.

Tony pushes, and pushes. Sweat drips off his face, mixing with the tears and blood on her face which is turning from red to purple. Tears, snot and blood from her split lip run into her hair. Suddenly there's a snap, like the sound of a small twig breaking. Cara quits struggling. She's gone limp and is no longer crying.

A couple of heartbeats pass before Tony realizes Cara isn't moving anymore and has finally stopped bawling. That's when he smells the pee and something worse—shit.

"Shit. What's that fucking smell?"

THE WAYSTATION

He scoots across the bed and presses up against the headboard, staring at her in horror and revulsion. He kicks at her shoulder trying to get her as far away from him as possible. Cara rolls limply over on to her face displaying a large wet spot on her butt. He kicks her again and again shouting, "What the fuck is wrong with you?" She flips off the bed, landing on the floor with a meaty thump.

Reaching above his head and grasping the headboard, he stares in stunned disbelief for several moments at the pee stain on the sheets where Cara has voided her bladder. He nervously licks his lips as reality finally sets in. "Oh, fuck me," he whispers.

RACHEL

She can't help but smile as she glances at herself in the mirror for one last check. Last week she'd finally gotten up the nerve to cut her hair short and she thinks it looks great. It's a cute, spiky style that emphasizes her eyes and cheekbones. She keeps finding herself staring at her reflection in awe every time she passes a mirror, amazed at what a difference it makes in her appearance. Even Marco told her she was hot before, but now she's "smoking hot."

She admires her hair one last time and goes back to making the bed, running her hand over the new top sheet, and admiring the deep cinnamon color. Her mom was right. It was definitely worth the extra money. A higher thread count makes all the difference. They feel smooth as silk.

The house phone begins ringing. She's still thinking about the sheets and debating if she should go ahead and get the new comforter she's had her eye on. She reaches for the phone, assuming it's either her mom or maybe Todd. They're the only ones who ever call her on the house phone anymore. She always gives out her cell number to friends, and as far as she knows, the only people who would call Marco would be his parents. She's about to say hello when she realizes he's picked up too. It's Tony on the other end and he sounds almost hysterical. She knows it's not right, but she can't help listening in. She's always been too nosey for her own good.

Tony is babbling hysterically about Cara and totally freaking out. "Holy shit, I think I really fucked up this time. I lost it man and…and now, well, she's not moving and I don't know what to do. Dude, just get over here. Please, you gotta help me man!"

THE WAYSTATION

Those few seconds of eavesdropping are enough to terrify her. She just talked to Cara yesterday. Oh, my God, what did he do? He must have really hurt her this time.

You bastard, Tony. She better be okay.

Her heart pounds uncontrollably and the fear makes her stomach churn as she struggles to hold on to its contents. Finally, Rachel can't take it anymore. She's heard enough. Her hands are shaking and she fumbles the phone as she struggles to hang it up. It clatters against the charger. Panicked, she immediately starts praying that Tony and Marco are too busy yelling at each other to notice the noise. Her heart beats relentlessly in her ears and her fingertips prickle from the adrenaline that's been dumped into her system.

She feels like she can't catch her breath and knows she's about to throw up. She makes a mad dash to the bathroom, barely making it in time. Dropping to her knees, she wraps her arms around the toilet seat and everything she's eaten for breakfast comes up in a stinking, steaming rush. She retches a few more times until there is nothing left, then wipes her mouth with toilet paper. She flushes the toilet and clings to the side, too shattered and shocked to even try and stand. Tears pour from her eyes and she begins to sob, "Cara, Cara, oh my God, Cara. What has he done to you? Please be okay. Oh God, please let her be okay."

It suddenly occurs to her that if Marco comes in, he'll want to know what's wrong. She doesn't want him to know she overheard the phone call. She's not sure why she's worried about Marco knowing she eavesdropped, but something in her gut tells her it would be dangerous. Forcing herself to get up, she staggers to the door to see if he's still on the phone. He is, thank God, and still yelling at Tony too from the sound of things.

"Dammit, Tony, why are you calling me here? Cops can trace land lines you fucking idiot." He pauses, listening to Tony's excuses, "I don't give a shit. If I don't answer, you leave a fucking message for me to call you back." Marco pounds his fist on the table, "Don't move, I'm coming over right now, and you can explain everything to me when I get there. Jesus, Tony, I can't believe you're this stupid."

Rachel runs for the bathroom again and quickly sprays air freshener to cover the smell of vomit. She turns the water on in the sink and rinses out her mouth to wash out the foul taste. Then she sticks her head under the faucet to wet her hair and face so Marco won't see the tears. Grabbing the shampoo bottle from the shower, she pours a blob into her hand and tells herself to pull it together.

Take long, slow breaths Rachel. You've got to be calm or he'll know. He can't know you heard.

She lathers up her hair and waits to see if Marco will come in. A couple of minutes later he does, leaning against the door jamb and affecting an air of nonchalance. "Hey, babe?"

"Yeah," she says, trying to control the shaking in her voice and fervently hoping the sound of the water will help disguise it.

"Why are you washing your hair again? Didn't you just do that last night?"

Frantically coming up with what she hopes is a believable lie, she responds, "Yeah, I did, but I put a bunch of product in it when I styled it this morning and I didn't like the way it came out. So, I have to wash it out and start all over again."

"Oh, man, sucks to be you." He laughs then says, "I need to take care of some stuff. I'll probably be gone for a few hours."

"Okay."

"How about I bring back a nice bottle of wine or maybe some of that almond champagne you like? We can fire up a joint, have a few glasses and relax in the Jacuzzi tonight. What do you say?"

"Sounds great," she answers from under the stream of water. "You want me to make something to eat?"

Oh please, please leave.

"No, don't bother. We'll call for takeout or something. Give me a kiss, I gotta go."

Rachel turns her head sideways but keeps her eyes closed. Her hair is lathered up and she has her eyes squeezed tightly shut to presumably keep the soap out, but it's simply to keep Marco from seeing how red they are. She puckers up for him. He laughs again and tells her, "You are seriously cute." Then gives her a quick kiss before disappearing out the door.

She waits until she hears the front door slam before hurriedly rinsing out the soap. Grabbing a towel, she quickly dries her hair, and throws it on the floor before running for her purse and keys. No way is she staying here worrying about what's going on. She's going to follow him and find out. Cara has been her dearest friend since she was five, and she means more to Rachel than anyone else. Like Cara said, sisters take care of each other.

MARCO

He can't believe he has to deal with this bullshit. When did he become Tony's babysitter? It's not like he has any choice though. Obviously, this is not a situation that's going to go away on its own and it could have a direct impact on him and the business. He needs to deal with it, if for no other reason than to protect himself. He needs to have a plan.

He mulls over the possible scenarios and hopes this doesn't mean what he thinks it means. Cara might be dead. He has to admit there's a chance that's what he'll be dealing with. Tony never came straight out and said it, but it sure sounded like a definite possibility. Marco never should have answered the phone.

How did I wind up here? I had a normal life once. For God's sake, I was an altar boy as a kid and everybody in the parish loved me. I was a damn good tight end and had scouts coming to check me out. All the top schools were kissing my ass. If I hadn't blown out my knee senior year, I'd be in college playing ball right now. My life would be totally different. I sure wouldn't be on my way to help this idiot bury his girlfriend.

God, he hopes that isn't what he is on his way to do. Hopefully they're only looking at a trip to the ER and getting Tony out of town where he can lay low for a while. Once Marco gets through this he can decide where to go from there. Right now, it's all about protecting the business and by association, his own ass. A career in meth distribution is risky enough without adding domestic violence or possibly murder to the mix. This shit has to go away quickly.

He's driving to Tony's as fast as he can without drawing any unnecessary attention. The last thing he needs right now is for some cop to remember he's been in this neighborhood today. Somehow, he's going to have to get this crap cleaned up. If news of this gets back to his boss, Monkey, he's a dead man. Monkey won't tolerate anyone drawing the interest of the cops, and this is some seriously bad shit that could bring down all kinds of heat. His head spins with unsavory possibilities.

He pulls into Tony's side drive, and after opening the gate, drives directly into the back yard. As he closes the gate, he casually glances up and down the street. The neighborhood looks dead. That's good. Hopefully it stays that way long enough for them to get out of here.

He makes note of the big trees, which do an excellent job of screening the back yard from the neighbors. All that overgrown shrubbery in front of the garden walls doesn't hurt either. He's happy Tony is a house tweaker. If he was a yard tweaker there wouldn't be any bushes left for cover; they'd all be cut back to bare branches. With any luck, they might be able to carry her out of the house without anyone seeing them. It remains to be seen if that is going to be a trip to the hospital or an unmarked grave.

Marco marches in the back door and through the kitchen where he notices the dented wall, and the shattered toaster lying in pieces all over the floor. It's another sign that Tony's lost it. He can't even keep his temper in check with small appliances.

He finds Tony sitting on the couch, elbows resting on his knees, holding his head in his hands, a cigarette burning between his fingers. Tony gazes up through the smoke and shakes his head, "This is really fucked up Marco, really fucked up. What am I gonna do?"

"Well, for starters, you're going to pull your head out of your ass, and stop acting like a little bitch. Tell me exactly what happened and then I'm going to help you clean this shit up."

"Okay. Thanks man."

"I seriously hate that your fucking problems have become my fucking problems. Where is she?"

Tony has the grace to look ashamed. "She's in the bedroom. Look, shit, I didn't mean to…I mean, I just fucking blew up and it happened. I, I don't know how. It was an accident."

Marco's stomach sinks. It appears as if his worst fears are confirmed. "When I walk in that room, what am I gonna see? What did you do to her?" He clenches his fists and tries to keep his temper under control.

Tony closes his eyes and draws a deep breath before answering. "I lost it and I choked her out man. She's not breathing and she pissed her pants. I think she shit too, it sure smells like it."

"Are you fucking kidding me?" Marco roars. "This is what you've drug me in to?"

"I'm sorry man."

"Shut up Tony, I don't want to hear your lame-ass apologies. This kind of shit doesn't just fucking happen. I'll help you get out of this mess, and then you *will* do whatever I tell you and not give me any shit."

"Yeah, shit dude, I get it, I get it," Tony mumbles, staring at his hands and watching the smoke from his cigarette curl up and drift away. "I know this is a fucking mess, okay? I've done some stupid shit before, but this is insane. I know that. But how am I gonna hide this, dude? What am I gonna tell people when they realize she's missing? 'Cause sooner or later somebody's going to notice she's not around. She's supposed to be back to work in three days. I need to come up with a good story. I can't believe I fucking did this. Rachel's never gonna forgive me. I'm totally fucking screwed."

Marco stares at him in complete disbelief and doesn't even bother to respond. What bugs him the most is Tony doesn't even seem to be bothered by the idea that he's killed Cara. All he's worried about is his own ass and how to cover it. Marco turns away and walks into the bedroom where he spends several moments gazing at Cara. She lies face down on the floor at the foot of the bed. Her head is turned away from him and one of her arms is bent under her body. A large wet spot is spread across the seat of her pants and the room smells like a dirty diaper. He feels bad for Cara; he genuinely liked her. She was a sweet girl, and Rachel loved her.

What a way to die. This is going to kill Rachel. Thank God I don't have to look into Cara's eyes; I'm not sure I could handle that.

Pulling himself together, he yells, "Tony, get your ass in here and help me with this."

THE WAYSTATION

Reluctantly Tony shuffles into the room. He glances at the bed, at Marco, at the window, anywhere except on the floor where Cara lies. He's finding it hard to breathe and feels dizzy. "Oh Man, I think I'm gonna blow chunks."

Bam! Marco punches him in the shoulder—hard. "Fucking pull yourself together. We don't have time for that kind of bullshit. Get your ass over there and grab one end of the comforter and let's roll her up in it. We need to get her out of here."

Tony takes one last hit of his cigarette before walking to the bathroom and tossing the butt in the toilet. He watches it float in the water for a second before raising his eyes to meet Marco's. He wears an expression of regret, like a little kid who expects to be punished. Drawing a huge breath and then immediately regretting it because of the smell, Tony drags himself back into the bedroom and reluctantly looks at Cara. He immediately shifts his eyes away and focuses on the bed instead, picking the comforter up and silently holding it out to Marco. Marco shakes it out over Cara, and together they roll her up and haul her out of the room. Along the way, they manage to bounce her against the doorway and almost every piece of furniture in their path.

As they carry her past the decimated toaster, Marco tosses his head at the mess and says, "That shit needs to be cleaned up as soon as you get back." Tony only grunts in response.

"I mean it dude. This house needs to look perfectly normal. When Cara turns up missing the police are going to come here and question you. I don't want them to have any reason look at you twice."

"Okay man, I'll clean it up."

"I also want the shit moved tonight. Sell what you can and give me the rest. I want this place clean. You hear what I'm saying?"

"Yeah, yeah, I'm all over it."

Marco stops near the kitchen door, "Okay, put her down here and let's get the mattress."

"What? Why?" Tony bitches.

"Because I'm not going to prison because you're a fucking idiot. This is not just about you. It affects me too. I know we're friends man, but you work for me, remember? This is my product you're selling. I've got

Monkey watching every move I make, and I am *not* disappointing this man or giving him any reason to doubt my ability to manage my end."

"Ah, come on man. You know I'm not gonna fuck you up."

"You've already fucked me up by getting me involved in this. So, you're going to take that mattress to the dump. Then you're going to Sears and buying a new one *and* a new comforter. Make sure you get one that looks as much like this one as possible. Oh yeah, and get new sheets too. You come home, wash the new sheets and make the bed, nice and neat just like Cara would do it. Then you go and find a dumpster some-where and toss those dirty ones. After that, you get out there and move the shit, and then you come back here and sit your ass in front of the TV like it's a regular day. I don't want to hear from you until that's all done. Can you handle that?"

"Yeah, but Jesus, why a new mattress?" Tony whines. "I can under-stand getting a new comforter, even sheets, but a mattress too? That's a fucking pain in the ass and seriously expensive."

"Holy shit Tony, don't be stupid. Everything's got evidence on it. She pissed all over the sheets and the mattress. If you want to get out of this, do what I say and keep your mouth shut."

Marco angrily roots through the kitchen cabinets until he locates the trash bags. Slamming the door closed, he takes one with him to the bed-room and Tony follows dragging his feet.

RACHEL

Catching up with Marco is not difficult since she knows where he's going. She parks a little way down the block, behind a large moving van that completely hides her little car. She ignores the movers, and weaving her way through furniture scattered over the grass and sidewalk, she jogs up the street as quickly as possible. She hesitates at the house next door and peeks cautiously from behind a large shrub, catching a glimpse of Marco as he closes the gate. Fortunately, he doesn't lock it. She makes herself count to 100 before running up to the gate and quietly opening it, all the while praying Marco has gone straight in the house. She sends up a quick prayer of thanks when she sees the yard is empty and the back door closed. She latches the gate as quickly as possible, wincing at the loud click it makes.

There are plenty of things to hide behind on the side of the detached garage, and she chooses a spot that still allows her a view of the back door. She doesn't have to wait long. Through the kitchen window she hears Marco order Tony to put her down, and it's all Rachel can do to keep from crying out when she hears the thud on the kitchen floor.

She only hesitates for a moment, because it won't take them long to go back for the mattress. She runs to the door, pressing her face up against the window. A person-sized bundle is lying on the floor wrapped in a comforter. Rachel recognizes that comforter, and a heavy weight settles on her chest. She may have only seconds, but she needs to be certain. Opening the door as quietly as possible, she reaches for the comforter with trembling hands and pulls it back.

Cara's face stares at her. Her bright blue eyes are wide open and unblinking. Rachel nearly screams. She backs away in horror throwing both hands over her mouth, unable to tear her eyes away.

25

LAURIE JAMESON

OhmyGod, ohmyGod, ohmyGod. She's dead. She's really dead. Oh God, my poor Cara.

Marco's voice floats through the house, "Come on Tony, help me pick this thing up so we can get going. I don't have all fucking day."

Rachel's paralysis breaks. She flips the comforter back over Cara's face and closes the door with a soft click. She runs around the corner of the garage, crouching down behind the trash cans and unused garden equipment, her breath coming in harsh gasps. Her head is spinning and she's starting to see little sparkles floating around the edges of her vision. At this rate, she's going to pass out, knock crap over and totally give herself away. She sits down as quietly as possible and puts her head between her knees until the feeling passes. But that doesn't block the sound of Marco and Tony loading Cara's body into the back of the truck. Rachel forces herself to focus on keeping her breathing slow and steady, and tries not to let it get to her. She needs to keep it together until they're gone, then she can break down as much as she wants once it's safe.

MARCO

Marco shoves the soiled sheets inside the garbage bag and tosses it out the bedroom door into the living room. Then he opens the window to let out some of the stink. Lifting the edge of the mattress he yells, "Come on Tony, help me pick this thing up so we can get going. I don't have all fucking day."

Skirting the bag of sheets, Tony grudgingly re-enters the bedroom from where he had been hovering right outside the door, and picks up his end. Together they wrestle the mattress out the door and through the house, throwing it in the back of Tony's truck, then go back in for Cara.

As they carry her down the steps, the comforter shifts and Cara's face is once again staring up at the sky. Neither Tony or Marco can look at her, and both make a concerted effort to act as if it doesn't bother them. They lay her on top of the mattress, and Tony looks to Marco, waiting for further instruction.

"Shovels," Marco growls. "Do I have to spell everything out for you?"

Tony shrugs and trudges off to the garage to get shovels. When he returns, he notices that Marco has put the comforter back over Cara's face. This suits him just fine, because he can't bear to look at her again. He tosses the shovels in the back, closes and locks the cover. After checking to make sure the back door is locked, they drive away without bothering to close the gate.

RACHEL

Once Tony's truck pulls away and disappears down the street, Rachel rises from behind the trash cans. Dirt covers her hands, knees, and the butt of her pants. She had been quietly crying the entire time she was hiding and her face is streaked with tears. Trying not to sob out loud, she slogs back to her car absently wiping her hands on her pants. She ignores the curious looks from the movers, and spends a good thirty minutes sitting in her car crying because her heart is broken. Exhausted, she finally runs out of tears and turns the car around, heading for home.

She has no idea what she'll say to Marco when he gets back. What can she say? If she confronts him, he'll know she followed him. If she doesn't say anything, it will eat her alive. Fighting the urge to start balling all over again, she concentrates on driving and tells herself she can figure it out later. For now, she simply needs to get home before she completely falls apart. She can have a full-on panic attack there if she needs to. This is not the place to lose it. She needs to be at home where Marco left her. He can't know she was here. No one can know she was here.

TONY

Tony smokes furiously as he drives down his street. He keeps hoping he's going to wake up and this whole fucking nightmare will be over. He can't believe he's gotten himself into this mess. Marco has made it clear he's pissed, and Tony wonders how long it will take before the fallout from this shit goes away.

He can't come to grips with the idea that Cara is dead and it's his fault.

Aw, that's fucking bullshit. It isn't my fault. The bitch pushed me to it. She's been giving me shit for weeks and not supporting me the way she fucking should. She hasn't lived up to her end of the deal in a long time. Her job was to look good and keep me happy, and what does she do? She lets herself get fat and rubs my nose in it like I'm supposed to fucking like it. Then she goes and runs her big, fat mouth and complains to Rachel. Yeah, that's right; the bitch brought it on herself.

Satisfied with his conclusion, he glances at Marco and casually asks, "So, where are we going?"

Marco casts a disgusted sidelong glance at him and flatly states, "We're going to a place I know off the 15 freeway. It's called Lytle Creek. There's a lot of open space and not too many people. It should be easy to find a good spot to bury her out there. If we're lucky, no one will ever find her body. Then you can thank me for pulling your ass out of the fire."

He stares out the window and avoids making any more eye contact with Tony. "And dude, use your turn signals, don't fucking speed and try not to do anything stupid. Drive like there's a cop in front of you and a cop behind you. We don't need to be stopped for *any* reason."

"Yeah man, no problem," Tony mumbles and rolls his eyes at the offense. Marco is treating him like a little kid and he doesn't deserve it. It was an accident.

After what feels like an interminable amount of time, but in reality, is probably only 15 or 20 minutes, he takes a quick glance at Marco. He still looks incredibly pissed, but Tony is bored, and the freeway traffic is heavy. He decides to try again to get some conversation going. "So, how do you know about this place? Was it like some kind of hot party spot or something?"

Marco continues to ignore him, and lowers his window a couple of inches. He shakes out a cigarette, pauses to light it up and blows the smoke out in a thick stream through the opening. He watches the passing traffic and flicks the ash out the window, still refusing to look at Tony. Then he finally snarls out directions. "Get off here and turn left. It's about three and a half miles down the road. Don't forget what I said about speeding. The cops have radar all over this area."

"Yeah, I know, I got it," Tony answers peevishly.

He finally accepts that Marco isn't interested in making small talk, and because he can't think of anything else to say, reaches over and turns on the radio. AC/DC pours out of the speakers and helps to blow away some of the awkwardness he's feeling.

Fuck man, this isn't fair. We've always been friends up until now. Once again that bitch has fucked up my life, and now she's come between me and Marco.

He squeezes the steering wheel harder and struggles to get a grip on his rising temper. Pulling out a cigarette of his own, he smokes in silence while the sound of drums and screaming guitars fill the smoky cab.

CARA

Swimming to the surface of consciousness, Cara senses time has passed, but isn't certain how long. She thinks she might be drifting in and out every few minutes but can't be sure. She can hear traffic noise and is startled by a loud blast from a horn. Sounds like a semi, she thinks drowsily and wonders if she's in the trunk of a car. It's hard to breathe in here, the exhaust fumes are awful. Darkness silently pads in on fat, little cat feet. She fades away and remembers.

It was the day she and Rachel met and formed the perfect friendship. They were five years old and it was their first day of kindergarten. It was as if fate had decided they were meant to be together, even though they were physically nothing alike. Little elfin-like Cara with her long blonde hair and bright blue eyes, and long-legged, green-eyed Rachel who always wore her hair in braids. Holding hands and standing side-by-side in line, they gave their full attention to the teacher as she explained that this was the person who would be their line mate for the school year.

Pointing to Cara and Rachel, the teacher said "These two girls are together because Cara Healy and Rachel Henderson fall together alphabetically. How many of you know your alphabet?" She and Rachel immediately shot their hands up in the air smiling proudly at each other. It sealed their friendship and they became inseparable.

Years went by and they managed to remain line mates all the way through elementary school, laughing and giggling at all the things little girls do. Cara was always trying to make Rachel laugh by blowing her bangs up off her forehead while crossing her eyes. It gave Rachel the giggles every time. By the time they reached the fifth grade, Rachel was the tallest kid in school. This lasted until the boys finally started catch-

31

ing up during their junior year in high school. Her grandmother always referred to the two of them as Mutt and Jeff. Cara had no idea what that meant, though it always seemed to make her grandmother laugh.

Cara is aware of sounds. She has time to register the low humming of the tires on pavement, and decides that they're not on the freeway anymore. Then she's gone. Her memories begin to play again.

Sophomore year, after their first school dance of the year.

"Cara. Oh, my God, you are not going to believe what happened," Rachel hissed as she grabbed her by the arm.

Cara juggled her books, using her hip to pin her geometry book against the edge of her locker to keep it from crashing to the floor, while carefully extricating her arm from Rachel's vise-like grip.

"What? Holy crap Rach, let go before I drop everything."

Rachel snagged the geometry book in one hand and Cara's purse in the other, "Seriously. I've got to tell you this. You are going to freak out because it's just so gross!"

Cara finished jamming the rest of her books and loose papers into the locker and slammed the door shut, knowing that it would all probably fall out anyway when she opened it before next period.

"Okay, you got my attention; spill it."

"Well, you remember when I danced with Charlie Atkins during that slow song right at the end of the dance?"

Yeah, and?"

"Oh, man, Cara, you know he's way shorter than me."

"So are all of the guys you danced with. What else is new?"

"Yeah, but this was a slow song." She paused for effect, "You know, up close and personal?"

Cara leaned against her locker, raised an eyebrow and waited for the rest.

"It was totally embarrassing. His nose hit me right in the chest and he rested his cheek on my boob like it was some kind of pillow!"

Cara burst out laughing.

THE WAYSTATION

"It's not funny. He got this huge boner and was rubbing it up against my leg for the whole dance. I kept trying to shift away from him but he wouldn't let me. It was totally gross. I think I'm scarred for life."

Cara laughed and laughed, and started to do the pee-pee dance before finally begging, "Stop already. I'm going to wet my pants. Oh, man, I'm sorry, but that's hysterical. You've got to admit that you'd laugh like crazy if it happened to someone else."

Rachel gave her a dirty look before finally conceding that she was probably right. She wound her arm through Cara's and they hurried off to math class still talking about how disgusting guys could be. Not one to pass up a good opportunity, Cara spent a good part of that period whispering "boner" in Rachel's ear so she could watch her turn red.

৯ ৯ ৯ ৯ ৯ ৯ ৯ ৯ ৯ ৯

That memory morphs into the day before prom night of their junior year.

"Holy crap Cara, I'm so glad Charlie finally hit his growth spurt. You know he shot up to 5' 11" right? For once I won't have to worry about having a guy's nose pressed into my boobs. He'll probably want to dance every slow song. Now the only thing I have to worry about is a slow dance stiffy bouncing against me all night."

Cara laughed so hard she was almost crying. "Stop it. Oh, my god, stop it. I'm seriously going to ruin my makeup if you don't quit."

৯ ৯ ৯ ৯ ৯ ৯ ৯ ৯ ৯ ৯

She continues to float in and out of reality riding the waves of her memories as they travel toward their destination.

TONY

They drive without speaking until an old banged up gate appears off the road on the right. Next to it stands a battered brown sign on a rusted, buckled pole reading:

NO TARGET SHOOTING
STREET LEGAL VEHICLES ONLY
NO VEHS OFF ROADS
PENSTOCK to 2N79

"Turn in here," Marco says.

The road is twisted and rutted with visible signs of run-off revealing washed out sections in many places. Everything is damp or muddy. Rocks of all shapes and sizes can be seen in piles or lying alone on the side of the road. They bounce along listening to mud and small pebbles pinging off the undercarriage, the bushes and trees occasionally brushing the sides of the truck. In the bed, the comforter which had begun shifting as soon as they pulled out of Tony's back yard, no longer covers Cara's face and shoulders.

After about half a mile, Marco points to a turn off on the right and Tony complies without comment. They appear to be on some sort of a service road for a massive electrical tower he can see in the distance. Dark, ominous clouds hang in the sky, lending the impression they are pressing down on them. The air smells of rain, ozone, mud and wet plants.

Up ahead a wide area comes in to view off to the left. It looks big enough to accommodate the truck without a problem. Marco says,

"Here looks good. Back up to those trees over there and let's check it out."

The ground is muddy, but packed down reasonably well where they park. The space behind it appears perfect though. There are all types of bushes and small trees. Water glistens off the leaves and wild flowers. The abundance of blossoms is impressive. Purple, yellow and white blooms are arrayed in water drops like jewels, glistening as they raise their faces to the weak sun.

"There; that's perfect," Marco says pointing to an area of decomposing plant life under a section of deadfall that has been left behind from a lifeless tree. "The ground should be nice and soft in there."

Tony nods and heads for the back of the truck thinking to himself that this miserable day is never going to end. He unlocks and lifts the cover to the bed. Cara's face stares up at him. He jumps back with a yelp, eliciting a withering stare from Marco.

"What the fuck is your problem Tony? Why are you being such a pussy?"

"Sorry man, the comforter came off her face and, well, I just wasn't expecting it, that's all. I mean, fuck man, her eyes are open and it's kinda creepy."

He steels his nerves and avoids looking at her face as he reaches in to grab the shovels, wanting to get this over with as quickly as possible.

CARA

She fights her way out of the darkness once more. She has no way of knowing how long she's been out this time. She doesn't hear other cars anymore, but does notice the sound of the tires crunching on gravel and what she thinks must be rocks and dirt hitting the underside of the vehicle. She's bouncing around a lot and wonders where she is. Eventually they stop, a door slams and she hears two men talking, realizing with a surge of horror that she recognizes the voices.

Tony…and Marco.

When the trunk opens, and light fills the space, she knows where she is. She's in the bed of Tony's truck, and not in the trunk of a car. His truck has a cover on it. That's why she thought she was in a trunk. She watches his face in stunned disbelief as he yelps in surprise and Marco chews him out.

Oh, my God.

Everything comes rushing back to her all at once. She needs to do something. She needs to get out of here, but how? She can't move. Tony pulls two shovels from the bed next to her and he and Marco begin to argue, disagreeing on how deep to dig. Panic sets in as the truth hits her.

They must think I'm dead. No, you can't bury me, I'm alive! No, please stop.

Her heart is beating frantically, slamming into her ribcage like a piston, her thoughts skittering around in her head like a moth trapped in a jar. Too soon Marco seizes her by the arms and Tony by her ankles pulling her from the back of the truck and dropping her on the ground as if she were a sack of dirty laundry. The weird thing is it doesn't hurt when she hits.

I must be in shock.

THE WAYSTATION

She tries and tries to get their attention. She is desperate to be noticed, but nothing seems to be happening. She can't make a sound or move. Can't they see her panic, her fear? Surely it must show in her eyes.

Time skitters away again. She can hear the droning of bugs, and smell the recent rain and the fragrance of the plants surrounding her. Through the curtain of her hair, she can see a huge bush covered with big stalks of purple flowers that remind her of hyacinths. Drops of water are sparkling like diamonds all over the leaves and blooms. A cloud of butterflies flutter and crawl across the purple stems. She can't see much more from where she lies, but she does notice that droplets of water are everywhere and they create a beautiful, shining panorama out of simple weeds. It's stunning. She's terrified and yet at the same time she is surrounded by all this beauty; it's surreal.

They look sweaty and tired. Tony looks thoroughly pissed, his eyes throwing daggers at her as if this is all her fault.

How can you do this to me? Do you hate me this much? I loved you and once I thought you loved me too.

Out of nowhere, a memory of happier times plays in her head.

∽　∽　∽　∽　∽　∽　∽　∽　∽

They were cuddled together on the couch and Tony held her in his arms while he told her a silly story about ducks and a disappearing lake.

"There was this beautiful lake and it was a favorite spot for all the ducks in town. All summer long they would hang out there diving for bugs and taking handouts from kids who would bring bags of bread to feed them."

"Oh, how sweet," Cara interrupted. "Rachel and I used to do that too. We loved feeding the ducks."

Tony squeezed her tighter and kissed her forehead saying, "I bet you were the cutest one there too." He paused for a moment to nibble on her ear before continuing with his story. "So anyway, the ducks loved this lake and came back to it every year. One year when winter was coming and it was starting to get cold, the ducks started migrating south. This huge flock was passing through and landed on the lake to rest. While they were resting, this huge storm moved in really fast and the lake totally froze. The ducks were trapped. Then I guess they decided that they wanted out of there, so they all started flapping their wings at once and because there were so many of them, they actually lifted the frozen lake up and took it with them. They flew away heading south and no one ever saw that lake again."

Cara punched him in the arm and giggled. "That's stupid and lame. You totally made that up."

"Yeah, but you're still laughing. You can't say it's lame if you laugh."

Then he flipped her onto her back, pinned her to the couch and started tickling her.

"Stop," she screamed, kicking her legs and squirming. "Oh, my God, Tony stop." Tears formed in her eyes as she laughed and screamed for mercy.

He finally stopped and kissed her eyes, cheeks and lips repeatedly while he whispered silly nothings.

     ℛ   ℛ   ℛ   ℛ   ℛ   ℛ   ℛ   ℛ   ℛ

I know you loved me. I know it. What happened to you? Where did that person go? Why would you do this to me?

Their hands roughly grip her ankles and arms again. She is unceremoniously dumped in the hole and the comforter carelessly tossed in on top of her.

Lying there waiting for what she knows is inevitable, she can hear music coming from the truck. Beautiful guitar and haunting words float tenderly from the speakers in bizarre accompaniment to her situation.

Christine Myers; how fitting. She lost her baby before it was born too.

    I won't hold you in my arms.
    I won't see you when I wake.
    If you don't look into my eyes,
    How will you know me?
    How will you know me?

The scent of the rich, damp earth, normally a comforting clean smell that she loves, now smells only of death and decay. It smells of finality and lost dreams.

    You know I loved you from the start,
    I never doubted, never feared.
    Our time together was too short,
    I'll always love you.
    I'll always love you.

THE WAYSTATION

She wants to cry, scream, beg, or plead, but can speak with nothing but her silence.

> **Will you wait for me?**
> **Will you watch from up above?**
> **When we meet again, I'll surely know your face,**
> **'Cause I'll see Heaven in your eyes.**

What she doesn't realize is that she *is* crying. Tears are slowly leaking from the corners of her eyes, trickles of liquid sorrow that leave little trails in their wake. They pool in her ears, mixing with the dirt and forming small puddles of salty mud.

> **Heaven must be kind; they say that it is so.**
> **Heaven must be sweet, and soon we both will know.**
> **I will look for you.**
> **Will you look for me?**

Tony and Marco take a few minutes to rest, leaning on their shovels and smoking but not talking, not even acknowledging each other.

> **Beyond this place, is only love.**
> **Beyond this time, peace from above.**
> **There's no more pain.**
> **There's no more pain.**

My poor baby, I'm sorry you won't get a chance to live. I'm so sorry I can't hold you. Will I know you in heaven? Will I know your sweet face?

She fervently hopes so.

Will I be at peace? Oh, God, please help me, please save me. I'm not ready to die. I'm scared. I'm really, really, scared. Please do something.

She struggles unsuccessfully to get a grip on her anxiety as the panic pounds away relentlessly in her mind.

> **Will you wait for me?**
> **Will you watch from up above?**
> **When we meet again, I'll surely know your face,**
> **'Cause I'll see Heaven in your eyes.**

She longs to place her hands protectively over her stomach to bring comfort to her baby, but her arms won't obey.

Marco and Tony finish their smokes and flick them into the earth next to her, then bend to their vile task once again. Clods of dirt, small rocks and bits of leaves are pitched on top of her. As her view of the flowers and trees gradually becomes obscured, her terrified heart beats out its final frantic rhythm.

God help me. Why won't you help me? I'm scared, oh God I'm so scared. Please help me not to be afraid.

The last bit of oxygen in her lungs is depleted. There is nothing but darkness and she can hear her heart slowing, the echo in her ears becoming a faint tattoo until it ceases to beat entirely. She has time for one last thought before she disappears forever into the darkness…*please take care of my baby.*

MARCO & TONY

When the hole is completely filled, they throw leaves and some bigger rocks on top of the grave. It should be easy to place those large dead branches back on top, but because they buried her under several overhanging low trees, shoving them back under there is a lot harder than it should be and is in fact a major pain in the ass. It's one more thing that aggravates them both. Eventually they're able to get all the limbs back in the space reasonably close to the way they first found them and then stand back to survey their handiwork.

"Looks good," Marco says wiping the sweat from his forehead. "You can't even tell we've been here."

He picks up a couple of stray branches with the leaves still attached and swipes them back and forth across the ground erasing all traces of their footprints and evidence of where they piled the dirt. Once he's finally satisfied, he tosses them out into the brush and Tony throws the shovels in the back of the truck, slamming the tailgate and lid closed. They take off in a spray of mud and rocks, neither one looking back. They don't give another thought to who they are leaving behind or even consider the tire tracks left to dry in the mud.

As the truck disappears around the bend in the road, the breeze blows softly across the tops of the trees and bushes shaking free the accumulated rain drops and releasing a cascade of tears to mourn for Cara and her baby. Under the trees, the skeletal fingers of the branches gently stroke the flesh of the earth as if to comfort her in her sleep as night slowly begins to descend.

TONY

After what feels like an endless and almost silent drive back to his house, he and Marco finally pull into Tony's back yard. Marco angrily takes off his muddy shoes and unsuccessfully tries to beat off the caked-on mud. He finally throws them in his trunk before hastily taking off, leaving Tony to face the list of chores Marco assigned to him.

The mattress is still in the back of his truck because the dump had already closed by the time they made it back to town. He'll have to deal with that later. Kicking off his muddied shoes on the back steps and brushing as much dirt off his pants as he can, he enters the kitchen and sticks his head under the faucet to wash the grime and sweat off his hair, neck and hands.

Drying his head with a dishtowel and chugging a bottle of water, he leans against the counter and resentfully reviews his "to do" list in his head. He picks up the garbage bag Marco stuffed the sheets into earlier, and proceeds to crawl around on the floor collecting bits and pieces of the toaster, that are scattered all to hell and back. After gathering up what he feels is enough, he ties the bag closed.

He finds himself staring at the bedroom door. It's shut. But that's not right. He is almost positive they left it open because they were carrying out the mattress and their hands were full. His heart begins beating a little faster as he tries to decide what to do. He hasn't been all that quiet since coming home. If anyone is in there, they know he's out here. Slowly lowering the trash bag to the floor, he lights a cigarette while mulling over the possibilities. Finally deciding he is agonizing about nothing, he marches over to the door and flings it open.

THE WAYSTATION

The light is still shining from the bathroom, left on from his frantic search for Cara earlier. The indirect light shines on what remains of the bed. The box spring is still there (though he is having a hard time even glancing in that direction), but the rest is gone. Why then is the smell of shit and underlying that, her perfume, still so prevalent? The window has been open for several hours. The room should have aired out by now. The window. Of course, that's why the door was shut. A breeze must have pushed it closed. Figuring out that little mystery immediately makes him feel better and lightens his sense of anxiety.

"Be cool dude," he tells himself, and spends a few minutes in the bathroom taking a quick shower to wash off the rest of the dirt and sweat. He grabs some clean clothes and is pulling on his pants when he thinks he hears a soft step behind him. Whirling around, he expects… what, he doesn't know. Even though there is nothing there, all the hair on his arms feel like they're standing on end.

"What the hell," he yells. "This is bullshit!" He is not going to stay in here any longer so he can be creeped out. Hurrying to the closet, he grabs his shoes and the bag with all the dope in it. As usual, it has already been pre-measured and bagged, giving him the ability to take it and run if he ever has to, a plan he is extremely grateful for today. At this point, anything that expedites his departure is a plus.

Lastly, he pulls a pair of socks from the dresser and shoves them inside his shoes. He tries to walk as normally as possible from the bed-room and through the living room, affecting an air of nonchalance in an effort to convince himself he isn't frightened. He snags the trash bag with his other hand and immediately exits through the kitchen. Despite his jangling nerves, he feels fairly-good about how calmly he managed to pull that off. He makes a determined effort to ignore the sense of watching eyes that he's convinced are following him the whole time. He pauses to take one final look over his shoulder before resolutely slam-ming the door shut.

He jumps in his truck with a pounding heart and a need to put as much distance between himself and his house as fast as possible. It's going to take him a while to get everything done. Maybe by the time he comes back he won't have such a raging case of the willies and that feeling of being watched will be gone.

He doesn't stop to put on his socks and shoes until he is halfway down the street. As he's tying them, he decides to go straight to the nearest apartment complex. There is one a couple of streets over. They always have big dumpsters and there should be a lot of garbage from a bunch of different people. He figures it's as good a place as any to dump the trash bag. What's one more sack of trash among many?

When he arrives, he's pleased to find the dumpster is inside of a big trash enclosure and apparently, people make a habit of discarding large items there, as witnessed by a broken bookcase and nightstand piled off to one side. "Sweet, that'll save me a trip to the dump tomorrow since it all goes to the same place anyway."

He hurriedly offloads the mattress, wedging it between the dumpster and the wall, and gives it a kick for good measure. "Fuck you Marco, it's done." After tossing the trash bag in the container, he hops back in his truck and heads for the store to purchase a new mattress.

As he pulls away, a ragged man and an unkempt woman break away from the shadows where they had been hiding, and eagerly begin rummaging through the trash. Finding and rejecting the urine-soaked sheets, they are thrilled when they examine the relatively new mattress. They've hit the jackpot. Together they pull it out and awkwardly load it on top of their two overflowing shopping carts, taking the time to balance it carefully to keep it from falling off. As they companionably roll away side by side down the street with their prize, they grin at each other. They will sleep comfortably tonight, sheets or no sheets.

It's already 7:50 and Sears is closing at 9:00. He's cutting it close. An hour and forty minutes later he pulls back in his side drive and backs up to the door. Struggling to haul the new (and rather expensive—fuck you very much Marco) mattress into the house, he uses his elbow to flip on lights as he goes and leaves it leaning against the living room wall while he goes back out to retrieve the bags containing the new sheets and comforter.

The sheets and comforter don't look anything like the old ones, because who the hell knew where Cara had gotten them. However, it's the most he's willing to do at this point. The sheets go straight into the washer as instructed. "There ya go Marco," Tony says while dumping in detergent, "I hope this is good enough 'cause I'm done with this shit."

After shoving all the trash from the packages of sheets into the garbage can, Tony decides he could use a drink and another smoke. He pulls a Corona out of the fridge and downs half of it all at once, then lights up, all the while watching the bedroom door. He still has a raging case of the heebie-jeebies, but that's probably normal since he's never killed anyone before. Hopefully it's just temporary.

He nervously wipes beer off his upper lip and struggles to get his anxiety under control. It's going to be a long night; he has a lot of shit to move and Marco wants it done immediately. Figuring a little pick-me-up won't hurt the cause any, he chops up a small rock and lays out a couple of lines on the counter. He would prefer to smoke it, but his pipe is in the bedroom and he can't force himself to go back in there right now.

He feels re-energized after snorting it; more focused and clear-headed. This is going to be no problem he thinks. It's Friday night, party night. I can move this shit easy. With that happy thought, he heads back out the door to check one more thing off Marco's "to do" list.

RACHEL

The rest of the day crawls by stretching into eternity. She can't manage to find anything to focus on and instead wanders aimlessly through the house and back yard randomly picking things up and putting them down again, while a continuous trail of tears runs down her face. She can't turn off the sound track in her head either. Over and over it plays; Tony's panicked, "I fucked up, Marco," only to be followed by the thud of Cara's body being dropped on the kitchen floor. It's like the sound of flies buzzing around a huge pile of shit and is gradually driving her insane.

She finally decides that enough is enough, and sets out to do whatever it takes to numb the pain and stop the noise in her brain. Thankfully, Marco always keeps a healthy stash of excellent weed and is not stingy about sharing it. She usually only smokes it when she's with him, but today is most definitely an exception to the norm.

She proceeds to roll herself a joint as big as her little finger and intends to smoke it down to a roach. After getting three Heinekens out of the fridge and turning the stereo to the local classic rock station, KLOS, she cranks up the sound of Rush. She plops down in Marco's favorite chair, a brand new black leather massage chair (which cost him $3,000 and he is damn proud of it), and fires up her doobie. Toking long and hard, she concentrates on holding it in and not coughing it out. If she is going to do this, she's going to do it right.

Thirty minutes later, the roach lies in the ashtray and all the Heinies are gone. Rachel stares glassily at her and Cara's cheerleading picture from the activities section in her senior yearbook. She feels numb from her head to her toes and plans to stay that way for the rest of her life if that's what it takes. She no longer feels like crying; in fact, she feels virtually nothing. Except, she needs to pee very badly; beer always does that to her.

"Bladder the size of a walnut," she mumbles, and when she tries to stand up, tumbles to her knees, dumping the yearbook to the floor. "Whoa, I'm shit-faced," she says laughing at herself. "Good."

After retrieving the yearbook and several failed attempts to get back on her feet, she finally manages to stumble/lurch her way in to the bathroom and pees for what feels like hours. "Oh man, that feels awesome," she sighs. After flushing and giving her hands a token pass under the faucet, she staggers her way to the bed where she crashes down face first. Clutching Cara's picture to her chest, her last thought before passing out is, I wonder where they're taking my poor Cara.

As Rachel lies sleeping, the sun continues its slow journey across the sky and shadows creep in to cover her with a soft blanket of darkness. The day draws to a close. Marco is coming home.

MARCO

He finally pulls in to his driveway, and sits for a few minutes thinking about what a shit storm this whole thing is. He thinks he's done a decent job of dealing with the immediate crisis, but isn't sure about Tony's ability to follow through on everything that still needs to be done. But whatever, worrying about it isn't going to change anything. He's done dealing with Tony's shit for today. He's had enough.

He wants nothing more than a hot shower, food, a glass of wine and some time with Rachel in the hot tub, in that order. He picks up his bottle of wine and Rachel's favorite champagne he'd bought on the way back to the house. As he gets out of the car, he steps on a rock and it hurts like hell. Now he's pissed about taking off his muddy shoes at Tony's place. He thought keeping the mud out of his car was a good idea, but now he's regretting that decision.

He sets the car alarm and limps up the walkway only to realize that Rachel hasn't turned on the porch light for him. That isn't like her. He opens the door and not a single light is on inside the house either. The smell of weed is intense, immediately putting him on alert.

He turns on the living room light and sees two Heineken bottles lying on the carpet and one on the coffee table. Something is wrong. He cautiously scans the rest of the living room, then makes his way quietly to the kitchen. He sets the bottles down, and pulls a gun from the top shelf of the cabinet, thumbs off the safety, and chambers a round before heading to the bedroom. Rachel is lying across the bed on her stomach, her arms flung out above her head, out cold and snoring lightly. A book lies open beneath one of her hands. Moving quietly so as not to wake her, he leans over to see what it is. To his surprise, it's the cheerleading

48

section in her yearbook. He lets out a breath he didn't realize he's been holding, puts the safety back on and considers the situation.

Things begin clicking into place. Thinking back to the events of the afternoon, he zeros in on the panicked call from Tony. It didn't clearly register with him at the time, but now he realizes Rachel must have been listening. During the call, he'd heard an odd sound on the line, a kind of clatter, but was so focused on dealing with Tony and his bullshit that he hadn't processed it. Now it all makes sense; the weed, the beer, everything. This is not normal behavior for Rachel. In fact, it is so far away from normal she might as well have hung up a big flashing sign saying I know.

He continues to stare at her while formulating a plan. He finally decides to be cool for a bit and see how she plays it. If she owns up to it and comes to him for comfort and support, then maybe they can work this out. If not...well, there's no sense in panicking and jumping the gun.

In the meantime, he feels nasty and is in serious need of a hot shower and shave. If she's still asleep when he's done, he'll wake her up and they can continue with their evening as planned. However, he'll be watching her closely. You can bet on that.

RACHEL

What time is it? Her neck feels horribly stiff, and her tongue like a dried-out piece of leather. Dang, smoking weed gave her terrible cottonmouth. She rolls stiffly over on her back and lays that way for a little while letting her eyes play across the ceiling and fantasizing about a cold bottle of Dasani. Finally accepting that the water won't come to her, she tries to work up the energy to make the trek into the kitchen. She can hear the shower running in the bathroom and realizes Marco is home. She bolts upright. Oh, crap, did she clean everything up?

That thought gets her up and moving in a hurry, though her head feels incredibly fuzzy, like she is still half-asleep. She grabs the yearbook and stumbles her way into the living room. The beer bottles are gone, but the roach is still in the ashtray. She can't remember if she picked them up and guesses it doesn't matter at this point because the smell of weed is strong, and she's convinced Marco wouldn't have missed the smell or the roach either.

All righty then, what are you going to tell him you were up to? He's probably not going to accept the idea that you just had a sudden urge to party all by yourself. Think Rachel.

Unfortunately, nothing comes to mind. Shoving the book back in its place on the bookcase, she continues to make her way to the kitchen. She opens the fridge and snags a bottle of water, then stands there with the door open downing half of it all at once.

"Oh, my God, that's better," she gasps, and finishes off the rest with a few more swallows.

THE WAYSTATION

Now that her tongue is no longer stuck to the roof of her mouth, maybe she can figure a way out of this mess. She wipes her lips with the back of her hand and takes another bottle before closing the door.

The sound of the shower has stopped and Rachel knows she has only moments to come up with a story. Though she is still drawing a blank, she hurries back to the bedroom hoping for inspiration. Perching on the edge of the bed, she continues to sip from her bottle, watching the bathroom door anxiously and waiting for Marco to emerge. She wills herself not to think about Cara because she will only start crying again and that is the last thing she needs right now. How would she explain it to Marco anyway? Instead, she agonizes over what he is going to say to her. Will he seem any different after what he's done? He helped to dispose of her best friend's body, how could he not be different? How can she not act differently?

The door opens and Marco exits in a cloud of steam, smelling of soap and coconut scented shampoo. He has a towel slung low around his hips the way he always does, knowing he looks good naked. Gazing at her with his incredibly beautiful eyes, he gives her a slow smile full of promise, which has never failed to make her weak in the knees until today.

"Hey babe," he purrs. "How're you feeling? Did you have yourself a little party while I was gone?"

Rachel manages to put on a sheepish expression and smiles back at him making an effort to act contrite, yet still unconcerned at the same time. "No, not exactly. Todd showed up, and, well, you know how that goes." Yes. Now that is a story she can work with.

Her brother, Todd, is a bit of a leach. Holding down a job has never been a top priority for him and he makes a habit out of dropping by the houses of friends and family members who might have the means to provide a little herbal and/or liquid entertainment. He isn't a bad guy, just a major underachiever and hopeless pothead. The possibility that he had stopped by to mooch a little weed and beer was totally believable.

"He needed to borrow a little money and then he hung out for a while. You know, same ole, same ole."

Marco flashes his breathtaking grin at her, and chuckles, "Yeah, I kind of figured it was something like that. It's not usually your style to party all alone." That startles her since she'd had that exact same thought only a minute ago. He reaches out and strokes her hair, running his thumb across her lips. "Are you still up for our plans tonight or did he burn you out?"

"Of course, I've been looking forward to it all day. Besides, I had a nice little nap. I'm good to go." She forces herself to gaze at him sweetly, "Are we calling Chang's for takeout?"

"Sure babe, whatever you want."

As Marco heads for the dresser to get some shorts, Rachel could swear the smile fades from his face and is replaced by an expression of doubt, but when he turns around, it's back in place and he has a twinkle in his eyes.

TONY

Three days have come and gone since Cara's death and he's starting to lose it. He easily sold most of his supply to random people within about four hours of hitting the street Friday night. He held some aside for his personal use and passed the remainder of it on to his street slingers knowing it wouldn't take them long to get rid of it. Speed on a Friday night was always a hot commodity since everybody was up for a party. Normally he would have held some back for a select group of people he usually deals directly to because the profit is so much greater, however, he hadn't been willing to stress over that and instead opted for the quickest method of disposal.

Marco is leaving him to his own devices since he turned over his share of the sales and confirmed all possible evidence of Cara's murder is disposed of according to his instructions (well, relatively, but Marco doesn't need to know the details). In fact, Marco has straight up told him he doesn't want to talk to him or see him until things, "Cool way the fuck down."

Luckily, no one has called looking for Cara yet. He knows, because he's checked her cell phone. But it's only a matter of time before she's missed. She's supposed to go back to work tomorrow. Her supervisor will probably call to find out where she is, then the lying will begin.

But that's the least of his concerns at-the-moment. What's worrying him right now and making him paranoid are the shadows. Each time he goes into the bedroom there are shadows where shadows shouldn't be, even during the day. It's getting to the point where he's terrified simply being in the room. He's finding he can't even breathe very well in there.

These days he sleeps in the living room (what little bit of sleep he gets) on the new mattress so he can keep an eye on the bedroom door, and showers in the second bathroom. He can't even bear to leave the bedroom door open because it's like looking at a large, accusing eye; one that is always trying to lure him in. He swears there is movement in there and he often hears stealthy, slithery sounds coming from behind the closed door.

His appearance is deteriorating at a rapid pace since he hasn't bothered to shave for the last five days. His beard grows fast, and consequently he's starting to take on the appearance of a homeless man. It itches constantly. He nervously picks at it and spends hours in the bathroom in front of the mirror trying to dig out ingrown hairs. Even though he's succeeded in tearing a sizable hole in his right cheek and is beginning the same process on his left, he is completely oblivious to it. He's been using little wads of toilet paper to stop the bleeding, and their bloody remains are scattered all over the bathroom floor, though a few managed to make it into the trash can by sheer chance.

He's currently sitting on the couch smoking and staring at the bedroom door thinking furiously, picking at his chin and scratching his neck. He needs to get some clean clothes out of there, but is having trouble summoning the courage to even open the door, let alone walk in. Finally working up the nerve, he picks up the ashtray from the floor, grinds out his cigarette and stands. He can't seem to make his feet move and tries to give himself a pep talk. Just fucking do it, he thinks. Don't be such a pussy. Just run in, grab the clothes, and run out. Seriously, how fucking hard can that be?

He stands in front of the door, forces his hand to grab the handle and braces himself. Taking a big breath, he pushes the door open, runs in, yanks open the closet door and grabs an armful of clothes, pulling some off the hangers in the process. Throwing them out in the hall, he runs back and wrenches two drawers out of the dresser that contain his socks, underwear and some t-shirts, and sprints back out. He drops the drawers on the floor and in one continuous movement, snatches the door knob and slams the door shut. The whole operation can't have taken more than thirty seconds but felt like an eternity, as if he had been moving under water or in slow motion. He's convinced he heard voices whispering his name and calling to him the entire time he was in there.

THE WAYSTATION

His heart pounds and rivers of sweat run down his face and chest as he stands in the hallway and tries to get his breath back. Once he's breathing normally again and his heart is beating in a relatively ordinary fashion, he begins to gather up his clothes and put them away in the extra bedroom. The voices continue to whisper his name, but he refuses to listen.

When that's all done, he cranks up the stereo in the living room and settles in a chair to resume his watch on the door. The music manages to drown out the voices, but Tony can't drown out his imagination or his thoughts of what dwells in the darkness behind that door making those terrible sounds. He downs another beer, fires up a joint, and leans back focusing on the sound of guitars, refusing to think about it anymore.

RACHEL

Cara has been dead for five miserable days now. The police have been looking for her for only two days, and so far, haven't managed to come up with any leads. Of course, she doesn't think they're trying all that hard. Cara is an adult, and without any evidence of foul play, there is nothing they can do. Apparently, they accept Tony's explanation that she's taken off and will come back when she's good and ready. However, Rachel's having a tough time believing they accepted his story this easily. If they took the time to investigate, they would find out that type of behavior is totally out of character for her.

Rachel sits in the big, soft, dark brown leather chair she always chooses at the Starbucks on Ontario Avenue. Since it's only a couple of miles from their house, she usually comes here. She likes this corner because it's shadowy and feels a little bit sheltered from the hustle and bustle of the rest of the coffee house. Here she can attempt to pull herself together in relative privacy. Running her fingers across the arm of the chair, she notices that it has become worn in places from so many other fingers brushing over it day after day, fingers that belong to people whose lives probably haven't turned to shit. The cushion is nice and broken in too, and she can feel the dent forming itself perfectly around her butt in a comfortable embrace.

Cradling her cup of coffee, she takes her time inhaling the aroma, enjoying the feel of the warmth on her hands. A good cup of Starbucks always makes her feel better, and she savors the feeling of normality, even if it's only for a minute. Each day has been harder than the day before. She misses Cara so much it's a physical pain, and she thinks about her almost every minute of the day. The tears begin to well up again and she makes herself breathe slowly, trying to consciously relax so she can remain calm. But if she's honest, nothing in her life is ever going to feel normal again. Everything has been forever changed.

Cara's mom reported her missing two days ago, after trying to reach her to schedule a dinner for her dad's birthday. When she called Rachel to see if she had any idea where she was, it had taken everything in Rachel to claim ignorance and not burst into hysterics and confess what she knew. Since then she's been continuously beating herself up for not having the courage to speak up; for waiting for someone else to discover the truth. She's such a chicken. All it would take is a phone call, but she can't do it. She's terrified that Marco will do something to her, or his boss will. The man he works for likes his business to be kept very private. He wouldn't welcome trouble in the form a murder investigation.

She could call the police and leave an anonymous tip, even though she doesn't know what she could safely say. Maybe she could suggest they take a closer look at Tony. Tell them he's a freaking meth-head psycho and can't be trusted. But if she does that, won't she be complicit as well? After all, she knew the truth and hid it from the police. That thought makes her feel like a horrible person. How can she be more worried about herself than she is in getting justice for Cara?

Rachel vigorously shuts out that accusing voice and instead chooses to observe all the different groups of people scattered throughout the coffee shop…students and business people with their laptops, caffeine junkies, and teenagers huddled together sipping their Frappuccinos with extra caramel and whip cream, trying to play it cool. These are people who don't seem to have a care in the world. She feels jealous. She wishes her life was a bad dream.

She rolls her shoulders and neck trying to ease the tension, and closes her eyes letting her thoughts wander aimlessly. She rests her head against the back of the chair, and finds her mind fixating on the dream she had last night. It was so intense—so real. She dreamed she'd murdered a woman; she strangled her. She had no idea why. That was bad enough, but then it got even stranger when she realized the woman could be her twin and she was in her own bedroom. What did that mean?

In the dream, she was paralyzed with terror; unable to do anything but stare at the dead woman. She finally managed to work up her courage, and dragged the body down a set of stairs, bumping it on each step. She shoved it in the trunk of her car and drove out to a deserted part of the highway between Baker and the border of Nevada. Then she left the freeway and traveled down one of the long dirt roads she could see off in the distance. It was the perfect place to dump a body. She figured between the animals, the bugs and the heat, there wouldn't be much evidence left for the cops to work with once someone eventually stumbled on it. They wouldn't be able to tie the murder to her. When she got to a place that seemed safe, she pulled the body out of the trunk and dropped it on the ground. She slammed the trunk closed and rushed to get in her car, but then realized she hadn't driven out to the desert at all. Instead, she had wound up in a run-down neighborhood, and was dumping the body in a vacant lot. That's when she realized there were a couple of guys standing next to their car watching her.

She woke up covered in sweat thinking, what the hell was that all about? There was a phrase that kept rolling around in her brain – "the body of death." The body of death, and it wore her face. She had no idea where that came from or what it even meant, but needed to find out. Since going back to sleep was totally out of the question anyway, she checked to make sure Marco was still asleep and quietly slipped out of bed closing the bedroom door softly behind her. She went to her computer to see if she could find anything on the internet about it and finally found it in a quote from the Book of Romans.

"Oh, wretched man that I am! Who shall deliver me from the body of this death?" Romans 7:24

It turned out that it was part of a letter written by the apostle Paul, referring to a legal situation regarding murder and one of the most severe punishments of Roman law. What it literally meant was that the body of the murder victim was tied to the murderer, face-to-face, hand-to-hand, toe-to-toe. The condemned man was sentenced to go through the remainder of his life coupled to this decaying corpse. The smell would grow worse every day, causing him to become even more isolated because no one would be able to stand being near him. There would be no way to escape from the reminder of his crime. The murderer couldn't avoid continuously breathing in the reek of the rotting body. He would probably lose his mind and certainly die from exposure to the bacteria.

Talk about letting the punishment fit the crime. It made her head reel to think of all that gross decomposing flesh pressed up against hers. The smell would be horrible and the germs would be everywhere. Her skin crawled at the notion.

She continued to surf around the internet for a while and eventually found out that Paul used this particular illustration to address the issue of sin. He tried to live a sinless life, however, the harder he tried, the more frustrating his failure became. Though he was eventually made a saint, even he failed at remaining sinless. That caused her to question her own chances of salvation.

Damn, what chance do I have? My life, my sins are much worse than anything he could have done. I was indirectly responsible for Cara's death because I didn't do enough to help her. Now I'm lying to cover up the truth. How can God ever forgive me for that? I can't even forgive myself.

She suddenly had an epiphany.

I can't hide from or cover up my sin. That's why I was dumping the body in plain sight. That's what it meant. It's obvious—you can run but you can't hide. I think my lifestyle is catching up to me. No, I know it is.

Her breath caught in her throat. This was a warning from God, or her subconscious, whatever she wanted to call it. She didn't want to get all overly-spiritual and weird like those bizarre, big-haired TBN people. "That's all I need," she murmured, "to go all Tammy Faye and start bawling my head off with long runny streaks of mascara pouring down my face." She gave a little hiccup of a laugh and felt better. Darting a quick peek at the bedroom door to be sure it was closed, she went back to her research.

Rachel opens her eyes, shakes the memory away, and studies her coffee cup. This is her first opportunity to truly reflect on the dream and what she's learned. She's always believed in God in some remote man-on-the-mountain or Santa Claus-like kind of way, but ever since Cara's murder, she's actively begun to search Him out.

Lately, she finds herself spending time searching for answers more and more in the Bible and the teachings of pastors like Max Lucado and Greg Laurie because they're easy for her to understand and explain things in plain English. They don't come across like some preachers who make you feel crappy about yourself or feel like you're a horrible person, destined to go straight to hell. She's keeping all that hidden from Marco of course, since he won't understand her sudden interest, or maybe he will and the consequences of that might be even worse. Fear stabs at her heart, and her eyes began tearing up again. She scolds herself for being such a baby.

She rubs her eyes realizing she has a dull headache. She needs to get some decent sleep for a change instead of the alcohol or drug-induced comas she's been resorting to lately.

She drains her cup, sets it down on the table, and once again gazes around the Starbucks thinking her life has been so freaking hard ever since...well, ever since that horrible phone call. Then seeing Cara lying there dead and realizing she was gone; that she would never talk to her again. She fights back the tears and bites at her lower lip until she's able to get her emotions under control.

After getting a fresh cup of her favorite, skinny hazelnut with no foam, she sinks back in the chair and takes the lid off blowing across the top. No way is she taking a big gulp yet. She's made that mistake before and it's always much hotter than she expects. She inevitably winds up burning her mouth and tongue. She tentatively takes a small sip, then spends a few moments listening to the sound of Nora Jones floating from speakers mounted in strategic places on the ceiling. Though she fights it, tears begin to trail down her face. What if she's next? She hurriedly wipes the wetness from her cheeks. The last thing she needs is for someone to see her crying and get curious. Noticing that her hand is trembling, she cautiously sets her cup down and carefully replaces the lid, clasping both hands in her lap and locking her fingers together. She studies the room to make sure nobody is taking undue notice of her case of nerves. She feels paranoid. How did she get here?

Truthfully, that isn't too hard to pinpoint. It all goes back to the first day they met Marco and Tony. She and Cara were both attending

THE WAYSTATION

Riverside Community College a couple of days a week, and had a plan to one day run their own business. There was a lively ongoing debate as to whether it would be a clothing shop that served decent wine, or a pastry/coffee bar (which would be way cooler than Starbucks, of course). Either way, they intended to do it together just like everything else they'd done in their lives.

She and Cara were hosting at Claim Jumper four days a week and working at the college bookstore two days a week. The money wasn't great, but it paid the bills and was a lot of fun. There were always tons of guys to flirt with and they ate for free on the days they worked at the restaurant. They certainly couldn't complain about that because there were always plenty of leftovers. That kept their food bill way down, and since they shared a small apartment, they managed fairly well.

Things were going great until that fateful night Marco and Tony walked in the restaurant. They came in to watch the Angels' baseball game in the bar and started flirting with her and Cara the minute they strutted through the door. Cara (naturally) fell in love with Tony immediately because he was such a hunk. She'd always been that way, a sucker for guys who were totally buff, and Tony fit that description to a T.

Rachel blinked away her tears and nervously checked the room again to make sure no one noticed. She was still having trouble accepting the fact Cara was gone and that they'd never share anymore of those "girl" moments again. It seemed to sneak up on her constantly, making her feel like she was being slapped in the head repeatedly with a large fluffy pillow, taking her breath away and causing her mind to swim.

I wasn't any better. I was convinced Marco was the most beautiful guy I'd ever seen.

He was obviously Latino. He had thick, jet-black wavy hair that fell in a curl across his forehead and into his eyes in an adorable way. He was 6' 3" which made Rachel feel petite even though she stood 5' 9" in her bare feet. She loved that he was taller than her even when she was wearing heels. He had a beautiful dark tan which reminded her of someone who spent his days soaking up the sun on an exotic beach. His most attractive feature by far was his eyes. They were the color of caramel shot through with dark blue and had a rich green ring on the outside.

61

They were quite startling when paired with his deeply bronzed skin and dark hair. She'd been a goner the moment she laid eyes on him and she never looked back.

She should have remembered Todd's favorite saying, "Beauty is only skin deep, but ugly goes all the way to the bone." Lame, but true. He'd taken to quoting that because he tended to date so many beautiful (but psycho) girls and was convinced they gave up the sane part of their soul in exchange for their looks. Todd sure had that right; Marco turned out to be quite ugly inside. What kind of person would help hide a murder, especially the murder of his girlfriend's best friend?

When the game ended, Marco and Tony lingered at the front of the restaurant for the last thirty minutes of their shift and then they all went back to Marco's place to party and hang out in the hot tub. After that night, things kind of took off. Before they knew it, Cara was practically living with Tony and since Rachel was staying with Marco most of the time anyway, they let their apartment go. Neither one could see spending money on rent when they didn't have to. It made perfect sense at the time.

They gradually started working for Marco to make extra money. It was kind of scary at first, but exciting at the same time. They'd always been such good girls; it felt exhilarating to do something so amoral. Working for Marco was a breeze, and they were earning great money simply by picking up and making deliveries. It was all too easy. Cara kept working at Claim Jumper, but dropped her classes. Rachel was making such great money working for Marco she quit the restaurant, that way she could focus solely on school.

She chews on her full lower lip for a bit, pondering the stupid choices she'd made. Meth. They were all making a good living from selling lots and lots of meth. Why had it never occurred to her how dangerous this life could be? Why couldn't either of them see it? It was all about the money. What kind of person does that make her?

She picks dispiritedly at the lid of her coffee cup reflecting on how fast things progressed. They were couriers. They picked stuff up and dropped money off. That was it. She and Cara didn't get any deeper; no slinging on the street, manufacturing, or anything like that. They didn't have anything to do with guys higher up the chain because that was straight up scary and Marco didn't allow it anyway. But because they were so far removed from the ugly side of the business, it was easy to convince themselves it wasn't so bad. They were living a life that was cool and it came with lots of benefits.

It was all deceptively simple. They were free to make their own hours and the money was good, very good. They could afford to buy great clothes and shoes or whatever they wanted without giving it a second thought. She owned four pairs of Jimmy Choos. She was convinced it didn't get any better than that. They could hang out in all the hot clubs and never had to wait in line because people knew who they were. Everyone wanted to get close to them. They were in; they had made it to the big time.

If she had been honest with herself, she would have known it was only a matter of time until something bad happened. To someone on the outside, Cara's murder would simply look like a business casualty. That's what happens in the drug world, right?

But Rachel knows as long as she can keep her mouth shut, no one will ever know the truth. Tony killed her because he is a violent, unstable, steroid-fueled tweaker. Tony murdered Cara and Rachel knows it. How long will it be until Marco figures that out? How long will it be before Marco or Tony decide she is an unnecessary loose end? She shudders, imagining her body dumped in a ditch.

She's scared; very, very scared.

BILL & JOSH JAYSON

Father and son have been kicked out of the house for the day, and that's fine with them. It's a beautiful Saturday morning and the temperature is finally above 72 degrees with a clear and cloudless sky. Now that the rains are gone, Bill's wife, Lee, has decided it's time to shampoo carpets and clean out the winter funk that always tends to build up whenever the windows stay closed for too long. She told him in no uncertain terms that she has no intention of trying to do it with two "boys" and two dogs under foot.

With instructions to find something to do outdoors for the day, they plan on not coming home for at least six hours, though Lee said seven or eight would be better. Neither Bill nor Josh considers this to be a problem, and in fact, count it a blessing. She is no fun to be with when she gets in one of these spring cleaning frenzies, and husband and son are both grateful for the excuse to stay out of the way and off her radar. There is no telling what she would have them doing if they stayed. It's very possible she would have them moving furniture and cleaning out the garage. Yep, getting lost for the day is a much better proposition.

They're on the road headed for Lytle Creek. It was a favorite hiking spot of Bill's when he was young, and he likes the idea of sharing it with his 15-year-old son, Josh, and their dogs, Ruthie and Ozzie. The plan is to let the dogs run around in the hills for a bit and burn off some energy, then head down to the creek where they can splash about in the water until they are good and tired.

They brought along a cooler full of water and soda, chips, sandwiches, and to top it all off, Reese's peanut butter cups. There is nothing better than a half frozen peanut butter cup. Bill is feeling proud of himself for remembering to bring dog jerky, bones and peanut butter flavored treats for the dogs (this keeps them from drooling all over you when you're enjoying your own treat). It has all the makings of a perfect day.

Once they leave the highway, nature takes over. It only takes them about ten minutes to get through the few houses that are in this area, and soon they're traveling the road which runs adjacent to Lytle Creek. There is a great view of the water off to their left. Ozzie and Ruthie can smell it and dash back and forth in the backseat of the Tahoe, heads hanging out the windows, tongues flapping happily in the wind, slobber flying.

"Hey Dad, is that the creek down there?" Josh asks.

"Yep, that's it."

"It looks way too big to be called a creek. It's more like an actual river."

"That's because of all the runoff from the rain. The water isn't usually that wide. Don't worry though, there'll be plenty of areas we can hike around in down there. Trust me, it'll be great."

"Sweet. The dogs are gonna have a blast."

Eventually Bill turns on to a dirt road and rolls to a stop in front of an old beat up gate with an equally battered brown sign that reads:

NO TARGET SHOOTING
STREET LEGAL VEHICLES ONLY
NO VEHS OFF ROADS
PENSTOCK to 2N79

"Wow, that's a really old sign."

"I can't believe this road is still open. We used to come up here all the time when I was your age. For all I know that's the same sign from when I was a kid. It sure looks like it." Bill chuckles. "This area's great because there are access roads all through here that lead to those huge electrical towers you see way off in the distance. You can't get lost. If you get turned around, just follow almost any road downhill and you'll get back to this main road. The best part is you can be up here all day and never see another person."

Bumping their way through the gate, they travel up the hill until they find a wide place in the road where it seems safe to park and they all pile out. Ozzie, a big 110 lb. blockhead, chocolate lab practically tears the door off the hinges in his excitement to get out of the car with Ruthie hot on his tail. He and Ruthie, a lovable, brindle colored pit-bull, lab, terrier mix, bound off up the road while Bill and Josh try to keep up. Since Ozzie feels the need to stop and pee on every bush along the way, they can travel at nothing faster than a brisk walk. Ruthie, distracted by every butterfly and bee that buzzes by, manages to stay within shouting distance as well.

Eventually they come to a side road branching off to the right, and the dogs take off at a run with Josh close behind. Bill chooses to follow at a more leisurely pace, happy that Josh is staying with the dogs. It's dense through here, and he's concerned about losing Ozzie and Ruthie in the brush. Josh has already taken to calling him old man and teasing about his inability to keep up. This will simply give him another excuse to do more of the same.

Bill takes his time following, enjoying the sound of the birds and the light wind rustling in the trees and bushes. He can see a lot of areas where water from the rains has carved channels in the road, and he's grateful it has dried up enough that they won't be tracking copious amounts of mud home. That would set Lee off in the worst way. It will probably still get dirty inside the car, but since he's planning on taking it to the car wash tomorrow anyway, it's not a big deal.

Suddenly Josh is yelling at the top of his lungs, "Dad, holy crap, Dad, get up here. Oh, man this smells seriously gross. It's disgusting. Ozzie stop. Ruthie, come on stop, please. Daaad help!"

Bill immediately kicks it in to high gear and runs up the last of the road as fast as he can, arriving huffing and puffing to find Josh struggling with both of the dogs. Neither of them is cooperating with his attempt to rein them in, and they repeatedly escape. Each time they break free, they frantically start digging away in the dirt under some trees. It's an area where portions appear to have been washed away in the recent rain. As soon as Bill gets close enough, the stench hits him. Something is dead up here and the dogs are determined to get at it.

"Josh, hold them. They're going to be covered in that stink and we'll never get the smell out of the car."

THE WAYSTATION

"I'm trying, Dad, but they won't stop. Ruthie, Ozzie, come on, please, stop it. Crap!"

Bill frantically clutches at Ozzie's collar with both hands and tries to pull him back. While Ozzie, in a move worthy of a WWF champ, jerks his head and simultaneously twists, slipping right out of the collar. He continues his frantic digging, leaving Bill standing there holding an empty collar and feeling like an idiot.

Josh grasps Ruthie's harness at the neck and back and pulls her away. Unfortunately, his feet get tangled and he sits down abruptly pulling her on top of him. Ruthie continues to struggle and whine, clawing up his stomach and legs in the process. Bill seizes Ozzie again, this time by his harness, and pulls with everything he has, finally dragging him out from under the trees.

"Get the car," Bill orders digging the car keys out of his pocket and throwing them to Josh.

"But I only have a permit."

"Not an issue right now dude, just go get the car. I've got to hold Ozzie and he's too big for me to drag. Hurry."

Josh struggles to his feet, and fervently wishing he had her leash, drags Ruthie down the dirt road while she cries and fights him the whole way. After a few minutes, Bill finally hears the car barreling up the road and breathes a sigh of relief. Ozzie is wearing him out and he isn't sure how much longer he can hold him. Josh skids to a stop not three feet from where Bill stands, throwing a cloud of wet dirt and pebbles all over him. Ruthie is in the back seat barking and running wildly from window to window.

"Damn, Joshua, are you trying to kill me?" Bill wheezes, brushing a hand over his face to remove the grit.

"You said to hurry," Josh answers through the open window, not even trying to hide the big grin on his face.

Bill rolls his eyes. "Get some of that dog jerky out of my backpack. I think I can get Ozzie in the car if I bribe him."

Taking a second to put his window half way up to keep Ruthie from jumping out, he grabs the backpack from the floorboard and squeezes out of the car, shoving her back inside so he can get the door shut. She continues to paw and scratch, sticking her head out the window, whining continuously. Bill briefly worries about the scratches she's probably making on the door, knowing Lee will have kittens over it, then decides there's nothing he can do about it.

Josh digs through the backpack and hands his dad the jerky, immediately getting Ozzie's undivided attention. (Ozzie is passionate about food and will follow you anywhere if he thinks there is a treat to be had.) From there it's easy. He simply walks to the car, throws a handful of jerky in the back seat and Ozzie jumps right in. Bill tosses Ozzie's collar in behind him, slams the door shut and leans against the car in relief, wiping his forehead and winking at Josh as Ruthie enthusiastically licks his ear. Bill affectionately rubs her head and moves away from the car while absently rubbing his ear dry.

Josh runs over, leaps in the air and high-fives him. "That was awesome, Dad." He's riding high from his dash down the road to get the car and his dramatic skid. The best part is, they still get to investigate that awful smell. This day is turning out to be way better than he'd hoped when they left this morning.

Knowing exactly where Josh's mind will be, Bill claps him on the shoulder and says, "Well, come on let's check it out, kiddo."

Now that the commotion has died down, Bill can hear the buzzing flies and secretly dreads what that portends. As they pull aside branches and large pieces of dead tree, the smell washes over them in a putrid wave. Bill immediately pulls his t-shirt up to cover his nose and Josh, wisely deciding that maybe his old man is smarter than he usually gives him credit for, follows suit.

"Are you sure you want to do this?" he asks his son.

"Are you serious?" Josh stares at him in wide-eyed astonishment, tossing another piece branch off to the side. "I gotta know what this is."

"Okay, I hope you're ready. It's going to be pretty nasty."

Together they remove the last big branch and toss it into the bushes. Josh pulls his cell phone out of his pocket and gets his camera ready, preparing to take what he hopes is going to be the ultimate gross-out picture of all time.

THE WAYSTATION

"This is totally going up on my Facebook page. Angel and Simon are going to freak out when they see it. Just let them try and top this one."

When they turn back, what greets them will stay with them for the rest of their lives. They aren't prepared for what they find; how can they be? The corner of a comforter peeks out of the edge of a hole that was created by runoff, and has been enlarged by the dogs. A decaying arm and long blonde hair are visible. Josh stares at his Dad with horror in his eyes. This is no dead deer or coyote. This is bad, very, very bad. He slowly puts his phone back in his pocket.

Coughing and gagging, Josh lurches away and falls to his knees losing the breakfast burrito he'd eaten that morning. He retches up egg, cheese and potatoes until his throat burns and nothing is left except bile. Spitting repeatedly, he tries to get the taste out of his mouth crying and whispering, "Oh shit, oh shit, oh shit."

Bill can't turn away. He's mesmerized by her discolored fingers and the delicate twisted silver band she wears on the middle one. Chipped pink fingernail polish decorates her nails. As he stares, a trail of ants march across the back of her hand, climbing laboriously over crumbs of dirt. Several flies land on her arm and begin their search for a good location to lay their eggs. The thought of the maggots that will find a rich food-source almost causes him to join Josh. Bitterness burns the back of his throat and nose as he determinedly swallows and forces the contents of his stomach back down. Finally breaking his paralysis, he seizes Josh by the arm and urgently pulls him away from the burial site.

"Josh, come on, don't touch anything else. This is a crime scene and we've screwed it up enough already. We need to call the police, now."

Together they stumble away from the body and clamber inside the car. Bill rolls up the windows and cranks the air to high, trying to blow away the stench that clings to them like a second skin. The dogs are going crazy, sniffing their hair and smelling their shirts. Josh holds his face in his hands crying unashamedly. Tears leak between his fingers. Ruthie, worried over his cries, anxiously attempts to lick away the drops trickling down his hands. All thoughts of Facebook and one-upping his friends are gone.

Bill quickly backs the car far away from the make-shift gravesite, then cracks open a coke and hands him the can. "Here, swish this around in your mouth and spit it out. It'll help."

Josh's hands are shaking badly. He spills more on his shirt than he gets in his mouth. When he finally manages to get a mouthful, he swishes and spits it out the window. Downing the remainder, he lets loose with a huge burp and prays that he doesn't puke any more.

After driving a little further down the road, Bill gets out his phone and keeps rolling while watching the bars. Once he finally has a decent signal he stops and dials 911, thanking God for reception. He despairs over the loss of this beautiful day that has turned out to be a nightmare, one he is afraid he and his son are unlikely ever to forget.

Truthfully, he would have been a whole lot happier if he had stayed at home and helped Lee move furniture, clean carpets, dig holes, pull weeds, whatever she wanted. Anything would have been better than this.

CARA
(AT THE WAYSTATION)

She lifts her face and lets the breeze blow through her hair. She never tires of the sound of the wind singing in the trees, and makes it a habit to sit here every evening and enjoy the night music. The previous afternoon, as the sun was barely kissing the horizon, a butterfly had flown in the window and landed in her lap. She was surprised at his courage and excited to show him their kinship. "See, look little guy, we're related," she said, pointing to a birthmark on her arm. It was in the shape of a butterfly, and she loved showing it off. To her complete amazement, he crawled up on her arm and settled near the birthmark, almost as if he were examining it. She sat perfectly still for several minutes while he slowly flapped his wings and communed with his flesh-covered cousin. He eventually tired of this and flew off in search of the real thing.

The memory brings a look of happiness to her face. She shifts a little on the window ledge to get a better angle, and continues with her project. It's only a little piece of her usual graffiti to let people know she's been here. It isn't in an obvious place, so it's unlikely it will ever be seen by anyone. But that doesn't matter to her. She still wants it to look pretty. She puts the final touches on the butterfly as Sarah begins to call from downstairs.

"Cara. Supper's ready."

"Coming," she answers with genuine enthusiasm. She hops off the window ledge and makes her way down the stairs as quickly as possible.

Being dead has not done a thing to dampen her appetite. If anything, it has increased it. Besides, Sarah is an amazing cook. Since she knows it will be time for her to move on soon, she plans to consume as many

71

of Sarah's meals as possible before it's time for her to leave. She likes it here, and absolutely loves Sarah and Samuel. But if she is this happy here, she can only imagine how wonderful heaven will be.

As she heads for the kitchen to help Sarah bring the dishes out to the table, she pats her belly and asks it, "Are you as hungry as me baby? I smell something good. Let's pig out."

TONY

He is unraveling, piece by piece. It's been two days since Cara's body was discovered (shitty piece of luck that was), and he hasn't slept in at least four. He's been doing crystal for so many days, sleep is the last thing he's capable of. Besides, every time he tries to close his eyes the demons come, and he doesn't want to see the demons anymore.

He hasn't showered since the day Marco called him to say they'd found her body, because he's afraid to let his guard down long enough to undress and get in the shower. He's convinced that something is living in the bedroom where Cara died, and it's out to get him, to get even. In fact, it's several somethings which whisper and call to him night and day.

Yesterday, in desperation, he put a padlock on the bedroom door and sealed all the edges with duct tape, especially at the top and along the carpet at the bottom. He has spent the better part of today doubling and tripling up on the duct tape, getting it exactly right. It now extends out at least two feet from the base and edges of the door, and on to the ceiling. Piles of empty cardboard rolls lay in a heap on the floor. He doesn't know if demons can go through walls, but he's made certain whatever is in there is not coming out through the door.

He's currently sitting in the living room eyeballing the door and waiting, for what he isn't sure. His hands hang between his knees, loosely gripping a 45 pistol he picked up from some crack-head a couple of months ago. Anything that manages to ooze out through the walls is going to be filled with holes. It might not stop it, but he's dammed if he's going down without a fight. Besides, the simple act of holding the gun in his hands makes him feel better. The weight of it is comforting.

He brought a cooler in the house three days ago, and has kept it sitting right next to his chair fully stocked with beer, that way he doesn't have to go in the kitchen whenever he needs another. This makes it possible for him to keep his eyes on the door at all times. He reaches in to take one, only to discover they are all gone. Slamming the lid down in disgust, he realizes he's going to have to go out and buy more. Leaving the house is definitely not what he wants to do. But what choice does he have? Watching for demons is thirsty work.

It's late, but Circle K will be open. He'll have to run down there and get back as quickly as possible. Things have remained quiet behind the door for the last couple of hours. Maybe they're sleeping. Do demons sleep? He's not sure, but just in case, he decides to make as little noise as possible when he leaves the house and maybe they'll be fooled into thinking he's still standing guard.

He reluctantly makes his way to the kitchen and begins pawing through all the assorted junk that has piled up on the counter until he finds his keys. With one last worried glance at the bedroom door to make sure it's secure, he heads out the back door, closing it behind him as quietly as he can.

ANNE & DANNY CAMPBELL

It has been a perfect day and an even more perfect night. The wedding was everything Anne dreamed it would be, if you didn't count the fact that they had to have it on a Monday night. But in the long run it didn't matter, and they'd saved a ton of money by doing it on a weeknight instead of on the weekend. Since money is tight, the cost savings is especially important to them. It made the sacrifice worthwhile.

Anne and Danny dated through all the ups and downs of high school and fell in love in college. In their junior year, Danny romantically proposed with champagne, chocolate dipped strawberries and the perfect ring in a hot air balloon floating high over California's Temecula Valley during a wine tasting weekend. (Anne gave him major brownie points for creativity and imagination on that one.) As excited as they both were, they agreed to delay the wedding until they graduated and landed decent jobs.

Two years and fourteen days later, not that she'd been counting, their dream was finally a reality and it was amazing. They would have preferred to take additional time and save up a little more money, but neither could wait any longer for their life together to begin.

Since Anne's parents were killed in a car accident her freshman year in college, her dad wasn't there to give her away or pay for the wedding. Consequently, the burden of the cost fell mostly on their shoulders. Her parents' life insurance was what sustained her through college but, unfortunately, it was mostly gone now. Thank goodness Danny's parents generously agreed to cover the cost of the flowers, the minister, the DJ, and invitations. That was a huge help and took a lot of the pressure off.

Anne sighs and gazes at Danny, her face glowing with contentment and happiness. They left the reception 45 minutes earlier in a shower of birdseed and shouts of good wishes from all their friends and family. Anne had insisted on birdseed because she read on a bridal blog that rice could hurt the birds. Besides, with birdseed, no one had to clean it up.

Now they are on their way to San Diego for a one night stay at the Hilton and then will board a cruise ship early the next morning for a five-day cruise to Mexico. It's all they're able to swing right now. Nevertheless, they made a promise to each other that they will make it a priority to save up for a real cruise; something that lasts at least two weeks and goes somewhere exotic.

Danny's mom and dad have been kind enough to pack up all the gifts in their own car and are taking them home (along with Anne's dress and Danny's tux) so they can open them at their leisure when they return. Knowing Evelyn, they'll come back to their apartment to find fresh flowers and a delicious dinner in the oven as well. Anne finds herself constantly rejoicing in the knowledge that she's married into such an awesome family. It makes the loss of her own family much easier to bear.

Danny winks at Anne and reaches over to pull a stray safflower seed from her hair before taking her hand in his. "What are you smiling about, Mrs. Campbell?" he asks, running his thumb gently back and forth across her knuckles.

"I'm smiling at you, Mr. Campbell, and thinking about how happy I am. I keep picturing your face when I walked down the aisle. The way you looked at me made me feel incredibly beautiful. I don't think I'll ever forget that look as long as I live."

Kissing her fingers, he croons, "Well, that's because you are beautiful, honey. I am a very blessed man to be able to call you my wife, and I promise to try and look at you like that every day."

"Thank you, and yes, you *are* blessed. Don't you forget it," she answers pertly kissing his fingers in return. Those are the final words she ever speaks.

TONY & KEVIN

The Circle K is less than two miles down the road. Tony plans to race there, buy two cases of Corona, and head home in record time. Hopefully he won't be gone long enough for the demons to get up to any trouble. He flies into the parking lot, and with a squeal of brakes throws the truck in park and jumps from the cab, not even bothering to turn off the engine. He crashes through the door of the convenience store like he has a fire to go to. Ignoring the startled expression on the clerk's face, he marches straight to the beer and picks up two cases.

Assholes should keep this stuff cold.

The clerk, Kevin, according to his name tag, is giving him the evil eye like he's been doing from the minute he charged through the door.

Tony growls, "You got a problem with me, man? You got something you want to say?"

Kevin appears to shrink into himself as he shakes his head and takes a slight step back from the counter. However, he keeps his finger pressed firmly to the police alarm button in case this guy gets out of hand. He learned long ago that nighttime tends to bring out the assholes just like the cockroaches that live in the muck behind the dumpster out back. It's best to be prepared, because you never know if things will suddenly escalate. Kevin has kids to feed and he isn't taking any chances with this guy. He seems way too unstable.

Nervously eyeballing the cameras located in various locations around the store, Kevin makes a concerted effort to follow the rules and do his job. He tentatively speaks up, "Um, sir, I'm not sure you should be buying that beer. There are laws that I have to follow and it could cost me my job if I sell alcohol to someone who is already intoxicated."

Tony marches over to the counter and slams the cases of beer down hard enough to make the rack of sexual enhancement vitamins (what he and Marco jokingly call boner builders) fall over. Getting in the clerk's face, he snatches him by his shirt and spits out, "Are you kidding me man? I'm having a bad fucking day and I don't need your bullshit." Tony's eyes are practically spinning in his head and the veins in his temples and forehead pulse in time with his breathing.

Kevin shakes his head, wisely deciding that silence is probably not only his best course of action, but also the safest.

"Yeah, I thought so you little shit. Just keep your fucking mouth shut." Releasing the clerk's shirt, Tony gives him a shove and throws a wad of bills across the counter, then picks up the cases, angrily shouldering his way out the door.

As he's loading the beer in his truck, he briefly considers going back inside and beating the shit out of that minimum wage asshole. Although it would give him a tremendous amount of satisfaction, and his fingers itch in anticipation, he ultimately decides he can't spare another minute away from his demon watch. Demonic activity trumps asshole correction every time. Maybe he can come back later after the demons are gone and give him a little attitude adjustment.

Once Tony is out the door, Kevin gathers the bills from the floor and places them neatly in the register. As soon as he sees Tony get in his truck, he pulls out his cell to call his buddy. "Mark, man you are *not* going to believe this guy who was just in here. He was freaking huge and totally wasted, and he was tweaking like crazy. I don't know how he even drove here. I didn't want to sell him the beer but he didn't really give me any choice. He's probably going to kill someone. But dude, there was something seriously scary about him. There's no way I was going to tell him no. He probably would have pulled out a gun and shot me or maybe beat me to death. I mean he actually threatened me, you know what I'm saying?"

TONY

A s soon as Tony gets in the truck, he cracks open two beers, downing the first in one shot and lets loose with a massive burp. By the time he gets less than half a mile down the road, he's diligently consuming the second. He's only a block from his house when he runs the stop sign. The lighting is poor and he's very drunk. Truthfully, he never even sees the sign. As he flies through the intersection going south, a bright, blue Honda with a "Honk if You're Happy" bumper sticker crosses from the east. Tony's truck plows into it at over 50 mph, shattering the little car into pieces and sending debris flying in all directions.

Skidding to a stop, he dazedly shakes his head. The beer has flown all over the inside of the cab and is dripping down the windshield, though surprisingly he still holds the bottle in his hand. He absently wipes beer off his shirt as he opens the door and walks back to investigate. He cautiously approaches the remains of the little car and sees that someone has written the words **JUST MARRIED** across the cracked rear window and beneath that **ANNE & DANNY** with lots of hearts and curlicues decorating the edges. Unfortunately, the effect is rather marred by the bright red streaks, dots and clumps sprayed across it, but you can still see that someone has taken the time and effort to make it fancy.

Taking a deep breath, he forces himself to inspect the inside and gapes at what is left of the young couple, trying to grasp what's staring him in the face. Blood is spattered everywhere like a can of paint has been thrown all over the interior, the reek of it hot and metallic, smelling incredibly strong. He feels like he can taste it in the back of his throat.

The person in the passenger seat is almost indistinguishable as human and is obviously dead. Judging from the clothes, this must be Anne. The guy, most likely Danny, is in the driver's seat. His head is turned towards Tony at a vicious angle and his eyes are open staring right at him. His chest and side are completely crushed, his mouth opening and closing like a fish out of water gasping for air, his labored breath barely wheezing out between his bloody lips. Blood leaks from his ears, mouth and nose, and he begins to choke, coughing up even more.

He stares at Tony in desperation as if waiting for him to perform a miracle. Tony can't take his eyes off the blood as it runs from his lips and drips off the end of his chin. He's fascinated by the slow progression. After what feels like an interminable amount of time, Danny takes one final agonized breath, his ruined chest rising for one last time, then he falls silent. His eyes are still open yet they no longer see Tony; they no longer see anything. He's gone.

Tony grips the edge of the car so hard it's making his hand hurt. He feels rooted to the ground, unable to tear his eyes away from the sight until he hears movement in what little remains of the back seat. He jerks his head toward the sound. Sure enough, a dark shadow is slithering around back there making a whispery clicking sound and murmuring his name. That's it, he's had enough. He panics and throwing the beer bottle in the nearest bush, bolts for his truck.

Slamming the door closed, he tears down the street in a cloud of exhaust, never even noticing the neighbors who have come out of their houses in robes and pajamas to see what happened. He doesn't give another thought to the young newlyweds whose lives he cut tragically short. He thinks of nothing but those whispers speaking his name. Obviously, it's the demons, and they're following him wherever he goes. They must have escaped from the bedroom and are trying to take him down. He needs to get home and make sure the door is still secure. The thought of them all escaping is terrifying.

He enters the kitchen as silently as his sense of urgency will allow, not even bothering to close the door for fear of making too much noise. It never occurs to him that killing two innocent people on the way to their honeymoon is going to cause problems, let alone the fact that there must have been at least twenty witnesses who saw him take off from the scene and pull in to his own backyard. All he can think about is that slithery, whispering sound, the shadows, and the security of the bedroom door.

He left the kitchen and living room lights on when he left, yet the illumination barely manages to penetrate the thick pools of darkness looming in the corners and hallway. As he enters the living room, something goes thud behind the bedroom door. He jerks his head toward the sound, his heart pounding so fiercely he feels like his face is throbbing and he can't seem to catch his breath.

"Dude, get a fucking grip," he mutters, breathing hard and fast. He sets the cases of beer down next to his chair as quietly as possible and then can't make himself do anything else. The fear freezes him in place and he continues to stand there for several minutes, gripped by indecision and waiting for the next thump or bump to sound from behind the door. Nervous sweat trickles down his temples and pools in the hairs of his unshaven face. He swallows repeatedly, causing the drops of sweat gathered on his chin to tremble.

From the corner of his eye, he sees a flicker of movement outside the living room window. Did the demons in that couple's car follow him? Throwing himself flat against the wall, he stares out the window desperately trying to see the source of the activity. Unfortunately, he can't see a thing. The living room lights are reflecting off the glass making him virtually blind, and even worse, putting him in the spotlight for whomever, or whatever is out there. Reaching out, he flips off the switches with one hand, killing all the lights in the living room at once. The sudden darkness is terrifying, and it takes a couple of minutes for his eyes to adjust, but at least now he's on an even playing field with whatever is out there. It might not make a big difference, but he'll take whatever advantage he can get.

Now there is only a spill of illumination from the kitchen creating a thin finger of light through the doorway. Tony makes sure he's well hidden in the shadows as he reaches down and carefully plucks his gun off the top of the cooler where he left it. He checks to make sure a round is chambered, and holds it in both hands up near his head. Clearly this situation is about to explode and he's damn sure going to be ready for whatever comes next. His anxiety grows, and in frustration he begins to tap his forehead with the gun hissing, "Fuck, fuck, fuck."

He finally starts to relax, thinking maybe he imagined the movement outside, when he hears footsteps and muted conversation coming from the backyard.

Shit, I left the fucking door open!

Taking a chance, he peeks through the kitchen and sees movement out the back door. He presses himself against the wall and while he's trying to decide what to do, all hell breaks loose.

Voices start shouting at him from the back yard ordering him to come out. The demons choose that exact moment to burst through the bedroom door and attack, swarming all about, wrapping their arms around him and enveloping him in a misty cold that penetrates all the way through to his bones, making his teeth ache and his fingers hurt. The effect is overwhelming and he instantly goes numb from head to toe; unable to move. His mind becomes a kaleidoscope of sheer, uncontrollable terror and horrified screams are ripped from his throat.

When his paralysis finally breaks, he fires his gun at the spirits surrounding him. The sound of gunfire and shattering glass only adds to the chaos, confusing him even more. He falls to his knees and keeps squeezing the trigger, but nothing happens. He's out of ammo and they're still attacking. He isn't even aware that he's still screaming. He hugs the floor and crab crawls to his boxes of ammo, ejecting the spent magazine and slamming a loaded one home. Rising to his feet, he sprints through the kitchen attempting to make his escape, all the while screaming at the top of his lungs, "Get the fuck away from me. Just fucking die already!"

As he bursts through the back door, he is still firing at the shadows he's convinced are chasing him, and the two police officers standing outside return fire cutting Tony down in mid-scream, ending his terror in less than a heartbeat.

THE POLICE

Time momentarily comes to a stop, blanketing the yard in complete silence. Tony's body lays sprawled in the threshold half in and half out of the kitchen. Blood runs down the steps and pools on the ground, dripping off the edge of the concrete walk and seeping into the dirt and grass. Officer Manning cautiously lowers his weapon while his partner, Officer Sutter, keeps his trained on the back door. Manning kicks the gun away from Tony's outstretched hand and after reaching down to feel for a pulse says, "We should call an ambulance, but by the time they get here he'll probably be gone. Better call the ME too. We're going to need him."

The officers warily enter the house, being careful to step over the widening puddle of blood surrounding Tony's body. Spent cartridges litter the kitchen floor. They flank the door to the living room with their weapons at the ready. Sutter reaches carefully around the wall and turns on all the light switches. Light floods the living room, brilliantly displaying the evidence of the utter chaos of Tony's mind.

Cigarette butts overflow from several ashtrays and beer bottles are scattered around from one end of the room to the other. At least two dozen cardboard cylinders from spent rolls of duct tape lay in a heap next to the TV. The coffee table is littered with chopped crystal, a razor blade, a glass pipe and little plastic baggies. Two cases of beer are stacked next to a cooler.

Five full magazines, an empty one, and several boxes of ammo are piled on the floor next to a chair. One of the officers nudges the magazines with his toe and raises an eyebrow. Obviously, this guy was prepared to do battle with someone. In the middle of all this debris is a brand-new mattress wrapped in torn plastic. After clearing the house, they determine that no one else is hiding inside.

"Meth heads," Sutter says, gesturing to the bullet holes in the walls and the padlocked and taped-up bedroom door. "It never ceases to amaze me how crazy this crap makes these guys. What the hell is up with that door?"

Manning shrugs, "Beats the shit out of me, meth monsters maybe? Who knows? They're all whack jobs. That shit eats their brains. We need to get eyes in this room and make sure we don't have a hostage situation in there. Let's go outside and check the windows see if we've got any movement in there. If it looks clear, we'll wait to open it until backup arrives. I'm not cutting through all this and risk destroying evidence; the captain would have my ass. That call is way above my paygrade. I'll leave that decision to the sergeant."

It turned out they had a clear line of sight into the room. It appeared to be empty. A job made easier by Tony's choice to leave the bathroom light on.

"I'll go radio for the ambulance and the detectives," Sutter says. "I'll have them send the ME too. This is going to be one long-ass night."

Listening with half an ear to the call being placed, Manning pulls a pair of latex gloves from his pocket. After carefully fitting them over his fingers, he runs his hand across the duct tape sealing the edges of the door, wondering what on earth could have been going through this loser's head.

"Unbelievable. Christ," he grumbles, "This is going to be a shit-load of paperwork." He wants to pull out his phone and take a couple of pictures to show the chaos to his wife. She is never going to believe this one. But it's not worth the risk of invalidating the evidence. With his luck, some smart-ass attorney would get the entire case thrown out just because he snapped a couple of pictures. Bullshit lawyers.

MARCO

Something is wrong with Rachel beyond simple sadness over the loss of Cara. Whenever he attempts to touch or kiss her, she recoils slightly (almost imperceptible if you didn't know to watch for it).

The last time they had sex it was a nightmare. Rachel cried almost the entire time. She tried to blame it on her depression and the fact that she couldn't manage to get a handle on it since Cara's death. However, he knows what's going on; she's afraid of him. The trouble is he isn't sure how to deal with it. Normally he's a very decisive, no-holds-barred kind of guy, but this is different. He honestly cares for Rachel and keeps hoping a solution will present itself before he is forced to do something he dreads.

Unfortunately, the situation is worsening. She's completely falling apart and is drinking and smoking weed constantly. The smell of pot permeates every room in the house. It's as if the odor has been absorbed by the very walls themselves. She is stoned out of her mind by noon most days, and usually follows that up with four or five screwdrivers by 2:00. Then she'll nap until 4:00 when she starts the whole process all over again (with wine instead of vodka) until she passes out around midnight or 1:00 am. This is definitely not Rachel-like behavior. He's tried several times to talk to her about it, but his attempts are always met with tears and complete withdrawal.

Oddly, though, when she is sober enough, she always seems to have her nose in the Bible or reading blogs online by some guy named Max Lucado. It's all a bunch of religious blah, blah, blah, as far as he's concerned. She keeps trying to hide it from him, so he simply waits until she passes out and then checks the history on the computer. It's obvious she has become obsessed with religion.

LAURIE JAMESON

Yesterday, when he came home and told her Tony had been shot and killed by the cops, he could have sworn there was a flash of triumph in her eyes before she put her guard back up. Of course, she said all the right things and told him she was sorry that he'd lost his friend, but something was off. The look in her eyes didn't match her words.

He also makes it a point to check every day to see if she's visiting sites having to do with criminal tip lines or anything police-related, and checks her cell phone for calls or internet searches along the same vein. So far so good…she is being a good girl. Maybe she can get through this and they can salvage whatever is left of their relationship, but then again, maybe not. The jury is still out.

RACHEL

After taking what Rachel felt was way too long, the coroner finally released Cara's body to her parents. Once Cara's body was discovered and positively identified by her parents, Rachel was at last able to let go of her emotions. She was finally able to weep, wail and let loose with all the emotions she'd been forced to keep bottled up inside for so long. The pretending was done. Her true grieving had begun.

She completely lost it when the autopsy showed that Cara was pregnant. It also revealed traces of dirt in her lungs. The coroner's report said she had been strangled and her neck was broken, but that she was still breathing when she was buried. They buried her alive! Those bastards are even colder than she ever could have imagined. Her mind keeps trying to envision what it must have felt like for Cara to struggle to breathe while dirt was piled on top of her, knowing that her baby would die with her. That is the nightmare that drives Rachel to continuously drink every day until she passes out.

One of the things that helped the police make a positive ID was Cara's birthmark. It was in the shape of a butterfly on the inside of her right forearm slightly below the crook of her arm. Because of this birthmark, Cara proclaimed long ago that butterflies were lucky and made them her personal totem, even dotting her i's with tiny butterflies when they were little girls and then graduating to drawing a beautiful butterfly when she signed her name on notes or in the high school yearbook. A lot of their friends in high school even nick-named her Butterfly because of her obsession, and she loved it.

Once, when spending the night, she fogged up Rachel's bathroom mirror and drew butterflies all over it, that way when Rachel took a shower later, all those butterflies appeared as if by magic. This was the memory that did Rachel in, the picture of all those incredible butterflies left as a message of love for her.

Today, in honor of Cara, she got a tattoo of a butterfly in the exact same spot as Cara's birthmark, and had them color it in the same vibrant blue as her eyes. Rachel gazes down at her butterfly and slowly circles it with her finger. She feels better knowing she has something tangible to remind her of Cara. She can look at it and pretend they are still together.

These last two weeks have been the worst of Rachel's life. She feels like she's had to constantly watch over her shoulder, convinced Marco knows every thought in her head. She has never been a very good liar and is sure he can see her emotions play out as plain as day across her face.

When Marco came home yesterday and told her Tony had been shot and killed by the police, it had taken all the strength she had to keep her feelings in check. She'd wanted to jump up and down and scream, "Thank you, God! Thank you for taking that lousy excuse for a human being out of this world. I hope you have a special place in hell for him where he'll burn for all eternity." Instead, she forced herself to pretend she was shocked and sad, though she almost choked on the words. She's almost certain he didn't buy her act, but there's nothing she can do about it now except try to maintain the facade of concern.

She studies her face in the mirror and isn't surprised to see how tired she appears. She can't remember the last time she got a decent night's sleep. The days and nights have been one long alcohol and drug induced blur. It's the only way she can sleep anymore and it's starting to take a toll on her. Her hair appears dull and limp and there are dark smudges under her eyes. She hasn't bothered to put on makeup since the day Cara's body was found, because after all, what's the point? She's only going to cry it all off again.

Marco notices (she can see it in his eyes), but he hasn't said anything yet. She figures it's only a matter of time. However, she doesn't particularly care what he thinks. He may not have been the one who beat up and tried to kill Cara, but he helped that bastard Tony bury her while she was still alive, and that's just as bad. What he thinks of her and her appearance is not high on her list of priorities these days.

What worries her the most is the chance that he knows she overheard their phone call. She's positive neither of them saw her when she was hiding in Tony's back yard, but the constant anxiety that sooner or later he is going to confront her is terrifying. She feels like she is living with a huge rock suspended above her head and it's waiting to crush her at any moment.

She turns on the shower and waits for the water to heat up. At least she can feel clean even if she looks like shit. As she steps into the shower, Marco walks into the bathroom. Rachel doesn't hear him, and jumps when she sees his reflection in the mirror. She can't help it.

"Hey, honey, what's up?" she tries to ask as casually as possible.

"Just checking on you. How're you feeling today?" Marco leans casually against the wall and gazes at her through the shower door. He pulls a cigarette from the pack on the counter and lights up, blowing the smoke toward the ceiling where it mixes with the steam and swirls about before being sucked out by the fan. He doesn't want her to feel she's being stared at, so he watches her in the mirror's reflection. She seems shaky and scared.

"Oh, you know…it's hard to wrap my head around everything. I miss her so much and the whole thing is so…so awful, you know? Especially because of the baby and, well…" She trails off at that point, unable to articulate her horror at the thought of Cara being buried alive. She tilts her head up under the hot water and lets it pour down over her face while she tries to think of something, anything to say, but nothing is coming to her.

"Do you want to do something? You know, go to a movie or maybe, I don't know, take a drive down to the beach and go for a walk?"

"No, no, I can't," she says and breaks down. "I'm sorry, I …I just don't feel like I'm ready yet." She's crying hard now, though it's difficult to tell with water streaming down her face. She stares at him though the shower door keeping her back to the wall as if she is afraid to let down her guard. "I'm sorry," she whispers.

"Ok, no problem," he replies tossing his cigarette in the toilet. He can hear his cell ringing in the living room and as he's walking out the door, he glances in the mirror again. Rachel is watching him with a naked expression of fear on her face.

MONKEY

Monkey, known to his dear, sweet mama as Arturo Luis Arciero, is a man who feels comfortable with his place in the world and fears no man. He is a self-described big fat Mexican with a shaved head and a large and impressive, macho mustache. He favors cowboy hats, pointy-toed boots and Wrangler jeans. He can be found at least two to three nights a week at the Wild Horse Saloon, two stepping with as many fresh, young ladies as he can pour tequila into and lay his hands on. He isn't above waving around a fair amount of cash to loosen their thighs either.

The name Monkey, an intensely-hated childhood nickname, is never spoken in his presence by anyone who wishes to keep all their body parts intact. They all refer to him as Senior Arciero or simply Boss, though the young ladies at the bar call him Arty.

The despised nickname was given to him at birth by his older brother, Juan Jose, because he had, unfortunately, been born with an excessive amount of hair extending from the nape of his neck all the way down to his buttocks. His hairline had also traveled down his forehead to his eyebrows. The hair on his forehead disappeared quickly, but the hair on his back stubbornly refused to go away. Juan Jose had taken tremendous joy in tormenting him as a boy. The memories of the teasing still haunt him. One incident in particular sticks in his mind.

It was 1962 and Monkey had just turned six. He'd spent the entire summer running after Juan Jose and trying to keep up with the bigger kids. He did his best to run, jump and hit the ball as hard and as far as they did, though he always came up short.

One fateful afternoon while playing baseball in the empty dirt lot at the corner of their street, he tripped and fell as he tried to beat the throw to second base. When he hit the ground, his shirt rode up exposing the thick patch of hair at the base of his spine that stubbornly refused to go away. As Juan Jose reached down to tag him with his glove, he pinned him to the ground by placing his knee across Monkey's shoulders and yanked his shirt up uncovering his entire back.

Monkey cried and begged, "Juan Jose don't, please don't. Please let me up."

Juan Jose responded by pushing Monkey's face into the dirt and calling out to his buddies, "Hey guys, come over here and see this. Come see why I call this ugly little runt Monkey."

As the boys eagerly crowded around, they took turns making comments that stabbed at Monkey's heart like a knife.

"Holy cow! Look at that will ya."

"That's disgusting."

"Were you born in a tree?"

"I bet he has a tail."

"Yeah, if we pull down your pants will you have a tail?"

"Ooh ooh, ah ah, you want a banana little monkey boy?"

On and on it went. He cried in shame and lay in the dirt until his brother and his friends abandoned him in favor of more interesting pursuits. Once he was alone, he climbed to his feet and attempted to brush the dirt from his clothes and face, and wipe away the telltale signs of tears. He didn't want to walk home looking like a crybaby.

It is one of his worst childhood memories and one he has never forgotten. In part, it's this memory that has been his motivation to be so successful in life. He is determined that nobody will ever make fun of him again. Unfortunately, his back is still overly hairy, forcing him to have it waxed in secret on a regular basis; a painful process that inevitably leaves him in a foul temper for hours.

He knows people still call him Monkey, but *never* within his earshot. The last man to try it, more than fifteen years ago, met with the business end of Monkey's knife. Wet work doesn't bother him, and consequently word has gotten around. No one has ever made that mistake again.

He lives on a large property in San Bernardino County, in the heavily Hispanic city of Colton. It's a dry, desert-like area, as is most of the California Inland Empire, and its streets are crowded with older, but generally well-maintained, houses. His home is surrounded by tall, white, wrought iron fencing topped with spikes and fancy ornamentation. Dozens of well-tended rose bushes border the fence lending bright splashes of color to the yard and are the pride and joy of his faithful and devoted wife, Maritza.

His house blends in well (to the casual observer, though there are security cameras mounted in strategic locations all around the house) in a neighborhood populated primarily by lower income families who all lean towards the same type of garish fencing and yard decorations. Statues of saints, Mother Mary and bleeding heart Jesus occupy places of honor on most of the lawns and porches. Monkey's house is notably larger and more opulent than those of his neighbors, yet he prefers to stay in this less affluent neighborhood with people who fear and more importantly, respect him. He can count on their loyalty and knows no one can come near his house without him hearing about it. The eyes of his neighbors are a wonderful security system.

He keeps a low profile and, thanks to cell phones, his business operations are quite mobile and therefore difficult to pinpoint. Because he owns a window washing business and several other legitimate operations, it's a fairly-simple process to wash large amounts of cash. He's made a lifelong habit of putting at least three layers of protection between himself and actual product distribution. Normally there are very few problems that can't be resolved long before they become an issue he is forced to deal with personally.

Lately he's been feeling incredibly irritated by the trouble manifesting itself with Marco and his crew. Having two people within his organization die so violently makes him uncomfortable. He's starting to wonder if Marco has lost control of his end of the business. With all this attention focused on the murder of Cara Healy and now the cops shooting Tony Moretti, how long will it be before something happens that leads the police to his doorstep? This is unacceptable. Marco needs to get his ass in gear and clean house immediately or suffer the consequences.

Monkey calls out, "Maritza, un Cerveza por favor."

After thanking her with a kiss on the cheek and a dismissive pat on her butt, he closes his study door and takes his time lighting up a fat Cuban cigar, one of the many luxuries his money provides. He enjoys his little indulgences and has recently discovered that smoking a cigar while having his hands, feet and toes worked on by compliant little Asian women is almost as good as sex. He puffs away contentedly for a few moments, fantasizing about small hands soothing his aching feet, takes a large swallow of beer, and then, heaving an aggravated sigh, picks up his cell and punches the speed dial for Marco.

He's not a man who is big on discussion, and generally people are sufficiently afraid of him that only a few brief statements are ever required to make his point. He speaks with quiet authority into the phone, "Marco, I'm disappointed." He listens for a short time then speaks again. "I don't want this to be an issue anymore. I don't want to see this on the news or pick up a paper and read about you or anyone close to you or my business. This stops now. I don't have the patience for this. Do I make myself clear?" He listens again and says, "Gracias. I knew I could count on you. Adios, Marco."

Monkey presses the off button, drops the phone on his desk, leans back in his chair and blows smoke rings at the ceiling while he considers the situation. He'll give Marco a few days to see if he can make some progress in getting things cleaned up. After that, well, he'll do whatever needs to be done. He'll make that decision when the time comes.

Sitting up, he rises ponderously to his feet and hitches up his pants, taking a minute to make sure his shirt is neatly tucked in and his belt buckle is properly centered. He can smell dinner in the air and eagerly anticipates a good meal. That's one thing about Maritza, she might not be much to look at anymore, but that woman can cook, and he has his priorities.

Monkey lays his cigar in the dish and strolls out to the dining room, patting his ample belly in expectation, putting Marco and the whole mess out of his mind. Time enough for unpleasantness later.

RACHEL

Cara's funeral is incredibly painful—worse than she even imagined it would be. Rachel spends the entire church service feeling as if she can't breathe. Tears roll down her face continuously and her nose drips almost non-stop. Her purse is rapidly filling up with used tissues. She watches as pictures of Cara from birth through her adult years are projected on the screen while her favorite songs play as a sound track. It's almost unbearable. Many of the pictures shown are of Cara and Rachel together, and reliving those memories makes her feel as if her heart is being ripped from her chest. She cries until she feels sick to her stomach and her head pounds to the beat of a brutally relentless drum.

She'd had a painful phone conversation with Cara's parents yesterday. They wanted her to speak at the funeral. It broke Rachel's heart to hear them crying over not only the loss of their daughter, but their grandchild as well. She had to say yes.

She'd spent the last 24 hours agonizing over it. She had no idea what she could say, because she felt that she was partially responsible for Cara's death, though she could never tell her parents that. She'd let Cara down. Cara was murdered because she wasn't the friend, the sister she should have been. She should have checked on her more often. How had she let her drift away like that? She should have known how desperate her situation truly was. She should have felt it. She should have ripped her out of Tony's grasp as soon as Cara told her about the abuse. She hadn't been there for her in the end because she was selfishly wrapped up in her own life. How had money and stuff become more important than her love for Cara? When did she become that shallow? She failed her because she wasn't paying attention. That was the bald truth.

Now she stands at the podium clinging to the sides for dear life, sweat running down her sides and dampening her neck and armpits. Her knees are trembling badly and she is afraid she might fall. Through blurry, bloodshot eyes she contemplates the mourners, most of whom are weeping. She fixes her gaze on Cara's parents who each give her encouraging nods while they cling desperately to each other for support, and then she finally settles her eyes on the casket, staunchly trying to gather her courage.

The casket is covered in a huge spray of white roses and purple sweet peas that drape down the sides in a graceful fall of vibrant color. Cara's parents gave careful consideration to the type of flowers which would adorn it, finally deciding on the roses because they were her birth flower and sweet peas because they attracted butterflies. Cara would be thrilled by the idea of her grave being surrounded in a dancing cloud of butterflies. Rachel pictures her laughing and clapping her hands delightedly at the thought, and that momentarily brings a small smile to her lips, lessening the choking sensation in her throat, and giving her the courage she needs.

She unconsciously touches the butterfly tattoo on her arm. Taking a deep breath, she steadies herself and begins speaking in a shaky voice, "Cara was my best friend and the most amazing person I have ever known. We met when we were only five years old and we always told everyone we were supposed to have been born sisters. We used to joke around and say that our parents just hadn't planned appropriately or we really would have been sisters." That got a small chuckle from the crowd.

"I can honestly say she was the sister of my heart and always will be." In desperation, she grips the edges of the podium, willing herself to speak while the tears pour down her face. Angry at her inability to hold it in, she wipes them away and continues. "She was kind and loving. She was funny, and she made this world a better place simply because she was in it. I'm jealous of the angels in Heaven because they get to be with her now and I don't. It's not fair."

She sobs unreservedly for a minute, blows her nose and struggles to regain her composure. "If you take a good look at the pictures up there on the screen, you'll see we were always together. When we were kids, we matched our clothes, and our hairstyles, and even our Barbie lunch boxes. Our moms used to say we were like two peas in a pod. Well, my sister is gone now. She's been taken from me and I'm angry. I know you're not supposed to say things like that at a funeral, but I am. This isn't right and I'm pissed off! I ask God every day to help me not be angry, but it's not working. I struggle every day to get out of bed. I struggle to put my clothes on and go out in the world. The only thing I have to keep me going is the promise God makes to us in His word. The Bible says that one day we will all be together again in Heaven and we will know our loved ones. That's what I hold on to. I miss her every minute of every day, and I'm going to look forward to seeing her again because that's all I have left." She pauses as she tries to staunch the flow of tears, then shifts her eyes to Cara's parents and shoots them an apologetic look before lamely finishing with, "That's all I have to say."

She bawls openly as she stumbles from the podium to Cara's casket. She trails her fingers across the top of it, and since it's closed (for obvious reasons), settles for kissing the lid. She can hear Cara's parents weeping and feels guilty for not saying something more uplifting, but she honestly couldn't do it. They were lucky she hadn't started screaming and pointing to Marco, demanding that they ask *him* what had happened to their daughter and grandchild. Reluctantly she takes her seat next to Marco and tries not to flinch when he puts his arm across her shoulders.

The rest of the service passes in a blur. Other people speak, though Rachel couldn't have told you what any of them said. She remembers the pastor praying and Cara's family quietly filing out to the long, black limo. When Marco takes her arm to help her up and escort her from the church, it's all she can do not to shove him away.

They ride alone in his car to the cemetery. It's a strained and quiet ride. Marco finally clears his throat and offers, "I'm sorry, babe. I know this is really hard for you."

Rachel nods her head but doesn't meet his eyes. "Yeah, it is," she answers softly.

"You're going to get through this. I'll be there for you, whatever you need."

"Whatever I need?" Rachel questions. "Whatever I need? I need Cara back. I need my best friend. I should have been there for her. I knew she was in trouble. I told you she needed help. I knew Tony was way out of control. I should have done something more. I need to not have to hide the truth anymore. I'm tired of being afraid. I'm glad he's dead. I wish I could've fucking killed him myself!"

All of this pours out of her in a flood before she can stop it, and she screams the last part so loudly her throat feels raw afterward. She abruptly stops, wishing she could suck the words back in, but it's too late. The truth is out there, lying naked and vulnerable. She stares down at her lap and her clenched hands, knowing everything is forever changed. She has crossed an invisible line and probably sealed her fate. She buries her face in her hands and waits.

After a few moments, she can't take it anymore, and finally raises her eyes to see Marco's reaction. He's staring straight ahead intently watching traffic. Without taking his eyes off the road, he flatly states, "You were on the phone that day."

"It was an accident. I didn't mean to eavesdrop, I thought it was my Mom calling and I…I'm sorry." She doesn't add that she followed him to Tony's house. She can't see giving him something more to be angry about. That would be stupid.

Marco nods once, not bothering to respond, staying silent until they arrive at the cemetery. He focuses on following the other cars in the procession and parks. Exiting the car, he puts his jacket back on, shoots his cuffs, straightens his tie and walks around to open her door, offering his hand. She stares up at him fearfully trying to gauge his mood. His face gives away nothing.

He gives her a tight-lipped smile (almost like she has him by the balls) and with a "let's go" gesture, again offers his hand to help her from the car, finally speaking, "Don't worry, babe, I'll take care of you."

Rachel isn't sure what that means. With her heart hammering away in her chest, she reluctantly takes his hand and lets him lead her to the terrible empty hole that waits for Cara. Thankfully, the graveside service is brief. She pays close attention to what the preacher says and it makes a lot of sense. He quotes scriptures that seem to be speaking directly to her.

"In Isaiah 57:1-2 we read 'Good people are taken away, but no one understands. Those who live as God wants find rest in death.'"

That's right. What else is there to say? A beautiful person lived and then she was gone.

"God protects His children and takes them away from evil. This is the purpose of death. We know nobody lives one day more or one day less than God intends. Psalms 139:16 says, 'All the days planned for me were written in Your book before I was one day old.' This is what we must hold in our hearts."

That quote hits home with Rachel. She feels as if God has spoken directly to her.

He took Cara on purpose, because He knew from the minute she was born that her life was going to end this way. He planned for her to die. He was protecting Cara and her baby by taking them away. He did it because He loves them.

"But you do not know what will happen tomorrow. Your life is like a mist. You can see it for a short time, but then it goes away. James 4:14." The preacher looks up from his bible and meets the eyes of several of the mourners. "When we each look back on our own lives, and the lives of those we love, we can see that a person's days on earth are barely a tiny drop in the ocean of time."

Rachel sobs. *He's right. There is a lot of truth in that. Cara was here for such a short time, too short, and now she's gone forever. The dreams we had together are over.*

She feels confused and overwhelmed. She's in a daze as she stands next to Marco, consciously not touching him at all. Her head is pounding from all the crying, and she's afraid of what will happen next, even though she realizes it doesn't matter. Her life will never be the same, and her love for Marco can never be the same either. The question is where do they go from here? What is he going to do? Will he do anything? Does she even care?

MARCO

He stands next to Rachel during the graveside service and though they are no more than four or five inches apart, she makes no effort to hold his hand or turn to him for comfort. In fact, she appears to make every effort not to even allow her dress to brush up against him. That simple gesture speaks volumes. Once the service is finally finished, he says all the right things, shakes people's hands and gives all the appropriate hugs, never divulging the dark thoughts churning away behind his eyes.

He calmly and silently drives them to Cara's parents' house for the wake. He samples a few casseroles, refills drinks for the ladies and pronounces several babies beautiful. In short, he is the perfect gentleman. A couple of the older women even comment to each other that he is such a handsome man and how fortunate Rachel is to have him by her side during this difficult time. Young men of his age don't often display such lovely manners. His mother has obviously raised him properly. He is a real catch.

Throughout the entire afternoon, he turns the situation over and over in his mind. His suspicions have finally been confirmed; Rachel knows the truth. The fact that she hasn't acted on it is in her favor. However, Monkey made it very clear that all loose ends are to be taken care of without delay. He doesn't have much choice now. There is no doubt in his mind that Monkey won't hesitate to take him out if he screws this up.

Monkey doesn't know Rachel overheard my phone call with Tony, so that's something. But Rachel knows what happened. She's completely falling apart. How long can she continue to hide the truth? Tony getting shot and killed by the police turned out to be a blessing, otherwise I would have had to handle it myself eventually. At least his death is one less problem on my list.

100

THE WAYSTATION

He considers the situation, sipping from his cup of soda, nodding and smiling to various people and wondering if he's being too harsh. Despite everything that's happened, Tony had been his friend, although he was a weak and flawed individual. He mulls it over for a while, finally deciding no, he's justified in his relief. Tony had been way out of control for far too long. He'd been a danger to the business and that wasn't acceptable. The police have been all over Tony's place and Marco is convinced it's only a matter of time before they discover some sort of evidence to confirm Tony's involvement in Cara's murder. He feels confident that he hasn't left any trace of *his* presence at Tony's house. He should be in the clear with the cops. With Tony dead, the only person who can link him to her death is Rachel.

Fuck! What a mess.

He politely offers to refill Rachel's wine glass, giving her what he hopes will be perceived as a kind and loving expression. She doesn't return it, yet appears to be grateful nonetheless. He makes a mental note to ensure that her glass is never empty. The rest of this day isn't going to be pleasant, and it will be easier for them both if she is completely oblivious.

After several hours, they're finally able to take their leave of Cara's family and friends. He's obliged to hold Rachel up to keep her on her feet and walking out the door. He settles her in the car, carefully smoothing down her skirt and fastening her seat belt, making sure people note how well he takes care of her. Then he neatly lays his jacket in the back seat to keep it from wrinkling and waves one last goodbye before getting in. She considerately passes out before he even gets his seat belt fastened, giving him plenty of time to finish formulating his plan.

Thirty minutes later he pulls to a stop in front of Ricardo's place to pick up what he'll need. He's reluctantly come to the conclusion that he has no choice. Monkey has insisted on no loose ends, and that's exactly what Rachel is whether Monkey knows it or not.

Ricardo ushers him inside and they conduct their business quickly. Marco takes the paper bag containing what he needs, and then instead of placing the cash in Ricardo's outstretched hand, he rapidly puts two bullets in his chest, eliminating the potential for yet another loose end.

He doesn't feel even a twinge of guilt. In fact, he feels like he's doing the world a favor by getting rid of the worthless piece of shit. He's seen Ricardo deal smack to a pregnant mother of four and that's a sacred line Marco has always refused to cross.

Good riddance, you low-life piece of shit.

He pockets the gun while hurrying back to the car, thankful for the silencer Monkey gave him more than a year ago. At the time, he couldn't imagine why he would need it, but now he's grateful. He checks to make sure Rachel is still lights out, then leaves the neighborhood as quickly as possible, being careful to never exceed the speed limit. It will not be helpful if he's stopped by the police.

He makes a couple of detours before reaching the freeway. After exiting Ricardo's neighborhood, he pulls over to the curb, parking near a sewer drain. Yanking his shirt out of his pants, he rubs the silencer and the gun as thoroughly as possible, erasing his prints. Still using his shirt, he unscrews the silencer and tosses it down the drain, then ejects the magazine and places it in his shirt pocket. He drives a couple of blocks over, and after stealing a few tissues from Rachel's purse, he uses one to pick up the gun and drop it in a Dumpster at a McDonald's. It immediately sinks to the bottom beneath hundreds of bags of fast food trash. Once he reaches the onramp to the freeway, he uses another tissue to toss the magazine out the window where it lands deep in a tangle of overgrown bougainvillea plants. Satisfied, he picks up speed and heads for home.

When they finally pull into the driveway, he wakes Rachel and solicitously suggests she might want to relax in the Jacuzzi, even offering to roll her a joint and get her another glass of wine. She mumbles her thanks and a request for screwdrivers instead. He helps her to the door and holds her up with one hand while unlocking it with the other. She staggers through the entrance and immediately begins undressing, leaving a trail of discarded clothing behind her like flakes of dead skin as she makes her way toward the back yard.

He follows her a few minutes later carrying a pitcher full of orange juice and vodka, a tall glass of ice, and a freshly rolled fatty. He is as kind as he can be, filling her glass and lighting up for her. He sits in a nearby chair, thoughtfully observing but not drinking or smoking anything himself. It doesn't take long before she's out cold again. She's managed to smoke about a third of the joint and makes it through almost two screwdrivers before her body simply can't take anymore. Frankly, he is amazed she's lasted this long.

He glances around the yard thankful he spent the money to completely enclose it with good privacy fencing and large, mature bougainvillea plants and palms. It's completely screened and safe from the prying eyes of neighbors who might be home. Originally, he'd designed it this way to provide complete seclusion for late night interludes in the hot tub. He and Rachel have spent many spectacularly passion-filled nights out here. Now all that foliage means he doesn't have to worry about any potential witnesses getting an eyeful. He runs his fingers along her jawline and down and across her perfect breasts. Sighing, he shakes his head at the waste.

Rachel has conveniently provided the perfect scenario by blowing up at the memorial and getting totally wasted at the wake. He couldn't have planned it any better himself. Heroin has never been her drug of choice, but her family won't know that. Besides, it was painfully obvious to anyone who might be called to testify at an inquiry that she was not herself today and was incredibly distraught. Grief does terrible things to people and can cause them to behave in self-destructive ways.

He waits a few minutes before roughly shaking her shoulder calling, "Rachel, Rachel, wake up." When he doesn't get any kind of response, he goes back in the house to retrieve the paper bag from where he stashed it in the kitchen cabinet. He pulls on a pair of latex gloves and lays the contents of the bag on the counter and stares at it, trying to work up the nerve to go through with his plan. She's a beautiful woman and he genuinely cares about her; maybe even loves her. Killing her will be a real loss, but he can't think of any other way out. She'll never be able to keep this a secret. It will destroy her. He patiently boils the chunk of heroin down drawing the liquid up in the needle before heading back out to the Jacuzzi.

The autopsy will show massive amounts of alcohol, marijuana, and heroin in her system. There will be enough water in her lungs to generate a verdict of accidental drowning following what will be determined was a lethal dose of heroin. It won't be a stretch for people to believe she'd finally gone over the edge from grief. She made it patently clear today that she was stretched far beyond her limits and was out of control. Suicide, whether accidental or intentional, won't be hard for anyone to swallow. He should be in the clear.

As he walks out the back door and towards the hot tub, he's stunned to see Rachel floating face down in the water and bobbing around in the bubbles like a cork. Tossing the syringe into the nearest chair he rushes over and instinctively takes hold of her hair, pulling her face out of the water and clutching her to his chest, soaking his shirt and suit pants in the process. She is completely lifeless, her lips tinged a light shade of blue. He gently strokes her forehead and kisses her tenderly on the lips one last time.

"I'm sorry, babe, I didn't have a choice. Try and understand. It's just business."

He eases her back into the water and spends a few minutes watching her body swirl about and up and down in the bubbles before picking up the deadly needle from the chair where he had thrown it and returning it to the paper bag. He removes his gloves and places them in the bag as well.

Standing in the kitchen and grasping the edge of the counter, he hangs his head and fights the urge to cry. He'd been seconds away from killing her and she'd generously let him off the hook. This was so typical of Rachel; doing something nice to help him out.

He feels saddened by her death, but he also feels relief and that makes him feel shitty. He'd done his best to make sure she wasn't going to feel a thing because he felt he owed her that. That was an act of love. Why then did he feel so guilty that she accidentally drowned? Doesn't this solve all his problems?

Unwilling to continue this line of thought, he resolutely sets his mind to other tasks and begins to remove his wet clothing, dumping all but his suit pants in the washer. He throws on a pair of jeans, Nikes, and a button-down shirt, and gathers up Rachel's discarded clothing, redistributing them in a pattern leading from the bed to the back yard. Pulling back the comforter, he musses up the sheets and pillows a bit and then leaves the house locking the door behind him. He tosses the bag and his wet pants in the back seat, then calls Rachel's older sister while he's backing out of the driveway.

"Sylvia? Hi, it's Marco." He listens to her chatter for a couple of minutes before replying. "Yes, it's been incredibly hard for her the last few weeks. She's been drinking a lot every day and today was the worst. She's very depressed and drank way too much at the wake. She fell asleep a few minutes ago. Hey, could you do me a favor? I got a call about one of our LA high rise jobs. They're having some serious issues and I need to go deal with it. Could you let her sleep for a couple of hours and then maybe run by the house and check on her? I'm going to be tied up for a while and I don't want her to be alone when she wakes up."

He lets her ramble on for a little bit longer, responding when it's appropriate with "I know," and "Yes, it's awful," then hangs up after thanking her profusely and reminding her where the extra key is hidden. Managing a window washing company (one of Monkey's many ways to legitimize his income) tends to come in handy when you need to make excuses on the fly.

Now he can call Monkey and pass on the news. There's no need to go into detail about how much she knew. He'll just tell him that she had voiced her suspicions and he handled it. Then he'll make the drive to LA where he'll stand around and pretend to supervise the guys while they do their job, making sure he is seen by as many people as possible. His alibi needs to be solid. It's been a crappy day and will ultimately be a seriously shitty night once Rachel's body is discovered. There will be the police and her family to deal with, but he's mentally prepared for that. It won't be hard to act upset. He is upset, and fights the urge to cry.

Feelings of guilt begin to creep into his mind again and he doggedly pushes them away, convincing himself that now there is a light at the end of this tunnel. Eventually he is going to get his normal, albeit different, life back. Turning on the radio, he purposefully blasts a little old school Santana to lift his spirits, drumming along on the steering wheel.

CARA

Time seems to fly by and yet to stand still all at the same time. Peaceful, sun-drenched days blend together, but oddly enough she is never bored. Sarah treats her like a daughter and Samuel is the kindest man she has ever met. It occurs to her more than once that if Tony had possessed some of Samuel's loving and generous traits, her life would be completely different. She and Tony would be painting the walls of a nursery and buying a car seat and crib instead of their relationship ending in her death. These thoughts should make her sad, but oddly enough, they don't. Instead, she feels safe, secure and loved, and knows her baby will never suffer at his hand, or anyone else's for that matter. She won't be born in the conventional way, but she will still have life, albeit a different one. That's enough for Cara.

A few days after Cara arrived at the Waystation, Sarah told her that the baby was a little girl. Cara was delighted and promptly named her Wren.

"Wren? What a pretty name and so unusual. What made you choose that?" Sarah asked.

"Oh, there are a bunch of them that live in the tree outside my window. They sing up a storm every morning and I love it. There's one who seems to like me. He, or maybe it's a she, sits on my windowsill and watches me and I feel like we've become friends. He doesn't seem to be afraid of anything, and I have a feeling that my little girl will be like that—brave. I guess that sounds a little silly huh?"

"Not at all. I think it's very sweet. It's perfect."

She brushes her hair one last time and looks around to make sure her room is tidy. She wants the next person who sleeps here to feel as welcome and comfortable as she has. The sound of an arriving wagon drifts through the window and she knows it's time. This is it. She feels a little nervous, but excited. The competing emotions are all mixed up inside and make her stomach feel like it's filled with a bunch of dancing butterflies, a not altogether unpleasant sensation. It reminds her of the slight tickles she'd felt from Wren in the before time. She has taken to referring to the time before her death as the before time. It sounds nicer than saying, "when I was alive."

"Cara, they're here," Sarah calls from downstairs.

"Coming."

The sun is beginning to set by the time the travelers begin heading out the door and getting into the wagon for the rest of their journey. The sky is a massive colorful canvas, as if God has painted a masterpiece for her as a going away present.

"Will you look at that," Samuel says in awe. "That is a mighty pretty sky. The good Lord sure knows how to paint a picture."

"That's exactly what I was thinking. It's beautiful," Cara responds. "I'm so glad I got to see it."

"You know, I imagine that compared to the sunsets in Heaven, this is probably nothing," Sarah adds.

"Do you think so? Wow, I can't even imagine what it's going to be like," Cara says.

"Well, no sense stalling. Get yourself on up there and get comfortable," Sarah urges.

"Okay," Cara hesitates. "Are you sure Wren has to stay here? I really don't want to leave her. Can't she come with me and be born in Heaven?"

"No honey, God has a plan for her and it's very important. She needs to be here to help Rachel, then she'll join you. Trust me, you will never know she was gone. It will happen in the blink of an eye and the two of you will be together forever," Sarah answers.

"Promise?"

"I promise."

"What about Rachel? Will she be with me too?"

"Of course, she will."

"Oh, thank goodness. It won't be Heaven without her there. Okay, I think I'm ready. I'm going to miss you both very much. Please come and find me when you get there."

"We will," Sarah assures her.

"Yes mam, we certainly will," Samuel echoes. "Come on now." He holds out his hand and helps her up into the wagon.

As it slowly makes its way down the road, Cara can be seen waving, her voice floating in the breeze, "Good bye. I love you. Take good care of Wren for me. Tell her how much I love her."

Sarah and Samuel wait until the wagon is completely out of sight before heading back to the house to clean up. As they step up on the porch a little voice pipes up, "Hi."

A pretty little girl who looks to be about five-years old, is sitting on the bench with Lazy Boy curled up next to her. She is petting him, and his contented purring is loud enough to be heard by all.

"Well, hello there sweetheart. I think he likes you," Sarah says pointing at the cat. "You must be Wren."

"Yes," she answers as if this should be obvious. She jumps off the bench and dusts cat hair off her hands and dress, then holds one hand out to Sarah and one to Samuel, completely confident that they will take care of her. As they walk in the house together, Wren can be heard saying, "I'm hungry. Can you make me something to eat, please?"

Samuel chuckles, "Why Miss Wren, I believe you are going to fit in here just fine."

RACHEL

In the rich silence of the night, she hears the approaching sound of wagons accompanied by the jingling of harnesses, the clomping of hooves and gentle snorts made by several horses. When she hears the murmuring of voices, she opens her eyes and pads through a dark, unfamiliar room to pull back curtains and peek out an open window. Two wagons are parked below. Each of the wagons is pulled by a team of four horses and have open beds with benches lining each side. Several people are seated in the back of each one. Lanterns shine in the darkness and a tall black man and a smaller white woman dressed in a long skirt stand in the dirt drive talking with the riders.

The people begin to pile out chattering excitedly amongst themselves as they follow the woman and trail out of sight beneath Rachel's window. She hears the clomping of their feet on wood, and a door shutting below. The two drivers remain seated, reins held patiently in their hands, waiting, glancing neither to the left or the right. The black man speaks softly to the horses while he unharnesses them and then leads them away to a barn which casts its own golden glow in the distance. She drops the curtain and lies back down in bed. Closing her eyes, she drifts away again thinking dreams are strange.

Rachel can hear the excited, happy voices of birds twittering to each other and feels a light summer breeze caressing her face. It feels nice. The smell of frying bacon wafts on the air and she spends a nostalgic moment enjoying the safe, happy childhood memories the scent evokes. She gradually opens her eyes and examines a ceiling with which she is totally unfamiliar. It is tongue and groove with a light white washing. She realizes she's lying on a bed that isn't hers; that's weird.

"Where the heck am I?" she wonders aloud.

"Oh yay, you're awake," a little voice trills.

Startled, Rachel rolls to her side and sees a cute little girl standing in the doorway hopping excitedly from one foot to the other in the way only a small child will do. She appears to be about five or six years old with long, curly brown hair that falls nearly to her waist. Her bangs hang in little ringlets and curlicues, and she keeps blowing them out of her eyes. That gesture reminds her so strongly of Cara it gives her heart a little pang, instantly making her feel as if she knows the child. Her eyes are a chocolate brown fringed with long, dark lashes brushing cheeks shining pinkly with excitement. Her skin has the golden-brown glow that makes Rachel think of long summers at the beach. The whole picture is completed by adorable Cupid's bow lips and a pointed little chin.

Rachel tries to figure out where she can possibly be as she slowly takes in the room. She is in a bright, light-filled bedroom speckled with shade from a large tree she can see through the window. The window is open and white lace curtains blow gently back and forth in the sunshine-scented air. Her eyes travel from the window to an old-fashioned dresser with an ornately shaped mirror suspended from posts on either side. A runner with a rose pattern embroidered on it covers the top. Between the dresser and the window sits a comfortable looking overstuffed cream colored chair decorated in a pattern of faded pink roses.

Sitting up, she sees the floor is a honey colored oak that glows from the sun's reflection. She swings her feet to the floor, where they come to rest on a soft pink chenille rug. She wiggles her toes back and forth, enjoying the feel of the fabric brushing against her feet. Eventually Rachel drags her gaze back to the child again. The little girl smiles prettily at her, displaying dimples and making an obvious effort to stand quietly and wait patiently.

"Hi," Rachel says at last.

The little girl takes this as an invitation and practically dances into the room. She stops and places both hands on the covers next to Rachel's leg, grinning up at her as she says, "You're finally awake. I've been waiting all morning."

"Yeah, I am," she says stretching her arms above her head leaning first one way and then the other, enjoying the feel of the muscles pulling and stretching. It seems like ages since she's woken up feeling this good; well-rested and healthy. No hangover. No tears. "I'm sorry I slept so long. I must have been super tired."

"That's okay, everybody does when they first get here. Sarah says it's because the journey is very tiring and it takes your mind a little while to catch up to your body."

Rachel's head spins, with several questions vying for answers all at once until she randomly choses one. "Everybody? Who's everybody?"

"Everybody who comes to stay here are you hungry?" she asks, running the two thoughts together as if they were one.

"Um, yeah I am actually. Thank you, but, well, could you tell me where I am first?"

"Oh," the little girl giggles covering her mouth with both hands. "You're at the Waystation and I live here, and now you do too. Come on, Sarah and me made you breakfast."

"Wait, the Waystation? What's the Waystation, and what do you mean I live here?"

"It's the stopping place on the way to Heaven, silly," she states as if this is a simple fact she should already know.

With that question settled, the little girl grabs Rachel's hand and tugs. Rachel gets shakily to her feet and with a great deal of trepidation blurts out, "Oh God am I dead? I am, aren't I?"

The little girl nods vigorously, her curls bouncing against her plump cheeks. She squeezes Rachel's hand and stares into her eyes sagely declaring, "We don't call it that though. We say you've begun your journey."

Rachel feels the strength run out of her legs all at once as if it has been sucked out by a vacuum. She abruptly sits back down on the bed and feels a rush of vertigo when a flash of Deja vu hits her. This feels like a repeat of the day Cara died. The surreal quality is the same, but at least she doesn't need to puke; that's something.

Pieces of memory began to drop into place with almost audible clicks. She remembers lurching drunkenly through the house and pulling her clothes off. She vaguely recalls climbing in the hot tub. Her mind conjures up an image of a pitcher of screwdrivers. She can even see the beads of sweat running down the outside of the glass from which she was drinking. After that it's a blank until another memory surfaces. She sees a fuzzy picture of Marco's face as he strokes her forehead. He is whispering, "I'm sorry, babe, I didn't have a choice. Try and understand." She touches her fingers to her mouth reliving the feel of his lips on hers and then remembers his final words. "It's just business." The memory crushes her and she begins to cry.

Seeing the pain in Rachel's face, the child climbs up on the bed and onto Rachel's lap. She wraps her little arms around Rachel's neck in a big hug and nestles her head on her shoulder. She sits there patiently letting her cry. Then she tenderly pats Rachel's cheek and catching her eye says, "Don't worry, it'll be okay. You'll like it here. God promised."

She hands Rachel a soft, often-washed handkerchief that had been concealed in her pocket and continues to lean against her chest patting her gently. Rachel cries for a little while, eventually realizing the weight of the child on her lap and the little hand patting her is strangely comforting. Rachel hugs her back, resting her chin on top of the small head, and gradually feels her sadness slipping away. She gives a slight sniffle and wipes at her eyes and nose. "I don't feel dead," she tries to joke.

"That's 'cause dead's not really dead," the child answers brightly. "This is where your true life begins. At least that's what Sarah always says."

She gives Rachel a glowing smile which radiates pure happiness. "I'm so glad you're here, Rachel. I've been waiting for you forever."

As they continue to hold each other, Rachel asks, "What's your name?"

The little girl snuggles a little closer and answers pertly, "I'm Wren and I'm very pleased to meet you." Rachel has to laugh. She sounds like such a grown up and proper little lady.

Hearing her laughter, Wren beams at her saying, "You have a pretty laugh."

Rachel returns the smile. "Thank you, and you're very sweet. Thanks for making me feel better." She takes a big breath and bravely says, "Let's go get breakfast. I'm starving."

THE WAYSTATION

Wren eagerly hops off the bed and taking Rachel's hand again, pulls her towards the door. "Come on, we made fresh biscuits and we have honey too."

Rachel glances down, and notices for the first time that she is not wearing her own clothes. Instead she's wearing white, lightweight cotton pants with a drawstring waist and a matching tunic style shirt and is barefoot. It's not her normal style, but it's certainly comfortable. "Wait a sec," Rachel protests, "I need shoes."

"Oh," Wren exclaims. "Look under the bed, that's where I always leave mine."

Rachel bends down and lifting the edge of the bedspread, pulls out a pair of velvety, white moccasins. She's surprised to find they fit her perfectly when she slips them on. She takes Wren's hand and allows herself to be led out the door, all the while wondering who Sarah is.

The hallway is long and wide with the same golden wood floor as her room and has a cream-colored, thick wooden bannister on the right. She runs her hand across the top of it amazed at how big the building appears to be. Peering over the railing she sees a large common area arrayed with groupings of round tables and chairs that remind her of an old-time saloon from a western movie. She breathes deeply, inhaling all the wonderful aromas drifting up from below and her stomach rumbles in anticipation.

The stairs curve to the right as they descend and she keeps thinking, *I'm dead. Oh, my God, I'm actually dead. If I'm on my way to Heaven, what the heck am I doing here? What is going on? What is this place?*

Thoughts and questions tumble end over end in her head. Pondering them, she realizes she isn't feeling anxious or scared, simply curious and surprisingly, very hungry.

When they reach the bottom of the stairs, Wren guides Rachel to a long, highly polished wooden bar. They both perch on stools and wait.

Rachel glances conspiratorially at Wren and whispers, "Now what?"

"Breakfast silly," Wren whispers back. "I hope you like bacon. I *love* bacon."

SARAH

Sarah takes the last of the bacon from the frying pan and arranges it on two plates. She can hear Rachel and Wren whispering back and forth on the other side of the kitchen door and smiles knowing how excited Wren has been and how she must be talking Rachel's ear off.

She'd been underfoot all morning chattering away like a magpie, enthusiastically describing in detail all that she and Rachel are going to do together. After the third rendition of Wren's plans to take Rachel swimming and fishing with Samuel, Sarah finally put her to work kneading the dough for the biscuits. Then she had her stand on her little step stool so she could reach the sink and wash up a few dishes. This kept Wren busy for a little while until Sarah finally relented, and gave her permission to check on Rachel.

Wren had hastily dried her hands on her skirt and scampered out the kitchen door gleefully proclaiming, "I'm going to see if she's finally awake 'cause I know she's going to love my biscuits."

Sarah reaches into the oven and removes the now golden brown and fragrant biscuits. She places five of them on a plate and adds a crock of butter and a small jar of honey to the tray. She picks up the tray and is heading for the door when she stops, and setting it back down, adds a small glass vase of bright yellow freesia she'd picked that morning from the yard. She doesn't remember ever seeing it growing there before. She had picked it on impulse to add to Rachel's breakfast tray, not fully understanding why, yet feeling it would mean something to her. Sarah had long ago stopped wondering or questioning when these little insightful moments came. The good Lord had a way of speaking to her and guiding her actions, and He was always right.

THE WAYSTATION

She picks up the tray again, butts the door open with her hip, and walks through with a warm and welcoming expression on her face. She knows Rachel will have a lot of questions and she wants to make sure she feels comfortable right from the start. In Sarah's experience, a full stomach always makes things better.

MARCO

Marco sits on the edge of his bunk holding his head in his hands and trying to think. The cell block where he is housed is of the big open bay variety that they called a dorm. It is dingy and poorly lit, jam-packed with the dregs of society. Grime has accumulated in the corners and it smells faintly of bleach with an underlying aroma of piss and sweat. The noise level is intense which makes it difficult to keep a thought in his head. He wonders for the hundredth time how in the hell this happened to him. He thought he'd been careful, planned thoroughly and eliminated all traces of his involvement. There is nothing for him to do but wait, think, and hope his lawyer will have a brilliant piece of advice. He feels truly vulnerable for the first time in a very long time.

His heart beats a fierce tattoo in his chest, because he knows that he's screwed. Sooner or later he'll have to answer for this in one way or another. Monkey had long ago given him the name of a lawyer in the event he ever needed one. It was a good thing too, because Monkey completely distanced himself as soon as he got word of Marco's arrest. Marco hasn't heard one word of encouragement or even admonition from him. There will be no reaching out and certainly no help from that end. He is totally on his own.

The events of the last 24 hours are a blur in his mind. The situation spun out of control incredibly fast. He never anticipated things would play out like this. He always made sure the local cops were well compensated to look the other way. Those bastards should have warned him that things had gone south with that arrangement. It must have been one of the cops he didn't have in his pocket who managed to link him to Cara's murder. Assholes had even tailed him to her funeral. After that, they simply followed the trail of bodies he left behind. They arrested him when he stopped for gas; before he even got to the jobsite to set up his alibi. Fucking cops. So much for paid protection.

"Vicente." Marco glances up at the sound of his name. "Get off your ass, your lawyer's here."

The walk down the hall to the consultation room is one more depressing event in a never-ending series of depressing events. The clang of those steel doors closing behind him is unnerving. He wonders if he will ever get used to it. At least it's quieter in the hall. He hopes this guy is as good as he's supposed to be, or he's toast.

His lawyer stands when he enters the room and offers his hand. "Good afternoon, Mr. Vicente. My name is Daniel Stafford. I'll be representing you."

Marco shakes his hand and says, "I'm very glad to meet you Mr. Stafford. I've been told you're very good at what you do. But do me a favor and call me Marco."

"Of course, Marco, please, have a seat," he says indicating the chair across from him and giving him a moment to get settled before continuing. "I've been reviewing your case and I have to tell you, this is not going to be easy." He flips through a few documents before continuing. "Of course, I want to hear your version of events, however, I must be honest with you, they have a tremendous amount of evidence against you. I think our best option is going to be to try and plead some of this down."

"What do you mean by evidence?"

"Well, to begin with, they found tire tracks at the location where the body of Cara Healy was discovered. The impressions from those tracks match the tires on the truck owned by Tony Moretti."

"Hey, that's not my problem," Marco argues. "What do tire tracks from his truck have to do with me?"

"I understand your confusion Marco. I realize this particular piece of evidence does not implicate you directly. However, the type of mud and plants found at the burial site were also found imbedded in the soles of a pair of shoes the police found in the garage at your house."

Marco pales at this and struggles visibly to control his fear.

Shit, the shoes. I put those fucking things in the deep sink and forgot to clean them.

"Oh man, I didn't fucking kill her. That was all Tony. I just helped him get rid of her body. I'm serious, dude. I didn't have anything to do with her dying. I liked Cara. She was my girl's best friend. I came in after the fact because Tony begged me for help. They can't put this on me."

"Well, that's good to know, but it still leaves you in the position of accessory to two counts of murder."

"Wait. What do you mean two counts? Why two counts?"

"Marco," Stafford says patiently, "Because Cara was pregnant, the law considers the fetus to be a viable life and therefore the baby counts as a second homicide."

Marco is visibly sweating.

"Then there are the witnesses who saw you enter and leave the residence of a Mr. Ricardo Bastollo shortly before he was discovered with two bullets in his chest. Fortunately for you they haven't found the gun yet. They may not be able to convince a jury of your culpability on that one, though the circumstantial evidence is rather compelling."

"They also have latex gloves, rubber tubing, and a fully loaded syringe which were found in a bag on the floor in the back seat of your car, though we can reasonably assume that's just circumstantial evidence at this point. Until the toxicology screening comes back, we won't know if there are any traces of heroin in either Rachel or Mr. Bastollo's system. However, …" He lets the thought hang there and watching Marco's face for his reaction.

Marco manages to keep his expression neutral, so his lawyer continues. "And last, but certainly not least, the body of your girlfriend, Rachel Henderson, who was discovered by her sister, Sylvia, floating in your hot tub a mere twenty minutes after you left your house. Coincidentally, the police also found a pair of wet pants that smelled of chlorine in the back seat of your car. They appear to be the same suit pants you were wearing at the funeral service earlier in the day." Raising an eyebrow, he asks, "Is that enough or should I keep going?"

Marco's stomach churns and he can feel sweat accumulating on his scalp and under his arms. His fingers tremble as he runs them through his hair. "No, I've heard enough."

"The only solid evidence they have right now is the mud and plants from your shoes, but that only links you to the deaths of Cara Healy and her baby." Marco swallows with an audible click. Stafford meets his eye before continuing. "However, as the investigation progresses, there is always the possibility they'll be able to find additional physical evidence to tie you to the other two deaths as well. Those wet pants will almost certainly come back to bite you. Please keep that in mind as we discuss your options."

Marco is beginning to get pissed off. "You don't sound like you're even giving me the benefit of the doubt. Aren't I supposed to be innocent until proven guilty?"

"Of course, Marco; that's the law." Daniel gives him a polite smile. "However, in my line of work, with the clientele I generally represent, it's usually not a question of innocence or guilt. Instead, as in this instance, it's more a case of how do we mitigate this situation to best serve you, my client? Now, if you would prefer to profess your innocence and claim that you're being set up, we can go that route. Truthfully though, I think our time would be best spent trying to minimize the damage, don't you?"

Marco stares long and hard at his lawyer through narrowed eyes, finally giving him a brief nod. "Fine. What are my options? Do I even have any options?"

Stafford closes the file, sits back in his chair and crosses his legs, taking time to smooth down his pant legs and folding his hands in his lap before speaking. "Certainly, there are always options." He pauses and flicks a piece of lint off his pants giving Marco time to reflect on what he's saying. "My advice is that you find something you can offer up as a bargaining chip. As I said, we can plead this down and keep you off death row. But, I must have something I can give them if you want to have some leverage; specifically, a person whose is a little higher up the food chain. Perhaps you should consider giving them a name of an individual in your, shall we say, business ventures."

"Are you kidding me? That's suicide. No fucking way. I'm not that stupid."

Stafford leans forward, "I understand your reticence, Marco, but you need to understand that you don't have much choice here. They *are* going to find you guilty and in all likelihood, you will eventually find yourself sitting on death row. We need to make a deal if you're going to have any chance of coming out the other side of this."

"Oh shit. I can't even wrap my head around this. I am seriously fucked." Marco rests his elbows on the table and hangs his head in his hands.

His lawyer waits patiently, then taps his hand on the table before adding, "Let me make a suggestion. You give some thought to this tonight and then tomorrow we'll meet again and you can give me a name, preferably the person with whom you deal directly. The DA is looking to put up a win. If you cooperate and hand them your distributor, they'll be very amenable to keeping you off the row. It's my experience that one should never underestimate the power of inside information. You have an opportunity to make this whole thing play out in your favor. Let's not throw away all our cards just yet."

"Yeah, yeah, okay. Tomorrow maybe I'll give you a name. I can't believe I'm even thinking about doing this."

"Don't worry, Marco, this will get easier. Once you've made the deal, I'm confident the DA will make sure you're protected. You'll be way too valuable for them to risk having anything happen to you. I've seen it before. You'll be their golden boy."

Standing up, his lawyer once again holds out his hand and they shake. Marco's fear is evident and his palms are sweaty. Stafford resists the urge to wipe his hand on his pants.

DANIEL STAFFORD

After exiting the building, Stafford pulls out his cell phone and punches in a familiar number, one that he has memorized so it isn't saved to his phone book. "Buenos tardes, Senior Arciero. I've met with Mr. Vicente and I'm afraid your suspicions are correct. It appears that he will be a problem."

He listens attentively then replies, "Gracias, Senior. It's a pleasure as always. Please let me know if I can be of any further assistance. You have a very pleasant evening and give my best wishes to your lovely wife."

Daniel ends the call and pockets his phone, striding quickly to his car. If he hurries, he can make it to his son's soccer game. He believes in being an involved parent and feels it's important to keep his children active in sports and other activities. It's the key to keeping kids out of trouble these days. His children are not going to wind up like the people he represents. He isn't averse to making a good living off drug dealers, in fact, he greatly appreciates it, but he feels his children are destined for better things, and Senior Arciero's money is going to be crucial to their success. He drives out of the parking lot with a satisfied expression on his face, pleased with how his life is going.

MONKEY

He ends the call and leans back in his chair puffing on his cigar for a few moments while mulling over the situation. As he has anticipated, Marco is going to cover his own ass and leave everyone else's hanging out in the wind. Daniel is a good attorney and tremendously loyal. He's well paid to stay that way. If he feels Marco is turning, then it's settled, and that's what contingency plans are for. Monkey is a big fan of contingency plans. That kind of thinking has kept him off the police radar and out of prison for a very long time, and he has no intention of changing his method of operation now.

Punching in another number, he speaks briefly with the person on the other end. "Buenos tardes, Albierto. I would like for you to take care of that little problem we discussed earlier. Have your guys create a distraction of some kind." He listens briefly before responding, "I don't care what, a little fight or an argument, you decide what would work best. Just do something to draw the guards' attention. After that, it's up to you how you handle it. I don't need to know the details. I have confidence in you."

Content with the arrangements, he knows Marco won't be a concern for much longer. It will be a loss, but the hard truth is Marco can no longer be a useful earner. Even if by some miracle, he can get out from under all of this, he could never be completely trusted again, and the police will always be watching him. When a tool fails, you discard it and purchase a new one. There are plenty of men in his organization waiting for an opportunity to move up. Replacing him will not be difficult.

Rolling the cigar back and forth between his fat fingers, he considers calling Maritza to bring him a Cerveza. However, his children and all the grandchildren are expected this evening for a big family dinner and she is busy in the kitchen preparing enough food to feed a small army. He decides to be generous and heaves his bulk up from his chair, laying his cigar in the dish and ambling towards the kitchen. Perhaps she can prepare him a plate to tide him over until dinner.

He calls out, "Maritza, your husband is coming and he is very hungry. Be a good wife and prepare him something to eat."

Chuckling can be heard coming from the kitchen. "Of course, my handsome husband should never know hunger. I do not like skinny men."

And that, Monkey thinks with a contented sigh, is why I love my wife. She understands me.

RACHEL

Even though she just arrived, all her anxieties seem to melt away almost immediately. Wren and Sarah make her feel so comfortable at breakfast, it's like she's come home. She eats like a lumberjack, and yes, Wren's biscuits are delicious just as advertised. She eats three with butter and honey in addition to the eggs and bacon. The size of her appetite is a little embarrassing.

Once they finish eating, Sarah, refusing Rachel's offer to help with the dishes, says, "I think Wren has plans for you," and waves them off as she carries the dirty dishes into the kitchen.

"Come on Rachel," Wren says as she eagerly grabs Rachel's hand and leads her to the barn. "There's someone else you have to meet."

Rachel falls in love with Samuel the minute they're introduced. He is very kind and gentle, especially for such a large man. When he takes her hands in his and holds them between his giant paws, she feels warm, safe, and protected; like she truly belongs here. Love and kindness radiate from him.

He gazes intensely into her eyes, and when he smiles at her it lights up his whole face. He says in his deep southern drawl, "Welcome, Miss Rachel, welcome. We have been waitin' such an awful long time to meet you, ain't we Wren?" He winks at Wren, eliciting a giggle. Returning his attention to Rachel, he continues, "I know this is all kind of confusin' at first, but don't you worry none. God always has a plan, and everythin' works out just fine in His time. You can have complete faith in that."

Still holding her hand, Samuel proceeds to give her a tour of the barn, introducing her to the barn cats, Caspar and Lulu. She happily spends several minutes petting and loving on them. She loves cats and has always wanted one or two, but Marco wouldn't agree to let her have any because he hated all the hair and was too worried about them clawing up his precious massage chair.

"And these," Samuel says with obvious pride, "are our horses, Tallulah and Belle. Ain't they beautiful? They are just as sweet as they look too. Neither of them have ever given me a bit of trouble."

Rachel, never having spent any time with horses before, delights in rubbing their velvety noses and lets them blow gently into her hair. Wren eagerly shows her how to feed them pieces of carrot, and after her first nervous try (being unsure if she was going to lose any fingers to those huge teeth), she feeds them piece after piece until Samuel politely clears his throat and suggests, "Maybe we should save a little for tomorrow, that way we don't spoil their supper."

"Oh, of course, sorry about that." Blushing a little she asks, "Samuel do you think you could teach me to ride one day? I've always wanted to ride a horse. I mean, you know, if you're not too busy and if it's not too much trouble?"

"One day? Well, Miss Rachel, I ain't got any pressing business today. What do you say? Would you like to try it now?"

"Could we really? Oh, yes, please." She glances excitedly at Wren. "What do you think Wren? Should we go riding?"

Wren is already running for the bridles. "Yeah, let's go Rachel. You're gonna have so much fun. We can ride down to the creek and I can show you the best places to catch fish."

Samuel saddles up Belle for Rachel, but only puts a bridle on Tallulah, explaining, "Now, Miss Rachel, we're gonna have you ride with a saddle until you get more comfortable on a horse. Once you get the hang of it, you can ride bareback like me and Wren. But for now, you'll feel safer if you have somethin' to hang on to and somewhere to put your feet."

He shows her how to mount and gives her a leg up, placing her feet in the stirrups and then demonstrates how she should hold the reins. Patting Belle on the neck he says, "Now try to relax, and keep yourself steady by gripping with your knees. Don't jerk on the reins any and trust that Belle knows what she's doin'. She's a gentle girl, but if you get scared or feel like you might fall off, then hang on to this here saddle horn. Okay?"

Rachel nods eagerly, wrapping her hands over the saddle horn and waiting with barely suppressed excitement while Samuel gets settled on Tallulah. Reaching down he gives Wren his hand and she scampers up his leg like a monkey in a tree, where she perches comfortably on Tallulah's withers. She grabs a handful of mane and waits patiently as if she's done this a thousand times before.

Rachel is thoroughly impressed. "Wow, Wren, that is so cool. You must have been riding horses for a really long time."

"Of course, I have. I've been riding since I was a little baby, haven't I Sam?"

Samuel chuckles and after getting Wren situated in front of him answers, "Yes, Miss Wren. You've been ridin' pretty near your whole life."

The rest of the morning is wonderful. Wren narrates their tour, with a little help from Samuel, and Rachel is pleasantly surprised to find that riding a horse is as exciting as she imagined it would be. But, her butt is getting numb, and she's relieved when they finally reach the creek. She climbs down from Belle's back and gratefully hands the reins over to Samuel. Wren, appearing to be unaffected by their long ride, hops down and runs to the creek where she plops down and immediately puts her bare feet in the water.

"Come on Rachel, try it. Put your feet in the mud and the minnows will tickle your legs and your toes. It's fun."

Rachel wastes no time in removing her shoes and joins Wren on the creek bank. "You know," Rachel says lowering her feet into the water, "I read in a magazine that there are women who spend a lot of money to go to special shops where they let little fish nibble on their feet to eat the dry skin. It's supposed to make them feel soft and smooth."

Wren looks at Samuel in disbelief, her mouth hanging open. She bursts into laughter and asks, "Why would they do that when they can just stick their feet in the creek?"

Samuel shakes his head and says, "Well I'll be dipped in wax and called a candle if that ain't the silliest thing I ever heard."

Rachel shrugs, "Who knows."

THE WAYSTATION

She drifts along like this for a couple of days, amazed at how different she feels without the weight of all the fears and pressures of life. She isn't even terribly worried about her family, because somehow, she knows they're fine. It strikes her as strange that she doesn't miss her huge closet full of clothes or her expensive shoes. In fact, she feels better without all that stuff; lighter somehow. She feels peaceful and happy in a way she has never experienced before. She doesn't understand it, but is grateful nonetheless. She can't help but wonder if Cara came through here on her way to Heaven. She hopes she did. She, of all people, deserves to be this happy.

Wren is such a ray of sunshine it's impossible to feel anything except cheerful when she is near; it's contagious. No matter what they are doing, Wren finds joy in it. In fact, much to Rachel's amusement, Wren is currently crawling around on her hands and knees in the garden with a mason jar searching for bugs to feed the baby bird she is nursing along.

After proudly showing Rachel her bird which she has named Snowball, for reasons unfathomed by anyone except her, she explains with great seriousness her need to hunt for quality bugs. "I'm his new momma and it's up to me to make sure he grows up to be big and strong. That means I have to find the best bugs to feed him. Samuel says one day he's gonna fly away and live with the other birds in the trees, but I know he'll always love me best because you always love your momma more than anyone."

Rachel laughs in delight at her explanation. Wren can be awfully earnest at times, it is one of her most endearing qualities.

Since Wren is actively engaged in pursuit of the birdie version of a gourmet lunch, Rachel decides this is a good time to talk with Sarah. She has a lot of questions and feels ready to try and process whatever the answers might be.

She meanders up the path from the garden and runs her hands along the tops of flowering bushes for which she has no name, yet thinks are gorgeous. As she draws near the house, she notices some yellow freesia growing right outside the kitchen door. They give off an amazing fragrance. Freesia has always been her favorite flower. She tried a couple of times to grow it at her house (well, Marco's house), but they never thrived and the blossoms always dried up on the stems. That memory causes her to frown. She still finds it unsettling to think back to her time with Marco, so she resolutely shakes it off. The blooms here however, are flourishing, filling the air with their sweet perfume. The smell of them makes her content in a way she can't describe. Pinching off a stem, she holds it in her hand and inhales the scent, reveling in the pleasure created by such a simple thing.

She tucks her hair behind her ear, carefully placing the flower there so she can continue to enjoy the fragrance. Wiping the dirt off her shoes before entering the kitchen, she finds Sarah putting a couple of pies in the oven and grins in anticipation. Sarah looks up at her and gives an answering smile of her own, noticing the flower tucked in Rachel's hair. Apparently, God does know what He is doing.

"Well hello there, Rachel. Did you get tired of hunting creepy crawlies with Wren?"

Rachel laughs and takes a seat on a stool. "No, I never even started. I left that entirely up to her. She's the expert and much lower to the ground than I am. Besides, bugs aren't really my thing. I don't think it would have been very helpful for me to be screaming and running away."

Sarah chuckles, "Mine either, though I assume the good Lord must have had a purpose in putting them here. But as long as they stay out of my kitchen, we get along fine. Would you like a slice of pound cake and a glass of milk? The cake's still warm and I've got lemon icing to drizzle on top."

Rachel's mouth immediately begins to water at the thought. She isn't sure if it's because she is no longer drinking and smoking pot, or if it's simply the rightness (she can think of no other word to describe it) of the atmosphere here, but everything tastes wonderful. In fact, food has never tasted or smelled as good as it does here. At this rate, she is going to gain twenty pounds before she knows it, and surprisingly enough, she is totally okay with that. It's worth it.

"Oh yes, please, that sounds fabulous. You're doing an awful lot of cooking and baking today. This is a lot of food." She waves her hand at all the cakes, pies and covered dishes lining the counters. "How are we ever going to eat all of this?"

"Well, honey, that won't be a problem. We'll be having travelers come through later tonight," she explains as she pours the milk and slices the cake, "and they always eat like a swarm of locusts. I've found it's best to be prepared. There's usually not a lot of leftovers."

"Travelers? From where? You mean people like me who, you know, died?" It was strange, but without her even noticing, it had become easy to acknowledge her own death. In fact, it felt almost normal now.

"Yes, exactly," Sarah answers pouring Rachel's milk and a glass of water for herself. After drizzling the lemon icing over the top, she nods towards the door and says, "Let's go sit in the dining hall and talk. There are a few things I want to tell you."

Rachel picks up the plate and glass, remembering at the last second to grab a fork, and follows her through the door, resisting the urge to lick the icing off the plate. She is more than a little curious. She's been hoping to have a chance to talk and here it is. She doesn't even have to figure out a way to start the conversation. It's almost as if Sarah has been waiting for her. Truthfully, nothing about this place surprises her anymore.

MARCO

The meeting with his lawyer was anything but encouraging. In fact, it sucked. His options are shit or shit on toast. He is royally screwed. Either he keeps his mouth shut and goes down in flames, lethal injection most likely, or he snitches off Monkey and gets some heavy-duty prison time in protective custody. Both of these options have zero appeal and frankly, the idea of giving up Monkey makes him feel sick to his stomach. He can't even begin to make a choice. He keeps hoping a third option will miraculously present itself.

He'd been escorted back to his dorm where he has been sitting for the last three hours fingering the plastic rosary the resident priest gave him. Hey, it couldn't hurt, right? Surprisingly, he finds it comforting. Before he was arrested, it had been years since he'd gone to confession or prayed, but the guilt over Cara and Rachel was causing a constant pain in his gut, and he was feeling a strong desire to confess and ask for forgiveness. The priest was a pretty cool guy and had listened to Marco pour out his heart without berating him. He had even offered a few words of comfort.

"My son, it has been my experience that men who find themselves in this place are not here because God is punishing them. Instead, they are here because He has removed His hand from their lives and is allowing them to suffer the consequences of their actions. You need to pray to the Holy Father, not only for forgiveness of your sins, but also that He would reveal Himself to you. It wouldn't hurt to appeal to the blessed Virgin to intercede on your behalf as well. I'm a firm believer in covering all the bases," he imparted with a small smile.

Marco is amazed by how much better those simple words have made him feel; like he has found his way back to a safe and familiar place. All the penance is a bitch, but that seems like a small price to pay for some relief and there is always a chance it might make a difference. Besides, he has a lot of time on his hands. It gives him something to do.

The block he's being held in has fifteen dorms, and each is packed with row after row of bunk beds. His seems to be populated by an endless variety of the worst humanity has to offer. He warily watches the assholes he shares space with, agonizing over his situation and his lawyer's suggestion. When they are finally called up for dinner, he still hasn't come to a decision, but is hoping he might have a better idea after a night's sleep.

He disgustedly pushes his tray away after only a few bites. This place stinks and the food is a joke. The prisoner sitting across from him, a heavy-set Mexican with a shaved head and an interesting array of bad tattoos, including a demon on his head and multiple lipstick kisses on his neck, points at Marco's tray with his plastic fork and asks if he's going to finish that. Marco waves his hand as if to say, go ahead. Mr. Shaved-Head-Tattoo-Guy wolfs down the rest of Marco's food as if it's ambrosia and this is the last batch to be found anywhere on earth.

Holy shit, life among the savages. I should have gotten Rachel some help for her depression and been honest with her. I could have convinced her that I didn't have a choice; that I had to help Tony. Even if she'd thrown me under the bus, it would have only been for accessory and not murder one. Granted they still would have counted it as two murders, but still as an accessory, right? I could have pled that down and then I wouldn't be in this awful situation. I could have made it work.

Thoughts and impossible choices swirl around in his head as he does his best to ignore the circus surrounding him. Oddly enough it occurs to him that he and Tony probably had something to do with a few of these men being in this place. He remembers reading in a magazine that the percentage of people in the prison system for drug related offenses is greater than 55%.

Yeah, it's a good possibility some of these guys can probably thank me for ending up in here. Hopefully that little tidbit never becomes common knowledge. Then again, maybe it would earn me some street cred.

Finally, it's time to exit the California State correctional system's version of a fine dining establishment and they all trudge off to their dorm again. Yeah, buddy, the convict shuffle.

Later while lying in his bunk, he tries to figure out who he can hit up to put some money on his books. He's dying for a cigarette and that shit doesn't come free. Until they decide he's trustworthy enough to be put to work, he has no way of earning money. When he was processed in, they gave him a personal care bag containing deodorant, shampoo, soap, toothpaste, a toothbrush, and a crappy plastic hairbrush and comb. They allowed him to keep his one precious pack of smokes, but he's burned through those in record time because in here, what else is there to do other than watch TV and smoke? He can't call his family because he hasn't told any of them he's been arrested. It isn't like they're all that close anyway; being in the drug business tends to put a lot of space between families. Still, he doesn't want to break his mamma's heart or see the shame in his father's eyes; that would kill him. He hopes his mom is still praying for him. Right now, he can use all the help he can get.

Being the new fish, he's trying to keep a low profile until he can get the lay of the land. There's no sense pissing off the Aryan Brotherhood or any of the other gang members strutting around this place. Sooner or later he's going to have to figure out whom to align himself with, though he doesn't exactly have much of a choice. It will probably have to be one of the Mexican gangs. With his face and a name like Marco Vicente, that's who will be recruiting him, though he has a hard time picturing himself with lipstick kisses tattooed on his neck. Once he settles in and gets to know people, he figures it will be safe for him to check out the gym and maybe join in on one of the pick-up games of basketball. Until then, he's on his own.

Time ticks by slowly, but eventually it's his dorm's shower time. Oh, joy. Slipping on his shower shoes (he's been warned extensively about the nasty things you can pick up on your bare feet in the shower), he wraps his towel around his waist, gathers his shampoo and soap, and steels himself for what he feels is one of the worst parts of the day.

His first day in he'd been completely unprepared for the experience. Getting naked and showering in front of a group of guys is bad enough, but doing it in front of bunch of guys who stare at him in a way no guy should have to be stared at by another, is a different experience altogether. Fortunately, no one has touched him or even approached him yet. Still, he figures it's only a matter of time. He doesn't try to kid himself, he knows he's a good-looking man and he looks good naked. Rachel and many other women have told him that enough times, so he has no reason to doubt it. Besides, some of these guys have been in here a long time.

He faces the wall while he showers, keeping his back turned to the other prisoners, trying to ignore them and wash as quickly as possible. He finishes rinsing the shampoo out of his hair and has just wiped the water from his face when he feels a hand caress his shoulder and slide down his back to encircle his waist. He jumps and immediately starts to turn around ready to break the nose of whoever this is, only to be stopped short by a very sharp object pressed up against his throat.

A voice whispers in his ear in heavily accented English, "No, no, my pretty one, you don't want to do that." The hand caresses him again and runs a line slowly down the bones of his spine. Cold chills run up and down his arms despite the hot water raining down from the shower head, and he does his best not to shiver or show any emotion at all while furiously running through his limited options in his mind.

Marco can feel the shank digging into his neck and it's beginning to sting. That means this guy has already drawn blood. To make matters worse, he can feel his assailant's growing erection pressing up against his ass causing him to involuntarily tighten up his butt cheeks in anticipation of what he is afraid might be coming. The man begins to rub up against Marco with an increasing sense of urgency making Marco feel like he's going to vomit. *Holy shit, where are the guards?*

A soft chuckle ripples in his ear. "Oh yeah," the voice breathes, "now what I want you to do is pour out some of that shampoo, and make your hand all nice and soapy. Then I want you to reach back and wrap it around my dick and start stroking, and you do a good job. Don't even think about squeezing me too hard though or I will cut you bad. Comprende, amigo?"

Marco nods his head carefully to keep the blade from digging in any deeper. Swallowing thickly and pouring out a healthy amount of shampoo, he reaches back with a trembling hand while frantically trying to think of a way out of this which doesn't involve his throat being cut.

"Oh, that's nice, nino, nice. A little longer on the strokes though eh. Oh yeah, you got it. Just like that. You're doing real good for a first timer. Though maybe this ain't your first time, huh? Good looking chavo like you must have guys crawling up your ass all the time."

After a few interminable minutes, the man finally convulses, squirting a warm, stickiness all over Marco's hand and butt causing him to shudder with revulsion. Shaking with relief, he takes his hand back and discretely rinses it off in the water, hoping the worst is over.

"Was it good for you too? Maybe next time I do you in the ass, huh? What do you say?" the voice murmurs.

"If it's cool with you, I'd rather skip that part man," Marco almost begs.

The voice laughs, "Aw, I'm just fucking with you man. Go ahead and turn around."

Reluctantly he complies, though it's difficult since the shiv is still pressed firmly up against his throat. Marco's not surprised to see the voice belongs to a Mexican who looks like a hard-core gangbanger. The man regards him from a height of at least 6' 5". He wears more ink than skin, including three teardrops trailing from the corner of one eye. He's scowling at Marco as if he has a score to settle with him, though he can't imagine what since he's never seen this guy before.

Marco's eyes skip around the shower room noting with increasing desperation that all the other prisoners seem to have to disappeared. That can't be a coincidence. He licks his lips as he tries to get his nerves under control. "Dude, I did what you wanted. Are we cool now?"

The banger reaches out and casually flicks Marco between the eyes, causing him to jump and the shiv to pierce his skin even more. "Naw, esse, we're not cool. I still got a message to deliver to you from Monkey."

Marco feels his bowels loosen and is surprised that shit isn't spewing down his legs. "Wh…what's the message?" he asks in a trembling voice, anticipating the worst.

THE WAYSTATION

"This, you fucking pocho," he growls, stabbing Marco in the neck once, twice, again and again. "You think you're better than me, huh, pinche wedo?"

The pain is immediate and immense, blossoming in an explosive burst and spreading throughout his body. Blood streams down Marco's chest, mixing with the water and flowing down the drain. He tries to cry out, yet only manages to create a strange gurgling noise. If the banger hadn't been pressing him up against the wall, he would have already collapsed to the floor.

The man finally allows Marco to drop to the tile and then apparently in no hurry, takes the time to thoroughly rinse the blood off his hands and chest, even helping himself to Marco's soap. Before he walks away, he pauses long enough to spit on him. "Hijo de La Chingada. Monkey don't like fucking snitches man." Then he saunters away as if he doesn't have a care in the world, secure in the knowledge that he has successfully completed his job and his standing will rise even higher among the prisoner population.

As his life snakes across the tile and slips into the drain, Marco has time for one final thought before he blacks out. *But I hadn't even made up my mind yet.*

RACHEL & SARAH

Sarah settles comfortably in a chair. Hooking another one with her foot, she slips off her shoes with a tired sigh and puts both feet up. "Oh, that feels good," she groans, rubbing her arches. "My feet are plumb wore-out. I love to cook and get a lot of pleasure from seeing folks enjoy my food, but it can be mighty tiring."

Rachel sits across from her and digs into the pound cake with enthusiasm. Sarah watches her with a contented expression playing across her face, sipping her water and waiting quietly.

"Did you enjoy it?" she asks when Rachel is finished.

"Oh no, I hated it," Rachel jokes as she unashamedly licks the plate for any orphaned crumbs or stray drippings of icing.

That reaction earns a smile from Sarah. "If folks don't want to lick the plate clean, I haven't done my job right."

"Oh, you got it right. You could open your own bakery and make a fortune. I'd be your first customer."

"Well thank you honey. I appreciate that." Sarah crosses her ankles and continues. "Since you've had a while to settle in and get your feet back under you, I think that maybe it's time to tell you a little bit about this place."

"That'd be great," Rachel says eagerly. "All I know is what Wren told me. She said this is the place between our life on earth and our life in Heaven, but I don't really understand what that means. Why is Wren here? Why are you and Samuel here? You're all such wonderful people, why are you stuck here and not in Heaven where you belong? Not that I don't like it here, it's a beautiful place. I just assume Heaven is even better since it's where all believers hope to go."

THE WAYSTATION

"Well, that's a lot of questions dear, and I'm going to get to all of them, but let me start with the simple things first. The Waystation exists as a stopping point for those traveling from death to their reward. You need to understand that reward can mean different things to different people. Some of the people who travel through here are on their way to Heaven to live forever with God in His kingdom. On the other hand, some are on their way to Hell."

Rachel is shocked, yet fascinated at the same time.

"Now, we don't get too many of those poor souls, thank goodness. Mostly, we get the ones who are rejoicing in their journey. It's our blessing to get to welcome them and give them a chance to rest for a bit and have something good to eat and drink before they begin the final stretch. Think of it as their opportunity to adjust to the idea that they have passed and maybe ask a few questions."

"Okay, that makes sense. It's nice that you can do that for them. But even if you only, or mostly, get the good ones, how do you handle that many people? People are dying every second of every day. That would mean thousands and thousands of people would be passing through here. Are there other places like this? There must be, right?"

"Oh, honey, good and bad are terms we don't use because everyone has good and bad in them. It's not up to you or me to determine who's good and who's bad. Only God knows a person's true heart and sees them for who they truly are. But to answer your other question, I don't know if there are other Waystations. He has never revealed that to me. I've always kind of assumed there are, but in truth, it doesn't matter. We simply do as He has asked us and take real, good care of the people when they come through here."

"Oh, my gosh," Rachel blurts out. "I get it now. It wasn't a dream."

"What wasn't a dream?"

"When I first got here, I mean before that first morning when Wren came to get me, I thought I was dreaming. During the night, I heard horses and people, and saw wagons out my window. I saw you and Samuel too, though I didn't know it was you at the time. You had lanterns and were out in the front yard. You brought them inside and Samuel took the horses to the barn."

"Yes, that was the last time a group of travelers came through. We usually get a group every three or four days, but sometimes it's longer."

"So, there are more travelers coming through tonight? How many? Where are they from? Do you know who they are?"

Sarah laughs, "Yes, there are more coming through tonight. I don't know how many or where they come from, and I don't know who they are."

"Sorry, this is really exciting."

"Good, I'm glad you're excited. I was hoping maybe you'd like to help me welcome them tonight."

"Yes, of course, I'd love to. What do you want me to do?"

"Just be friendly and help me serve. There's nothing like the joy of serving a person in need to bring you closer to God. Serving one another is what the Lord has called us to do. You know, Jesus even went so far as to wash the disciples' feet, and I bet they must have had some nasty feet back then. People didn't wear proper shoes in those days." Sarah grins at her own joke.

"Also, you need to keep in mind that time is an odd thing; it's not linear here like it is in life. You may feel as if you have been here for three days, but on earth it may be five years or you may not have even been born yet. My point is, sometimes we get groups of people who are dressed in a way to make you think they must have died a hundred years in the past, or fifty years in the future, yet in their minds they passed only a few seconds ago. You'll need to prepare yourself for that and try not to mention it because it can become a bit awkward."

"Whoa, seriously? That's so insane, it's hard for me to wrap my head around it."

"What does wrap my head around it mean? I've heard some of the travelers use it from time to time, but I never asked any of them to explain it."

"Oops, sorry, it's an expression we always use, er, used to use." She frowns. It was an expression she and Marco had always used, and she didn't want to think about him at all. Resolutely rejecting any thoughts of Marco, she continues, "It just means it's hard for me to…oh man, how do I explain it? It's hard for me to completely understand and accept that idea. It doesn't mean I don't believe you; it's just difficult to comprehend. Does that make sense?"

"Yes, thank you dear. I thought it must be something like that." She pats Rachel's hand. "My point is you need to keep an open mind, and even more importantly, an open heart. Some people will be rejoicing, and some will be timid or confused, yet they all need and deserve our love and understanding."

"I can do that."

"I know you can. I have complete faith in you."

"Does Wren help out too?"

"Occasionally, though not too often. Usually the wagons come through late at night; too late for her. Though the main reason is to protect her from the drivers and what may happen to them. I believe that may be why God chooses to usually bring them through at night."

"Why does she need to be protected from them? Are they bad people? Would they hurt her?"

Sarah sighs, "This may be a little difficult to explain. What is your version of Hell? What do you know about it?"

"Um, well, it has a lake of fire. Satan lives there and evil people go there to burn for all eternity. Oh, and there are many levels with different punishments—at least according to Dante. Is there more to it than that?"

"Everything you said is fairly accurate, however, there is occasionally a transition process before the sinners go to Hell, though that's not actually an appropriate name for them since we have all sinned and fallen short of the glory of God. However, for lack of a better word, I'll call them sinners. These sinners are sometimes called upon to be the ones who transport our travelers from death to their reward. They have to drive them to the very gates of Heaven and watch as they joyfully enter in, but are refused entrance themselves. It's part of their punishment."

"Oh wow, that's intense. How long do they have to do this, or is it only once and then they go straight from there to Hell?"

"It varies from person to person. We never know how their providence is determined. Some of these drivers make the trip time after time and some only once. Nevertheless, what Wren needs to be protected from is the chance that they are spirited away right here."

"Spirited away?"

"Yes. I've seen it happen several times. It's very frightening, and would be especially so for a child. The Lord opens the barrier He has erected between here and the underworld to protect us from Satan's minions, and allows the demons to enter and drag the sinner away to his fate. It's not something I want Wren to see."

"Oh man, that sounds awful. You're right. She does *not* need to see that; it would be way too scary for her."

Sarah nods her head in agreement. "One other thing, under no circumstance are you to speak to the drivers or offer them comfort or even a glass of water. Another part of their punishment is to be abandoned and rejected. God has forbidden us to speak with them and they cannot speak to us."

"Man, that sounds really harsh, but I guess they were very bad people in life huh?"

"The Lord can be terribly demanding and full of righteous anger. He doesn't take it lightly when people abuse His children, and we are all His children, old and young alike. We are precious to Him. The ones who have done harm to His children, and sometimes even the ones who may have been the cause of their deaths, are the drivers."

Rachel thinks about this for a moment then asks, "So, someone could be riding in a wagon driven by the person who killed them? Holy crap, that must be awful for them."

"Yes, that's possible, but the travelers won't suffer because of it. The Lord loves us so much that He blinds them to the driver's identity, but He does not blind the drivers to theirs. In this way, they're forced to face their victims and endure the guilt, and fear the coming of their punishment."

"Well, that's something at least. Is there anything else I need to know?"

"No. I think that's enough for now." Sarah reaches out and clasps Rachel's hand. "I simply want you to know how much you are loved and how important you are to Wren. She has been waiting a long time for you to arrive. You're very special."

Rachel jerks in surprise and tries to pull her hand away. "What? Why am I special?"

Sarah tightens her hold, "Because your arrival was necessary for her to begin her own journey."

"But why did God choose to keep her here? She died so young. It's unfair. She never got a chance to grow up."

"Oh honey, she didn't die. She was never born in the conventional sense. Her mother died while she was still carrying Wren in her womb. This is the only life—the only place she has ever known. She's never had to suffer at anyone's hand. She has experienced nothing but love and happiness her entire life."

Rachel stares at Sarah trying to absorb what she's said. "But, but, I mean, does she know that?"

"Of course, she does." She releases Rachel's hand and adds, "I know this is all a bit overwhelming at first. I tell you what, we're going to have a busy evening, why don't you go and lie down for a little while before supper. I'll call you when it's time to eat, alright?"

Rachel slowly gets to her feet, "Okay, thanks." As she walks away and begins to climb the stairs, she stops and grasping the newel post, she turns back. With a slight tremble in her voice she asks, "You said I was important to her. Is it possible, I mean, do I…um, did I know Wren's mother?"

Sarah is on her way to the kitchen with Rachel's dirty dishes when she stops and answers with great tenderness, "Why yes honey, you did. You knew her very well."

RACHEL

She sits in the rose-patterned chair in her room and tries to take in all that Sarah told her. As for the demons-dragging-the-damned-off-to-hell thing, okay, that's simple to understand even if it is a little scary. She doesn't want to witness it for herself though, because she's a little concerned she might pee her pants or something embarrassing like that. She's never been one for scary movies and knows dealing with that type of thing in real-life is not going to end well for her. But, she'll cross that bridge when she comes to it. No sense spending time worrying about it now.

Wren is another story. Rachel traces the rose pattern with her finger on the arm of the chair while she thinks about it. Wren has never been born. She came to be here when her mother died. How that works out she can't begin to fathom. But, if Sarah said that's how it happened, then that's what happened. She can accept that.

Restless, she stands up and wanders over to the window and sits on the sill, enjoying the feel of the breeze blowing through the trees. The windows are quite large and the sills are very wide, so she can fit comfortably in the opening without banging her head on the bottom of the frame.

Wren...Cara...could it be? The police said Cara was pregnant when she died and Sarah said I knew Wren's mother. Who else could it be? Wren must be Cara's baby.

As she wrestles with the possibilities, she happens to glance up at the edge of the frame above her head. There for the entire world to see is her answer.

THE WAYSTATION

 Cara was here

For a moment, she thinks her heart must have stopped because suddenly she can't breathe and her head feels light. She reaches up and tentatively runs her fingers across the words, tracing the edges of the butterfly. Her hands start to tingle and she realizes there is a good possibility she might pass out. Tumbling off the window ledge, she plops down in the chair and puts her head between her knees. After a couple of minutes of deep breathing, when she feels steady enough to stand, she approaches the window again thinking maybe she imagined it. But no, the graffiti is still there. She places her fingers over it, then looks down at her arm and traces her own butterfly, all the while grinning from ear to ear.

Rachel feels like dancing for joy. She spins in circles, throwing her arms out, laughing aloud and proclaiming, "You were here. You were here. Oh, my God, I knew it, I just knew it!"

She feels an immense sense of delight in knowing that she and Cara are traveling the same path once again, exactly as they did in life. She is ecstatic and can't contain it. Deciding that no one is going to judge her, she runs over, kicks off her shoes, climbs on top of her bed and begins to bounce up and down laughing and crying at the same time calling out, "Thank you. Thank you, God. Cara was here and she was safe and happy. Now I *know* I'll get to see her again. And her baby…her baby… thank you so much."

She continues to enthusiastically jump up and down until she hears an indrawn breath. Wren stands rooted in the doorway with her mouth hanging open, her jar of bugs wrapped securely in her arms. Rachel stops and asks, "What are you doing just standing there? Get up here and help me celebrate."

Wren wastes no time complying and after carefully placing her precious container of birdie snacks on the dresser, pulls off her shoes and climbs up on Rachel's bed to join in. They hold hands and jump up and down until they have no breath left, then collapse in a giggling, sweaty heap where they lay panting and grinning like lunatics. Wren has no idea what's going on, but that doesn't matter, she only knows this is the best time she's ever had.

Wiping her forehead and lifting her hair away from her neck, Rachel finally says, "Oh my goodness, I haven't done that in like, forever. It was awesome."

Lying on her back and staring at the ceiling, Wren answers with aplomb, "I do it a lot, but it's way more fun with you." Then she asks the obvious question, "What are we celebrating?"

Rachel grins at her, "I found a message from my friend today and now I'm positive I'll get to see her again. She was like a sister to me, so that makes me really, really happy."

Wren reaches over and puts her hand in Rachel's. "I love you, Rachel. Can I be your sister too?"

Rachel hugs Wren to her chest, feeling tears pricking at the corners of her eyes, and kisses the top of her head. "Of course, you can; you already are." Feeling such a rush of love and tenderness for this little girl is almost more than she can bear.

"Come here, I want to show you something."

Wren follows her over to the window and Rachel picks her up and holds her so she can stand on the window ledge.

"Now look up," she instructs.

Wren cranes her head up and immediately spots the butterfly and the note.

"Cara was here. Who's Cara? Is she your sister…I mean your friend?"

"She's the sister of my heart and the best friend I've ever had. I'm so happy she was here too. This butterfly means she slept in this room, in this very bed and she knew Sarah and Samuel and got to be happy here. I know in my heart that this is a message she left for me to find. She was always doing stuff like that. It's almost like we're here together. I'm so excited."

Wren reaches out to touch the drawing, flashing her dimples, "I like it. It's pretty. It's the same as your butterfly," she says pointing to Rachel's tattoo.

"Well, that's because I got this tattoo after Cara died. I got it because I wanted to remember her always, and I knew every time I saw it, it would remind me of her."

Rachel puts her down on the floor, then sits in the chair and holds both of Wren's hands. Hoping she is doing the right thing, she takes a fortifying breath and says, "I've got something else to tell you sweetie. It's kind of important and very, very special. I think it will make you happy. Cara is not only my best friend and the most wonderful person I have ever known, she's also your momma."

Wren's eyes fly open wide, her mouth a perfect O of surprise. "My momma? You know my momma?" She begins to bounce up and down in excitement. "You know my momma. You know my momma. Now we really are sisters!"

Rachel can't keep a huge grin from splitting her face while tears begin to spill from her eyes. She feels just as excited as Wren.

Wren drags Rachel back to the bed, and they begin jumping on the mattress again until Sarah calls from the bottom of the stairs, "Supper, girls. Don't let it get cold."

Wren abruptly stops and says, "Uh oh, we need to go and eat and I have to feed Snowball soon while his bugs are still fresh." She scrambles off the bed, grabs her shoes with one hand and her jar with the other. Turning back as she gets to the door, she favors Rachel with one of her dazzling smiles. "Come on, my sister, I'm starving," and is gone in a swirl of skirts. The pounding of her feet echo on the stairs as she hollers to Sarah, "I'm coming. Hey Sarah, Rachel knows my momma."

Feeling dazed but totally content, Rachel puts her shoes back on and takes her time walking back to the window, needing to touch Cara's words once more. She kisses the butterfly and declares, "See you soon, sister," and heads out the door and down the stairs to have dinner with the rest of her new family.

After cleaning up all the supper dishes, Rachel and Wren go out to the barn and feed Snowball his yummy, and still wriggling gourmet meal.

Well, Wren feeds him while Rachel stands by and applauds his healthy appetite and Wren's amazing foraging skills.

Wren is immensely proud of herself and as they walk back up to the house, she boasts, "He's going to be the strongest bird ever because he's getting the best food."

Rachel agrees.

RACHEL & THE TRAVELERS

It's 10:30. Wren has taken her bath and is, hopefully, asleep. Once she is tucked in, Sarah and Rachel begin a flurry of activity in preparation for the arrival of the travelers. Samuel heads out to the barn to make sure the feed bags are prepared for the horses that will be pulling the wagon, and the extra stalls are clean and ready in case they're needed.

She and Sarah light and set up six large lanterns along the railings of the front porch where they spread a mellow, golden glow down the steps and across the yard. The moon is full and sheds its own white light through the branches of the mimosa trees, casting a pretty, lacy pattern throughout the yard. Crickets sing their tune and are joined by other members of the insect choir, creating a joyful soundtrack to complete the concert.

Rachel arranges the sandwiches, cakes and pies along the bar while Sarah places glasses and pitchers of ice tea and water on the tables. As she carries platters and dishes from the kitchen, her mind races with thoughts and questions. Who will come through tonight? What timeframe had they lived in? What can she talk to them about? Will she say or do something stupid to hurt someone's feelings or embarrass herself? She desperately hopes not. Will they like her?

As she fans the napkins out in an attractive pattern and stacks the plates and forks nearby, the creaking of wagon wheels and the thud of horses' hooves float in through the open windows. Rachel's heart kicks up another few beats as she nervously follows Sarah out the door.

A big wagon sits in the yard. It's pulled by a team of four large cream-colored horses with long white manes. Rachel doesn't know what type of horse they are, but they seem to be very friendly. Samuel holds one of the lead horses by the bridle and talks to her while she nuzzles at his shirt searching for treats. Apparently, this horse has been here before and knows Sam. But then again, he has such a way with horses, he may not have ever seen this particular one before, and it's simply his gentle nature that won her over.

The wooden wagon is long and wide with benches running down each side. It has the appearance of being well cared for and seems sturdy. The seats are occupied by ten men and ten women of various ages who are surveying the yard and scrutinizing the house with unabashed curiosity. She's relieved to see they're dressed in a way to indicate that they are from a time-period relatively close to her own; maybe the late 1990's, judging by the hair and the clothes. That's a good thing, because she's been concerned about how she was going to handle it if they were from the future and whether-or-not she'd be able to hold up her end of the conversation. But then again, Sarah and Samuel seem to handle it fine, and they obviously come from times earlier than her own. She figures she probably would have worked it out either way.

As Sarah had warned, the driver sits alone at the front of the wagon, holding the reins loosely in his hands and staring straight ahead, not making eye contact with them. She briefly wonders what he's done to wind up in that position, but then decides it doesn't matter and eagerly goes forward to welcome the tired and hungry travelers.

Sam sets up a three-step platform to help the passengers disembark more easily. He stands near the steps to lend a hand in case anyone loses their balance, and as each person descends, Sarah greets them with a joyful hug and a gentle kiss on the cheek. Rachel decides to follow suit and taking each one of the travelers by the hands, she looks them straight in the eye, heartily declaring, "We're so happy you're here."

Rachel hopes she is doing the right thing, and glances at Sarah for confirmation. Sarah gives her a sunny smile and a brief nod indicating that she is doing fine.

After they're all safely down, Sarah links arms with one of the older women and leads her up the stairs and on to the porch, turning back to call over her shoulder, "Everyone come on in the house. We've got plenty to eat and drink. I'm sure you all could use a little something."

As the travelers troop up the steps, Rachel looks back to see if Sam is following. He waves them on with a cheerful, "Let me get these sweet girls fed and watered, and I'll be in to join y'all shortly." Unhooking the horses from the wagon, he leads all four gentle giants away to the barn for their well-deserved rest. Rachel brings up the rear and gently closes the door behind her to keep the moths at bay.

The room is alive with light and laughter. People are happily piling their plates with food and finding places to sit. Sarah glides effortlessly from table to table answering questions, patting shoulders, and sharing words of encouragement. Rachel contemplates the crowd unsure who she should sit with, until she sees a young woman close to her own age who is alone at one of the tables. She appears a little dazed and insecure. Her hair is dry and a little ragged, displaying the signs of too many bad blonde dye jobs with at least three inches of dark root showing. Her fingernails are bitten down to the quick and she keeps her dark ringed eyes fixed firmly on her plate. Anxiety rolls off her in waves. Deciding this is the person she is supposed to speak with, she resolutely strides over to her table and sits down.

"Hi, I'm Rachel. What's your name?"

The girl regards her with startled gray eyes. "I'm Lisa." Then she quickly lowers her gaze to her plate and begins to toy with her half-eaten piece of pecan pie.

Rachel decides to just go for it and asks, "Are you scared? If you are, that's okay. I was totally confused when I first got here."

Lisa slowly raises her eyes and whispers, "I don't know if I belong here, you know, with these other people." She waves her hand to encompass the room as-a-whole, swallows, and seems to work up her courage before continuing. "I did a lot of bad stuff before…you know what I mean…when I was alive."

Rachel takes her time pouring a glass of ice tea, giving Lisa a chance to regain her composure. After taking a sip, she says, "Oh, I wouldn't worry about that too much. We've all done things we're not proud of. There's no way to get through life without that happening every now and then." She gives her a friendly look to let her know she is sincere. "What happened? Do you want to talk about it?"

Lisa shrugs, and takes a deep breath before answering, "I was addicted to heroin. I stole shit, uh, I mean stuff, and turned tricks so I could get high, and like, you know, stay well." She begins to chew on the remains of a ragged fingernail before continuing. "I really hurt my family. I mean they tried to help me and everything, and I...I took advantage of them. They let me come home a couple of times and helped me get clean. They loved me, you know? Then I ripped them off and went out and used and started doing the same shit, oops, sorry. I mean doing the same crap all over again. I know I broke my mom and dad's hearts. I feel awful about that. They probably hate me and I don't blame them. I'd hate me too."

Rachel nods in understanding. "I get what you're saying Lisa, but they're your parents. I'm sure they don't hate you. God already knows about all of this, and He doesn't expect you to be perfect." She gives her a smile of encouragement, "I'm not, that's for sure."

"What did you do? I mean, you know, if you don't mind me asking."

"No, I don't mind. Let's see," Rachel holds up her hand and begins to tick things off one by one. "I lived with my drug-dealing boyfriend and helped him sell meth, probably to people just like you. I lied to my family and friends to cover up what I was doing. I gave up on all my dreams and plans for my future, and the worst thing was I wasn't there for my best friend in the whole world when she needed me the most. She was murdered and I feel like it happened because I wasn't paying attention. If I hadn't been so selfish and caught up in my own life, maybe I could have saved her." She chokes out that last part and starts to tear up. Once she gets her emotions back under control, she tries to joke, "Yep, I think that about covers it."

Lisa stares at her in amazement, a small giggle escaping her open mouth before she can stop it. Horrified, her eyes widen and she claps her hand over her lips to stifle it. "I'm sorry. I didn't mean to laugh. That's awful and so sad...I mean...I'm sorry...I mean, oh shit, I don't know what I mean. Oh God, I'm sorry. Is it okay if I say shit?"

THE WAYSTATION

That makes Rachel laugh…genuinely laugh. When the laughter finally runs itself out, she pats Lisa's arm and says, "It's okay. I understand. All I'm trying to say is everyone has stuff, you know, baggage they have to deal with. I'm not saying what you lived through or what I lived through wasn't important or painful, it was; it was tragic. It's just that now that's all history. The truth is you've already been forgiven for your mistakes. God loves you very much and wants to hang out with you, and that's where you're going. So, cheer up, it gets really good from here."

Lisa visibly relaxes. She reaches across the table, takes Rachel's hand and squeezes it. "Thank you. That's totally what I needed to hear. You're really good at this."

Rachel brightens, "Really? Oh wow, thanks. That's what *I* needed to hear." She decides to change the subject, "How's the pie? I've been smelling Sarah's baking all day, and I'm dying to have a piece."

"Oh, it's amazing! I haven't had pie this good since my grandmother died. Hey, do you think I'll get to see her, you know, when I get there?"

"I don't think, I *know* you will." Rachel trots off to get a piece for herself, glancing back over her shoulder to call, "I'll be right back."

For the next few hours, Rachel and Lisa eat, drink, and chat about life, death, and hope. Rachel feels good about how well it went and is pleased to see that when Lisa climbs back on the wagon, she does it with a sense of excitement and an expression of expectation. All her worries seem to have vanished.

As they drive away, Lisa looks back one last time and waves calling out, "Thank you, Rachel! I love you. I'll see you when you get there."

After the wagon is out of sight, Sarah gives a tired sigh, takes Rachel's arm in hers, and starts walking back towards the house. "I think that went well and you did fine. You seem to have a natural gift for hospitality."

"Thank you. I feel pretty good about it."

"Do you know that some people consider hospitality to be one of the spiritual gifts?"

"Spiritual gifts? Oh, you mean like healing or evangelism?"

"Yes, exactly. There are many gifts: mercy, prophecy, giving, leadership, teaching, faith, healing, discernment, tongues, and interpretation of tongues." She quotes, "'As every man hath received the gift, even so minister the same one to another, as good stewards of the manifold grace of God.' That's from 1 Peter, 4:10."

Rachel feels oddly pleased by this compliment. "Huh, I have a gift. That's cool. Are there any other verses about gifts?"

"Oh, several, but I can only think of one other right now. It's from Romans 12. It says, 'For as we have many members in one body, and all members have not the same office. So we, being many, are one body in Christ, and every one members one of another. Having then gifts differing according to the grace that is given to us.' There's more, but I think you understand what it says."

"I love that, grace given to us. You know what? I think I'm going to be okay with this."

"Yes, I believe you are."

SARAH

S arah and Rachel sleep in as late as Wren will let them, then spend most of the day getting everything cleaned up and set back to rights. After they wash, dry, and put away the last dish, fork, and glass, Sarah and Rachel settle themselves comfortably in the rockers on the front porch with glasses of sweet tea and a few left-over lady finger cookies. The cat, aptly named Lazy Boy, jumps up in Rachel's lap where he proceeds to industriously knead and paw until he feels her lap is comfortable enough to suit him. He then turns in a circle twice and flops down for a nap in a puff of cat hair. Leaning her head back against the rocker, Rachel gives a contented sigh as a light breeze caresses the hairs framing her face. She closes her eyes and strokes his back, being careful not to disturb him as she rocks back and forth. Sarah can hear the soft rumble emanating from deep within his chest and understands the pleased expression Rachel wears on her face. The purring of a cat is a soothing sound and always makes her feel happy as well.

Wren scampers about in the yard until she eventually decides to play on the rope swing. She amuses herself by twisting it around and around, then letting it go, stretching her legs out straight and leaning her head back to allow her hair to fly in a wave as she spins. She seems to find this endlessly entertaining and does it again and again. Apparently, it doesn't make her dizzy.

Sarah and Rachel watch her for a few moments before Sarah comments, "Lord knows, I love that child, like she was my own." She finishes eating her cookie, dusts the crumbs from her fingers, then clears her throat and announces, "I think this is as good a time as any to talk about how I came to be here; if you'd like to hear it."

Rachel's eyes immediately fly open and she sits up so abruptly Lazy Boy yowls in indignation and digs his claws into her thighs to keep from being dumped onto the floor. She, in turn, gives out a yell of her own and carefully pulls each claw out of her flesh as she tries to appease his hurt feelings by scratching behind his ears.

"Finally, oh, my God. Oops, sorry. I mean yeah, of course I'd love to hear your story."

Sarah smiles to show she isn't offended. She waits patiently for Rachel and Lazy Boy to get resettled and without any fanfare begins her tale.

"I lived a simple, ordinary life as the wife of a farmer. My married name was Sarah Eleanor Gilbert and my husband, Chester, was the love of my life. We were happy together. We married when we were fairly young and bought land in Harmony, Kansas. Chester had grown up working his father's farm and was quite an accomplished farmer." She says this with more than a little pride in her voice and slowly rocks back and forth, her eyes seeing something far away, lost in the memories.

Coming back to the present, she continues. "My sister, Amanda, always said Chester could grow corn out of thin air and in a way, I suppose he almost could. It seemed like everything he set his hand to blossomed; he had the touch. It was like he had a sense of what the weather would be or what the spring and fall seasons would hold. We had a wonderful life together. Our farm flourished, so much so that we eventually had to hire a man to help out at planting and harvest times. We had the horses, of course, but we also had pigs, chickens, and a few cows. Our life was good."

Rachel interrupts, "It sounds amazing."

"Oh, it was. We were very happy."

It was a good spring with plenty of rain, and harvest time would be busy. What a blessing, Sarah thought. The Lord has seen fit to bless us with good weather and plenty of rain again this year. He had done so for years. The farm was prosperous and they were doing well. At this rate, they would soon need to buy additional acreage. Then just when she felt she couldn't be any happier, it got better. After six years of trying, she was finally pregnant. Chester was beside himself with joy, and so proud. He was strutting around like a Bandy rooster.

He had even scolded her the previous morning for trying to carry a bag of potatoes up from the root cellar. The root cellar was dug into the side of a small hill and was only a few steps from the house, so the bag didn't have to be carried far, but that didn't matter to him. "I don't want you doing any heavy lifting, Sarah. You have to take care of yourself. You're carrying precious cargo now."

"Oh, Chester. You worry too much. I'll be fine."

"I mean it now, no arguing." Taking the bag of potatoes from her, he gave her a kiss and carried it up the steps and to the kitchen, calling over his shoulder, "Come on now, girl, get on up here. I don't trust you to behave."

He closed the cellar door and placing both hands on his hips, gave her a stern look, raising his eyebrows to emphasize the point. She laughed at him and patted his cheek before obligingly saying, "Yes, dear. I'll behave. I promise." Then she gave him a thank you kiss before he made his way out to the barn.

She looked out the kitchen door, and could see him standing at the edge of the field next to the wagon he was using to haul his tools. He was absently patting the neck of his horse and talking with another man who she figured must be Henry Porter. He'd taken up Chester's offer to go from part time help to full time help. He was now officially their hired man. She felt proud that Chester would take him on to keep her from doing anything that might harm the baby. He was awfully protective. It was sweet.

She had only three more months to go and so far, it had been a very peaceful time. She never felt sick or had a single day where she felt anything but joy and thankfulness. Each night Chester would place his hands on her belly and talk to the baby. He would tell her, "Hello, little one. I'm your daddy and I will always love you and protect you. Me and your momma can't wait to see you." Then he would kiss her stomach with great tenderness.

They were completely in love with their child before they ever laid eyes on her.

"You had a little girl?"

Sarah nods, her eyes shining with a few unshed tears. "Oh yes, and she was perfect. She came in to this world with little white blonde curls and the prettiest blue eyes you ever saw, blue like the sky on a cloudless, July day. We named her Abigail after Chester's mother, and she was the center of our world. Chester called her sunshine. He said it was because she was the light of his life."

She closes her eyes while a sweet expression of remembrance plays on her face. Rachel, watching the emotions flitting across Sarah's features, wonders where this story will go. She almost feels afraid to hear the rest. A tight knot of worry forms in her stomach.

"For the ten years after Abigail was born we were very contented. We had all we'd ever wanted; a prosperous farm, Chester was well-respected among the town folk, and we had a beautiful daughter. We felt blessed beyond measure. Then one day it all changed."

Rachel leans forward in anticipation, squashing Lazy Boy in the process. He finally decides enough is enough, and giving out an aggravated howl, jumps off her lap with an angry flick of his tail and stalks off to find a patch of sunshine where he can sleep without fear of being crushed. She mutters absentmindedly, "Sorry, boy," and brushing the cat hair from her lap, anxiously waits for Sarah to continue.

"That fall influenza swept through the town. Do you know about influenza?"

Rachel nods, "We called it the flu in my time, but I read about how horrible influenza was before people knew how to treat it and before they had discovered a vaccine."

"Oh, they have a vaccine now? That's wonderful; it must save a lot of lives. But yes, you're right, it was terrible. Whole communities would practically disappear whenever a bad epidemic hit. We lost so many good people that year, men, women and children.

On a warm fall day Henry fell ill, so all the work of harvest time fell on Chester. Sarah spent a great deal of time nursing him and the rest of the time she helped with the farm as much as possible. Abigail did her part as well, but she was only a little girl. That meant Chester had to carry the burden of most of the work. After three long weeks Henry finally recovered. He was one of the lucky ones, but by then, Chester was worn out and it wasn't long before he fell sick and was too weak to leave his bed.

Sarah never left his side, convinced that the power of her love alone would sustain him. But in the early hours on a Sunday morning, as she sat beside him holding his hand and listening to him struggle to breathe, she knew that his time had come. As the minutes ticked by, he became weaker and weaker, until he simply stopped breathing. His chest no longer rose and fell. One minute he was there and the next he was gone. She continued to sit next to him for a long time, knowing he was gone, but unable to let go. Tears dripped unheeded and soaked the front of her dress. She wasn't ready to say goodbye. She kept hoping he would open his eyes again and tell her it was all a mistake, that he would be fine. Perhaps tell her he was only teasing. It was a vain hope, and one she knew was probably held by many when they lost a loved one.

She finally released his hand, placed it carefully on his chest, and tucked the sheet neatly around him. She wiped her eyes and attempted to pull herself together. She forced herself to stand and walk calmly out the bedroom door. Abigail needed to be told. She would want to tell her daddy goodbye.

They buried Chester the next morning under an old white oak that stood a good 40 feet tall. It was one of their favorite picnic spots in the summer because it provided so much shade. Henry did most of the digging, though Sarah would spell him occasionally to give him a chance to rest since he was still weak from his illness. Then they grieved. Henry spent a couple of days carving a grave marker. Sarah cried fresh tears when she saw the inscription he had laboriously carved on the back.

GOD TOOK HIM HOME
IT WAS HIS WILL
BUT IN OUR HEARTS
HE LIVETH STILL

For a couple of weeks Sarah felt like she needed to remind herself to breathe. She lay in bed each night hugging his pillow to her chest and using it to muffle her sobs. Abigail had taken to sleeping with her and

Sarah didn't want to upset her any more than she already was. Each day she forced herself to bathe and comb her hair. She struggled to remain strong for Abigail. After a while she finally realized that this was not what Chester would want for her. She knew he would want her to carry on and not waste time mourning something she couldn't change. He would want her to dust herself off and get back to the business of living and raising their daughter.

So, she did what she had to do. She had a farm to run and a child to provide for. Life was still going on all around her and she didn't have the luxury of curling up in a ball and crying for months on end. She desperately wanted to, but she didn't; she couldn't. She owed his memory that much. His family and this farm were his dream. It was up to her to keep that dream alive.

Henry treated her kindly and took care of the animals and the crops without a single complaint until she was able to get her grief under control. They worked side by side for months doing what they could to keep things going. Eventually winter came on and there wasn't anything more that needed to be done in the fields, so Henry took on the job of hunting to keep them all fed. He kept the wood chopped and the fires stoked, and Sarah felt secure at night knowing that he was only a few steps away in his room in the barn. She was grateful for all he was doing and knew they wouldn't have made it through this time without him. Though they still mourned, the sun continued to rise and set every day, and eventually the cold, gloomy days passed.

Abigail grew tall and her blonde hair grew long. Her little girl prettiness began the process of changing into the beauty she would possess as a young lady. Sarah was proud of her and knew her daddy would have been too. She was Sarah's sunshine during those dark days. She was her only reason for living.

"Come early springtime the roads finally cleared enough for us to get into town. After a long winter, there are always supplies that need to be replenished first chance you get. So, we all piled in the wagon and made the trip. When we arrived, we found that gossip was going around

Harmony about me and Henry being out on the farm together and not being married."

Rachel stares at her wide-eyed. "But that's horrible. What was wrong with those people? You'd just lost your husband. What could they possibly think was going on? Sometimes people seriously suck."

Sarah gave a small cough to cover a laugh and explained, "Well, honey, when the snow is lying deep on the ground and the nights are long, people get bored. Tongues tend to wag and a good story, be it true or not, will blow through faster than a hard winter wind, and it always gets worse with every telling. I can't say I was truly surprised."

"That was awfully understanding of you. I mean seriously, I would have been super pissed off. I totally would have given those people a piece of my mind."

"Oh, I felt that way on the inside, believe me, but I managed to keep my temper. I had to. You see, I needed to be careful. I could live with the thought that they were spreading stories about me, talk is just talk and it can't hurt you if you don't let it. But I couldn't bear the thought of what it could mean to Abigail. I couldn't risk her being hurt by it. So, to put a stop to it all, Henry and I got married."

"Married? But...did you love him?"

"Of course, I didn't love him. But I respected him and appreciated all he had done for us. He was a hard worker and I knew he would be a good provider. You need to remember, Rachel, in those days a woman couldn't run a farm by herself, it wasn't physically possible. In fact, it hadn't even been too many years since the government passed a law that allowed a woman to legally hold property. I had very few options. It was either marry Henry or sell the farm. If I had sold the farm, Abigail and I would have had to live with my sister and her husband, and I simply wasn't prepared to do that. I wasn't willing to give up on Chester's dream either. I owed it to my daughter too. The farm was all she had left of her daddy."

"What do you mean a woman couldn't hold property? That doesn't make any sense." Suddenly it hits her, "Wait, when was this?"

Sarah watches Rachel's face while an amused expression plays around the corners of her mouth. "It was 1874 when Henry and I married."

"1874? Holy shit, er…I mean, wow. Wow! That's so freaking long ago. I had no idea."

"I told you, dear, time is a funny thing here. Take a moment to wrap your head around that," she declares with a sparkle in her eye.

Rachel begins to giggle and can't stop. Every time she thinks of Sarah saying "wrap your head around that" she starts up again. Sarah decides to give her time to recover, and goes back in the house to get the pitcher of tea. Lifting it in a question, she fills both their glasses at Rachel's nod. By then the giggles have finally petered out, so Sarah sits back down and resumes her story.

"It was a marriage of convenience, we both knew that, but we made it work. I felt that I brought a lot to the marriage, a dowry if you will, and I believed Henry was happy. In one fell swoop he had become a property owner with a ready-made family and a bright future. He had everything a man works so hard for simply handed to him. Unfortunately, it turned out that there was something broken in him. Something I never knew was there. I missed it."

Sarah suddenly stands to her feet and calls out, "Wren, sweetheart, could you please go on out to the barn and see if Samuel will take you down to the creek? I need you to catch us some catfish for supper. I have a craving for catfish and hushpuppies tonight."

Wren, who is on an upward swing, jumps free and in a swirl of skirts lands neatly on her feet, leaving the tree swing to complete its arc unencumbered. "Yum catfish, I love catfish. I'll go right now." She happily scampers off to find Samuel all the while singing, "I've got worms, really tasty worms, so get ready fishies 'cause here we come."

Sarah returns to the rocking chair, smoothing down her skirt as she sits and responds to Rachel's questioning look, "This part of the story isn't fit for little ears."

Rachel nods solemnly and waits in silence until Sarah is ready. She takes a big breath and continues.

Spring turned to summer and Sarah and Abigail were managing to get on with their lives. Sarah had even gotten better at keeping the grief at bay, believing it would help Abigail heal. One sunny morning their nearest neighbor, Marilee Martin, went into labor, so Sarah was away for the day to lend a hand and provide whatever help she needed. She chose to leave Abigail at home because Marilee had several other children, and Sarah felt that adding another child to the mix would only increase the chaos. Harmony's midwife, Alice Harper, was there to help with the birth. This allowed Sarah to focus on taking care of the children. She kept them fed and occupied while Marilee went about the business of having her baby. Her pains started early that morning and she delivered a fine, healthy boy that afternoon, a relatively quick birth for which all parties were grateful.

Because the birth had gone smoothly, Sarah made her way home feeling light hearted. A new life coming into the world was a thing to be celebrated. Marilee's brother, Joseph, gave her a ride back to the farm in their buggy, and Sarah asked him to drop her off at the barn thinking she would find Henry there. She wanted to share the news of the baby with him before heading up to the house to get supper started. When she didn't find him in the barn, she walked on up to the house. That's probably why he never heard her coming; he didn't hear the buggy.

She entered through the kitchen and the first thing she heard was Abigail crying. The sound was coming from behind the closed door of her and Henry's bedroom. She ran to the door and threw it open only to have her heart break into a million pieces. Henry had Abigail pinned down on the bed with her skirts shoved up around her waist. He was holding both of her small hands in one of his and had them trapped above her head. She was crying and begging him to stop. His pants were puddled around his ankles, his hips buried in hers, his bare buttocks rising and falling. He was telling her "You're my beautiful baby, you're so beautiful. Just relax and enjoy it." Sarah could tell he'd been drinking because the smell permeated the room.

Her paralysis finally broke and letting out a scream from deep within her chest, she launched herself at him. She landed on his back, knocking the wind out of him and causing him to lose his balance. She grabbed two fistfuls of hair and yanked as hard as she could, pulling him off Abigail. Because his pants were down around his ankles, his feet got tangled up and he went down on his side, banging his head on the floor, momentarily disorienting him.

Sarah pulled Abigail's skirts down and helped her off the bed murmuring, "My poor, sweet baby. Come on now sweetheart, let's get you out of here." She guided her out the door and pushed her towards the settee. Then she turned back to look at Henry. He was struggling to get up off the floor and looked mad as hell. Sarah started screaming at him again and kept screaming as she kicked him to keep him from getting up. She kicked him in the ribs and in the face. Later she would have no memory of what or how much she'd screamed, but her throat was raw for hours afterwards. She finally ran from the room to find Abigail curled in a ball on the settee crying her little heart out. She didn't stop to think, she simply acted. She did what she felt Chester would do.

She marched to the mantel, took Chester's shotgun down and calmly walked back in the bedroom. By then Henry had managed to get back on his feet, weaving a bit as he pulled his britches up. He was tugging on his suspenders and stared at her as if she were a crazy woman. "What do you think you're gonna do with that thing?" he asked.

Maybe she *was* temporarily crazed, because she never gave it a second thought. She simply shot him, right in the chest. She was standing so close to him that it blew his chest completely apart sending blood and pieces of him all over the room, painting the walls and floor a vivid red. His body was blown backwards and landed half on and half off the bed. There was no doubt he was dead. He would never lay a hand on Abigail again.

Sarah's ears rang so badly she was afraid she might have gone deaf, but then realized that she could still faintly hear Abigail's terrified screaming in the other room, "Momma, Momma, Momma!" An expression of pure panic came over Abigail's face when she saw the blood splashed all over Sarah, but when she realized it wasn't her mother's blood, she cried even harder, this time in relief.

Sarah dropped the gun and stumbled to the settee and sat down next to her. Sarah took her in her arms, not worrying about the gore she was smearing all over Abigail's dress. They held each other tightly, crying and rocking back and forth. Sarah stroked her tangled hair and tried to comfort her. "I love you baby. I love you so much. We're going to be okay, I promise. This is not your fault. There was nothing you could have done to stop him. The fault was his. There was something rotten and evil inside of him. You are not to blame for any of this; you need to believe that. You're still my good girl."

They sat there for a long time before Abigail finally calmed down. This gave Sarah ample time to think and come up with a plan. First, she heated some water and filled the washtub, bathing Abigail from head to toe. She washed and combed her hair, then dressed her in fresh underthings and a clean dress, and sat her down at the kitchen table with a glass of water. Abigail seemed to have completely cried herself out, and sat in a trance staring at the glass in her hand as if she didn't know what to do with it.

Sarah gathered up Abigail's soiled clothes and dumped them on the floor in the bedroom, knowing she would never want to wear them again. Sarah did her best to ignore Henry's body and all the blood that had pooled on the floor and run down the walls. But the sight gave her the chills, and she shivered, running her hands up and down her arms to warm them.

When Sarah returned to the kitchen, she managed to get Abigail on her feet, and together they carried the tub out of the kitchen and emptied it in the small vegetable patch right outside the back door. Then Sarah set Abigail to heating up some more water for her own bath. While Abigail did that, Sarah managed to get Henry's body laid out on the bed and took off his shoes. He was not a small man and his body was very heavy, but there was still so much adrenaline pumping through her system, she found the strength to do it, though she would feel it in her back for days.

She picked out clean clothes for herself and then stripped down to her shift, leaving her bloody dress on the floor with Abigail's. While she took her bath, she explained her plan to Abigail. Though she was only eleven going on twelve, she was a smart girl, and agreed that they should hide what had happened. No one ever needed to know the truth. It would be their secret.

Sarah finished her bath and quickly dressed. Then they emptied the washtub again and hauled it out to the shed where it was always stored. Things needed to appear as normal as possible. She went back in the bedroom, and had to search for a bit, but finally found the bottle of whiskey he'd been drinking; it had rolled under the bed. She put it on the bedside table because it needed to appear as if he'd gotten drunk and fallen asleep. She made sure his tobacco pouch was on the table too. Then she poured the kerosene out of the lamp, all over the bed and the floor and lit it.

"Holy cow, Sarah, you're so smart."

"No, not smart; desperate. It was my job to protect Abigail above everything else. If Chester had been there, he would have beaten Henry to death with his fists and buried him out behind the barn, of that I have no doubt. But being a woman, I didn't have that luxury. I had to come up with my own solution."

"Okay, you set the bedroom on fire, then what did you do?" Rachel is so anxious she's practically chewing her fingernails completely off her hand.

"Abigail and I planned to go out and tend the garden, we needed to look busy and be out of the house. I knew Silas Dorner, a neighbor from down the road, was expected that afternoon. He'd arranged with Henry to buy one of our milk cows and four of the piglets from our sow's latest brood. I knew he would arrive as soon as he finished his afternoon chores, so time was short."

"As we opened the door and stepped out into the yard, there came Silas with two of his boys in tow. My heart felt like it stopped beating and I couldn't get my breath. I couldn't think of what to do next."

"Oh, my God, no."

Sarah nods, "I knew if I didn't get him away from the house, then I was caught. I tried to draw them away as fast as I could, but Silas was a talker and insisted on chewing the fat even though I explained to him that Henry was resting. By the time I finally got him moving toward the pens, the smoke had started to escape from the bedroom. Of course, he and the boys rushed right in to help and found Henry's body. The fire hadn't had a chance to burn long enough to erase all the blood or destroy my bloody dress. Henry's body was fairly burnt up, but it was still obvious he hadn't simply fallen asleep. You could see the great big hole I'd blown in his chest."

"Oh Sarah, that's so unfair; you were only protecting your daughter. Did you try to explain? Did you tell them what he'd done?"

"No, I couldn't. I had to protect Abigail. I didn't want her to have to live with the shame of what he did to her."

"Shame? But she didn't do anything! She was just a little girl and he raped her. Surely people would have understood."

"I don't know if they would have Rachel. Times were quite different then. Instead, I made up a story about how he had beaten me and threatened me with the shotgun. I told them I had managed to get the gun away from him and shot him in self-defense. They didn't believe me, of course. After all, I didn't have a mark on me and besides, who would believe a woman my size could wrestle a gun away from a man as big as him? It was a poor lie, but it was all I could think of on the spur of the moment."

"Silas and his boys carried us to town and handed me over to the constable. I know Silas felt real bad about it, but he was an honest, law abiding man and felt it was the proper thing to do. I don't blame him. He had to live with his conscience. Also, he knew I was hiding something. I wouldn't have believed me either. I'm afraid I'm not a good liar. We had a small jail with only one cell in it, and that's where they put me until such a time as the circuit judge could come back around and I could stand trial."

"But, what about Abigail? What happened to her? They didn't lock her up too did they?"

"Oh no, I made sure they knew she had nothing to do with it, and I made her promise me that she would never say a word to anybody about what actually happened."

"Elizabeth, Silas's wife, was a wonderful woman, very kind and compassionate. She sent one of her boys to fetch my sister, Amanda, who lived about twenty miles out, and he brought her back to Harmony. I don't know what I would have done without Amanda. She was such a comfort to Abigail and to me too. What a blessing my sister was. She gave me the strength to get through each day. My poor girl would have been lost without her."

Sarah had a long time to wait because the circuit judge wasn't scheduled to return to Harmony for at least forty-five days. She sat in her cell day after day praying with her whole heart that God would forgive her for what she'd done. She also prayed that He would change her heart, because she knew if given the chance, she would do the same thing again without giving it a second thought.

They allowed her to have a Bible in her cell and she spent a great deal of time each day reading it and reflecting on the words. She felt a terrible conviction when she came upon a passage in the Book of Romans. It said "...avenge not yourselves, but *rather* give place unto wrath: for it is written, Vengeance *is* mine; I will repay, saith the Lord." She knew she had taken vengeance into her own hands that day and didn't wait for God to exact His revenge. Instead she'd acted as if her feelings and emotions were more important than God's will, as if she knew better than Him. She knew in that, if nothing else, she had sinned.

She prayed daily for a sign that He had forgiven her, but instead He sent what she felt was a sign of his wrath. Ten days after she was locked up, a plague of grasshoppers descended on Harmony and destroyed the town. At first it was only a trickle of hungry bugs, but then eventually the sky became so thick with them it was as if night had arrived in the middle of the day. The whirring noise terrified Sarah. It seemed as if a tornado had arrived in Harmony, bringing a rainstorm of unheard of proportions. They poured down from the sky in great waves, flying into her cell by the hundreds before she managed to close the window. After that, they beat endlessly against the glass creating a nerve-wracking staccato of sound. It was a nightmare come to life.

She could smell smoke and worried that the town was on fire and she would burn to death while trapped in her cell. Eventually Amanda arrived and assured her that the town was not burning, but instead the smoke was from fires which were intentionally being set by people desperate to fight the insects.

THE WAYSTATION

"Sarah, it's horrible out there. People are lighting fires with anything that will burn. The smoke seems to stun the creatures and they fall out of the sky by the thousands. Then folks pile up the bodies, pour kerosene on them and set them on fire as well. But it's not doing any good. They just keep coming. All the crops have been eaten down to the dirt. They've chewed the bark off all the trees and the wooden handles off folk's tools. They even ate the wool off Bob Sutter's sheep, and they're starting to eat the clothes off people's backs. I heard that the train can't make the run through town because the rails are too slippery from all the bugs. Without the train, how will we get supplies? I don't know what we're going to do," Amanda moaned. "It feels like the end of the world."

"It's what I imagine the Egyptians and Pharaoh must have gone through when the Lord sent the locusts to convince him to let the slaves go free," Sarah responded. "I guess people must be thinking this is a kind of judgement from the Lord. Are they spending a lot of time in church?"

"Oh, my goodness, yes. They have prayer meetings going on night and day. What else can we do but pray?"

'I don't know," Sarah answered. "I surely don't know."

After five days of pure misery, people had had enough, and in desperation took matters into their own hands. Friends Sarah had known for more than sixteen years, and had broken bread with many, many times, barged into the jail and dragged her from her cell. They were led by Bertram Millhouser, the same reverend who had baptized Abigail.

The reverend stood in the doorway and waved his Bible in the air, proclaiming, "You, Sarah Porter, are to blame for this plague. God is raining down His judgement on this town because of your sin. We are all being punished because you committed the sin of murder."

Sarah couldn't argue with him, because she had come to believe that very thing herself.

Her friends and neighbors hauled her from the cell, forced her into the back of a wagon, and took her far out on the plain. None of them would meet her eye or even speak to her. They all wore hats which were tied snugly under their chins. Their clothing was buttoned tightly at the neck and wrists, and they had twine wrapped around their cuffs as well.

167

Neckerchiefs were tied over their noses and mouths to keep the bugs off. Nothing was offered to Sarah, and she suffered the entire ride with locusts crawling all over body, including her face and down the neck of her dress. She did her best to brush them off, but there were simply too many.

Once they finally arrived at a location the reverend deemed suitable, they pulled her out of the wagon, and tied ropes to her wrists and ankles, then laid her on her back and staked her to the ground. As they were doing this, the reverend continued to shout his condemnation of the sin she carried in her heart.

"The only way Harmony can be saved is by the offering up of this sinner. God always demands a sacrifice and it is up to us not to question His word, but to do His will. Lord, we commit the fate of this sinful woman to Thy hands. Let Your will be done in this as in all things. Amen."

It was a scene straight from the depths of hell, as he stood there screaming to the heavens while thousands of locusts flew about creating a whirlwind with their wings. When the reverend was finished, he directed his attention to her. "Sarah, you are now in God's hands. He will decide if you live or die." Then without another word, they climbed back into the wagon and drove away, leaving Sarah to her fate.

"They left me there, pinned to the ground, all alone on the prairie to die. First the swarm ate the clothes from my body while they crawled up my nose and in my ears. After they started crawling into my mouth, my memory is mercifully blank. I think by then I may have lost my mind. Then just like you, I woke up here and have been here ever since."

Rachel is stunned beyond words. The horror of what Sarah had endured made own experiences pale by comparison. Tears run down her face and she isn't even aware of it. She realizes her hands are hurting and looks down to see she is gripping the arms of the rocker so hard her fingers have gone white. Slowly she relaxes her hands and brings them to her lap where she begins to massage out the cramps.

"Sarah, I don't even know what to say. I think that is the saddest and most frightening story I've ever heard in my life. I don't believe it was your fault the plague of grasshoppers came. I think it was just a coincidence and those people blamed you because they needed to pin the blame on somebody. You were an easy target; a scapegoat."

"I think perhaps you're right, dear. Since I've been here, I've had a lot of time to reflect on the events of that day. I've also learned to give myself a little bit of grace as God has given it to me, and have finally managed to find peace within my heart."

"Your poor daughter, she must have been devastated. Did you even get to see her one last time?"

Pain flashes across Sarah's face and Rachel mentally kicks herself, immediately feeling guilty for asking such an unfeeling question.

"No. I never got to see her sweet face or kiss her goodbye, though maybe that was for the best. I don't know what she was told, but I hope they were kind enough to spare her the details of how I died and not torture her with the same guilt they placed on me. I've had to trust that God protected her after I was gone. In my heart, I believe He did."

"I'm sure your sister took good care of her."

She gives a sad smile. "I know she did. I'm sure she gave her all the love I would have given her too."

"I feel terrible that you had to go through all that. I wish there was something I could do or say to make you feel better, even though I know there's nothing."

Sarah searches her countenance for quite a while before quietly saying, "Maybe it was better that it happened that way. If I'd been convicted of Henry's murder, they would have hanged me. That would have been a horrible memory for Abigail to carry with her for the rest of her life. Perhaps things worked out for the best. Anyway, that was all a long, long time ago and as they say, time eventually heals all wounds. I know I'll be with my precious girl and my husband again soon, and all will be well."

Sarah stands with determination, "Come on, let's get up and start getting things ready for supper. Wren and Samuel should be coming back with those fish any time now." She gathers up her glass and the pitcher and walks into the house without a backward glance.

Rachel wipes her face and picks up her own glass and the empty plate. She follows her into the house with the echo of Wren's excited laughter and Samuel's deep bass voice floating on the wind.

RACHEL

Time eventually heals all wounds. That's what Sarah said, and over the course of the next few weeks, she begins to believe it. People would come through on their journey every four or five days, or occasionally as much as a week apart, and each time a flurry of baking and preparations would begin anew.

Her days have developed a comfortable rhythm of periods of activity sprinkled with long lazy afternoons of fishing or riding Tallulah and Belle through the flower-filled fields embracing the house. She feels rather proud of the fact that she can ride without a saddle now. Wren showed her how to make daisy chain crowns for their hair and she has become quite adept at adding in different flowers to create intricate designs. They sometimes make large wreaths to hang around the horses' necks so Wren can pretend she is a fairy princess in a parade and wave at all the imaginary people who have come to admire them as they ride by.

Sarah is also teaching her to bake and she is pleasantly surprised to find that not only does she enjoy it more than she expected she would, but she is good at it. Wren has decreed that her lady finger cookies are just as good, maybe even better than Sarah's. She doubts if that's true, but she appreciates Wren's loyalty all the same. However, she does take a great deal of pleasure whenever one of the travelers comments on how delicious they are.

She spends many hours with Samuel in the garden tending the plants and harvesting the vegetables which are part of their daily fare. The exercise feels wonderful and eases a little of the guilt she feels for the massive amounts of food she manages to consume every day. She particularly enjoys taking care of the fruit trees. There is something very satisfying about tying up the heavy-laden branches and then picking each perfect piece. They're often destined to be baked into one of Sarah's delicious pies. The nectarines are amazing, but the peaches and pears are her favorites. Wren is usually right there doing her best to help, but can frequently be found perched comfortably on a rock wall eating the fruit she'd picked from the tree and unabashedly licking sticky juice from her fingers.

Rachel can't remember a time in her life when she felt this calm and safe. She is pleased to discover a new-found ability to see the joy in the little things she'd never taken the time to notice when she was alive. Things like the smell of the grass and flowers on a summer morning before the sun dries up all the dew, or the way the light shines through the stream like a spotlight in a theater, highlighting the fish circling lazily below. In this way, time passes peacefully and the world moves on.

SAMUEL

Samuel gently rubs Belle's nose and speaks softly to her, ruffling her forelock with his words. She has a few burrs caught in her tail from her last ride with Wren and Rachel and he wants to make sure she is calm and comfortable with him nosing around her backside before he begins the careful process of combing them out. Taking a hoof to his shin is not his idea of a pleasant way to end the day, and Belle will feel bad about it if she hurts him.

He hears a quiet step behind him at the barn door and without bothering to raise his eyes says, "Well hello there, Miss Rachel."

"Hi Sam. How'd you know it was me?" she asks as she enters. She hops up and sits on the workbench, giving him a sunny grin as she gets comfortable, perfectly content to watch him work.

Running his hand down Belle's back, he works his way towards her tail and answers, "Well, Wren woulda busted in here like some kind of tornado and Sarah woulda started callin' for me long before she ever reached the door, so that left just you."

"Ha. You know us pretty well. Face it, you're surrounded by women. But like my dad would say, you're a lucky man."

"Nah, not lucky, Miss Rachel, blessed. I am truly blessed to have so many beautiful women in my life." He works a stubborn burr out and turns to look at her. "I've always been blessed that way."

"Wow, I didn't know you were such a ladies' man. You're full of surprises," she teases.

Sam practically blushes and shakes his head in denial. "Nah, I ain't no ladies' man. But I did have a wonderful momma, though she died when I was still a boy. I also had a sweet sister by the name of Emma. She married a godly man named William and they had two girls. Then there were are all my aunties and cousins. My family had lots of girls." He grins, "I was blessed to have those women in my life then and I'm blessed to have y'all here with me now."

"Aw thanks, Sam, you're very sweet. We're blessed to have you too. You mentioned all those women, but you didn't say anything about a girlfriend. Did you ever have a girlfriend?"

"Oh, I had plenty of friends who were girls. Like I said, I was surrounded by women my whole life."

Rachel chuckles, "No, I mean someone who was your sweetheart."

He doesn't answer right away but instead takes his time and finishes combing the last burr out of Belle's tail before straightening up. He pats her on the back and walks to the workbench lost in thought. Carefully laying the comb and brush on the bench, he turns and finally meets Rachel's eye. "Well, yes, I did have myself a sweetheart. Her name was Loreli Shannon."

"Loreli, what a beautiful name. Was she a pretty girl? I bet she was, huh?"

He puts the grooming tools away and brushes a bit non-existent dust from the bench. "Oh yes, she was the prettiest girl I ever knew and not just on the outside, but she was pretty on the inside. She was awful sweet too."

She reaches over and clasps his hand, "That's awesome, Sam. I'm glad you had someone to love, you deserve it. Did you and Loreli get married?"

Tears form in his eyes as he slowly withdraws his hand from hers before responding, "No, Miss Rachel. I'm afraid it didn't end that way. We never got the chance to marry. In fact, we never woulda been allowed to marry."

Rachel is confused. "What do you mean you wouldn't have been allowed to marry? That doesn't make any sense. Why would anyone want to stop you from getting married?"

He rests both forearms on the workbench and clasping his hands together, hangs his head down as if he is deep in thought. After a brief pause he turns his head to look at her and answers, "It ain't a nice story and it won't get any better with the tellin' of it."

THE WAYSTATION

She thinks about it briefly, "I don't want to make you sad, and if you say it's none of my business, I'll totally understand. It won't hurt my feelings at all. I'm sorry if you feel like I'm being nosey, that's a bad habit of mine. If you want, just forget I even asked."

His face bears an unhappy expression. "Nah, I don't mind. Let's walk down to the creek and sit for a spell. I need to get out of this barn for a while and stretch my legs."

They make small talk about the fish and the singing of the birds for a few minutes after getting themselves settled comfortably on the bank, each finding a sturdy tree or rock to lean against. Eventually they run out of things to say and Samuel heaves a great sigh as if preparing to lift a heavy weight.

"I guess I might as well stop stallin' and start tellin' my story or we'll likely still be sittin' here come moonrise." He pauses momentarily to swat at a mosquito that is buzzing around his head. "Damn bugs."

Rachel waits for him to continue. Over the last few weeks, it has become easier and easier for her to be patient. When she was alive, it was never her strong suit, but with no real responsibilities or stresses in her life, being patient has become a simple thing. After all, it isn't like there's anywhere else she needs to be.

He takes his time gathering his thoughts while staring at the water, watching the bugs lighting and the fish nibbling at the surface. Picking up a leaf, he rolls it into a tube then lightly sets in on the water's surface, and with a gentle nudge, sends it floating away. He studies it for a few seconds before finally clearing his throat and beginning.

"I was born on April 13, 1906. My father was the head horse trainer for a rancher by the name of Richard Shannon who had a big spread in Hillsboro, North Carolina. He worked for Mister Shannon to make extra money so he could spoil my momma. We had a nice farm of our own, and daddy did well with it, but cash money was hard to come by and he loved her so much that he wanted the extra to be able to buy her anythin' she set her heart on. He surely delighted in surprisin' her every now and then with somethin' special."

"I remember one time he came home with a whole mess of dress fabric she'd had her eye on for a long time. Momma lit up like a candle at first, and then laughed herself silly 'cause he'd bought so much. You see, Daddy didn't know how much material it took to make a dress, and he bought a whole bolt of cloth. Momma had enough to make dresses for both her and my sister Emma, and she still had so much left over that she made dresses for three poor girls at our church whose momma had already gone on to glory. She said that there was no reason we all shouldn't share in daddy's generosity." Samuel grins at the memory.

Rachel smiles in return and nods her head in an encouraging way.

"When I was eight years-old my daddy finally decided it would be alright for me to start workin' with him at Mister Shannon's place. I managed to convince him that it was important for me to start learnin' about the world and takin' on some responsibility. I was going to be in charge of muckin' out the stalls, feedin' and waterin' the horses and helpin' with the groomin'. I didn't mind. I liked it, because anything was better than pullin' weeds in momma's garden." He joked, "When you're a boy, pullin' weeds is pure torture."

"I had been pestering him for months and was so excited when he finally agreed…"

SAMUEL
HILLSBORO, NC 1914

Eight-year-old Samuel Wellman ran through the front door and launched off the front porch in a burst of boyish energy, calling back over his shoulder, "Come on Daddy, hurry. We don't want to be late on my very first day."

His father, Isaiah, followed at a more sedate pace and spoke sternly to his son in his heavy southern drawl. "There's no need to holler at me Samuel. Those horses will still be there waitin' on us whether you're runnin' around like a headless chicken or not."

When Isaiah reached the bottom step, he turned around and gave his wife, Elizabeth, a goodbye kiss. "Now you and Emma don't spend too much time out in that garden today," he admonished. "It's gonna be a scorcher and I don't want to come home and find you both laid out flat on your backs out there. Stick to the weedin' between the peas and beans this morning while it's still cool. I'll get Samuel home in plenty of time for him to do his chores, so don't y'all feel like you haveta do everythin' yourselves now, you hear me?"

"Yes dear," Elizabeth answered gently in her flat mid-western accent. "Emma and I will limit ourselves to the early morning and late afternoon after you and Samuel return. I've already planned-out our day. We'll work on her studies and take care of the mending and other household chores and then sit here on the porch in the shade and shell peas during the hot part of the day. Don't you worry about us; we'll be just fine. Now quit your grumbling and both of you get on out of here before Samuel wears himself out jumping up and down like that."

"Samuel," she called out. "You mind your daddy and be polite to Mister Shannon. You're a good boy and you may know what you're doing with the horses, and that's all well and good, but that only goes so far. It's important to show him that we've raised you properly if you want to be invited back."

"Yes, momma," he answered, as he finished saddling up his daddy's horse before handing him the reins. "I will. I promise. And momma," he paused, "thank you for lettin' me go. I like workin' the horses ever so much better than pullin' weeds."

"I know son. Be a good boy and we'll see you this afternoon. Don't you forget though, after you get your chores done you'll still owe me ten pages of reading tonight and then your penmanship exercises too. We have an agreement." She waved goodbye as she and Emma pulled on their sun hats and began walking toward the large garden with baskets and digging sticks in hand.

"Bye daddy," thirteen-year-old Emma called out. "I love you."

"I love you too, punkin. See y'all this afternoon."

"Daddy," Samuel asked as they rode away, "why did you have to go and marry yourself a school teacher? I hate penmanship exercises. Nobody cares what kind of hand I write and horses don't read."

"I care Samuel," he answered gruffly. "Life as a colored man is hard enough in this world. There ain't no sense in makin' it harder by bein' ignorant. Bein' allowed to study and read and write is a gift boy and you should be thankful. In fact, you should be thankin' God every day for the privilege. You're lucky to have a momma who can teach you these things. Why your granddaddy could barely sign his name and couldn't read much more than a few words outta his Bible, even though he was the first man in this family who was born a free man. Your great grand-daddy was beat senseless by the overseer more than once after gettin' caught studyin' his letters in secret, but that never stopped him from tryin'. Knowledge is somethin' nobody can ever take away from you."

"Now before you go and say anythin' else, I know that your grand-daddy and great granddaddy both had a way with horses, and you and me got the same gift, but that ain't enough to get by in this world. I expect things are gonna change a lot by the time you're my age and I want you to be ready. Do you understand me?"

THE WAYSTATION

"Yes sir…but daddy, all I want to do is work with horses. I love them and they love me. Why would I want to do anything different?"

"Because son, I don't want you to just be the one workin' the horses, I want you to be the one who owns 'em. That's an important difference."

"Yes sir, I understand, but I still don't like it." With that pronouncement, Samuel dug in his heels, leaned in low over his horse's withers and slapped the reins yelling, "Race ya!" leaving his father behind in a cloud of dust.

Isaiah muttered, "Oh hell boy, I'm way too old for this nonsense," but chased after him anyway and eventually passed him grinning and waving his hat in victory.

When they arrived at the Shannon's ranch, Loreli, a red-haired, blue-eyed firecracker of a girl, enthusiastically greeted them. She was only seven years-old, but as Richard Shannon's only daughter, he openly adored her and allowed her to do almost anything she set her mind to. The stables were her favorite place to be and she had no intention of sitting around and playing with dolls up at the big house when she could be out grooming the horses or riding them.

As Isaiah and Samuel drew near the stables she came running out to meet them. "Hey, good morning y'all. Mr. Wellman, is this Samuel?"

"Why yes, he is Miss Loreli," he said as he dismounted. "Samuel, get offa that horse and say your hellos to Miss Loreli."

Swinging his leg over the saddle horn, Samuel leapt off his horse in what he hoped would be perceived as a dashing dismount, and sweeping his hat from his head, bowed low and said, "I am very pleased to meet you Miss Loreli." He'd been reading *The Three Musketeers* and had been practicing his bow in secret, hoping he would have a chance to use it one day. He lifted his eyes to take-a-peek at Loreli, and was pleased to see it had elicited the desired effect.

Loreli pressed both hands against her mouth and giggled, then curtsied and answered in her best Lady Guinevere voice, "The pleasure is all mine sir," causing her to break out in giggles again.

Isaiah reached over and lightly slapped Samuel on the back of his head and scolded, "Don't be acting like a fool, boy. That's how people get hurt," then led his horse into the barn leaving Samuel and Loreli to get acquainted.

It was the beginning of a beautiful friendship.

Months went by and the relationship flourished. Loreli made it a point to always be at the stables whenever Samuel was there. She followed him around in an attitude of complete adoration, pestering him with an endless variety of questions and insisting that he allow her to lend him a hand no matter what he was doing. Because her brother, John, thought he was already a man at thirteen, and there were no other children on the ranch for her to play with, she was thrilled to have the company of someone near her own age. John treated her like she was a burr caught under his horse's saddle, and did everything he could to avoid her. The fact that Samuel was a boy meant that she finally had a friend who would teach her interesting things like how to bait a hook and climb trees.

Samuel continuously tried to discourage her from mucking out stalls and doing the dirty work, but she always insisted. Her response was inevitably, "Sam, you are my friend, and friends help each other. Besides, the sooner you get your work done, the sooner we can go do something fun."

"Loreli, your daddy is not gonna like you gettin' all dirty. I tell you what, you sit down there on that bucket and keep me company while I finish up here and then if my daddy says it's alright, I'll take you fishin'."

"Really? Promise?" she asked brightly.

"I promise."

"Okay then, but hurry up," she said settling on the upturned bucket, and folding her arms across her skinny chest while impatiently tapping her foot.

As Samuel worked, he watched her out of the corner of his eye, marveling at his good fortune in not only having a paying job that he loved, but having a job that provided him with his best friend too. Since they were always together, Mr. Shannon trusted him to watch over her and keep her safe, and that made him feel important. She was such a little thing, but she wasn't afraid of anything and had quickly mastered the art of tree climbing just as good as any boy, and she didn't shy away from digging up the fat worms they used for bait. She could even clean a fish faster than he could and wasn't above pelting him with fish guts when she was feeling sassy.

That day she had plaited her long hair in braids to keep it out of the way, and was wearing a pair of boy's overalls in anticipation of climbing creek banks and digging in the mud. At first, Mr. Shannon had strenuously objected to her dressing like a boy no matter what her justification was. But over time she had worn him down with her persistent begging and had even resorted to intentionally skinning her knees and tearing holes in several of her dresses as proof that she needed to be dressed more appropriately for her daily activities.

After waiting impatiently for all of five minutes, she jumped up and grabbed a shovel stating, "Sam, at this rate the sun's gonna be too high and the fish won't be biting anymore. I'm helping you whether you like it or not. I promised daddy I'd bring him catfish for dinner and I imagine your momma would like some too."

Samuel raised his hands in surrender and quit arguing; with Loreli there was no point, because he was going to lose anyway.

This was the nature of their days together and ten good years flew by. Samuel, now a young man of eighteen, already stood almost 6' 3" with the promise of more to come. His chest had broadened, and his arms had grown muscular from years of hard work. He rode the familiar path to the Shannon's ranch and tried not to worry. Several weeks ago, his momma had come down with a racking cough that simply wouldn't go away. She was having trouble breathing and had constant pain in her chest and shoulder. It had gotten so bad that his daddy quit going to the ranch so he could stay home and nurse her, and had given over all the responsibility for the care and training of the horses to Samuel. He was glad to do it because it made him feel like a man to do a man's work and provide for his family. The money from this job was more important than ever since no one could spare the time to work the farm properly. Emma, who was now a married woman with a daughter of her own and another child on the way, also spent most of her days at the house helping their daddy care for their momma.

Daddy had finally asked Doctor Monroe to come out to the house the day before to take a look at her. She'd been running a fever on and off for almost a week and was now coughing up blood. After the examination, he'd shared the bad news as gently as possible, but it was a terrible blow nonetheless.

"Isaiah, I don't want to add to your worry, and I can't be certain yet, but it looks like Elizabeth might have lung cancer. We'll know more in a couple of weeks if she doesn't start improving. If the pain continues at this level and she's still losing weight, I'm afraid there won't be much I can do for her other than to keep prescribing laudanum for the pain."

"Cancer," Isaiah whispered collapsing onto a chair. My Elizabeth has cancer? No, she can't. Are you sure?"

"No. As I said, I'll know more in a couple of weeks if she isn't getting better. I'm leaving you medicine for the cough and the laudanum, but there's not a whole lot more I can do. Try your best to get some food in her so she can keep her strength up and as much water as she can keep down. She can't afford to lose any more weight and she's already weak enough without being dehydrated on top of everything else."

"Yes sir," he answered in a daze. "We'll take real good care of her. Emma will be here to help me so we'll make sure she eats and drinks."

"I'll be back in a few days to check on her. In the meantime, don't assume the worst and try to keep a smile on your face as much as possible. It's important that she doesn't see you worrying. Do whatever you can to keep her spirits up. The laudanum will make her sleep quite a bit, but when she's awake and feeling up to it, read to her and talk with her. Get Emma to talk about the new baby. Try to keep things as normal as possible, alright?"

Isaiah, unable to speak, simply nodded. The doctor awkwardly patted him on the shoulder in an attempt to comfort him. Isaiah finally stood and shook the doctor's hand. "I want to thank you for takin' the time to make the long trip out here. We'll do just what you told us to."

The doctor picked up his bag and as he was leaving, turned and added, "If y'all need me or if she takes a turn for the worse, you be sure to send Samuel to town to fetch me. I'll come as quick as I can, and Isaiah, it wouldn't hurt to pray." With that, he quietly closed the door leaving

THE WAYSTATION

Isaiah alone to fall to his knees and sob unreservedly into his callused hands as he begged God for help.

Six weeks later Elizabeth was dead.

Samuel sat on the creek bank and cried on Loreli's shoulder. She hadn't seen him since the day of Elizabeth's funeral which happened to fall two days before Sam's nineteenth birthday. She could only imagine what a somber and miserable occasion that had been. More than a week had passed since the burial, and she felt an immense sense of relief in finally being able to hold and comfort him. She murmured quiet words while rubbing circles on his back as she tried not to cry. She understood exactly how he was feeling because she could still remember the unbearable pain she'd felt when her mother died. She'd gone from an almost uncontainable excitement at the prospect of a new little brother or sister to complete devastation in the span of one day. She'd been only six years old when they buried her mother and still-born sister, but the memory of that day was forever lodged in her heart. It was a like a block of ice that never melted and never left her.

"It clean broke daddy's heart, Loreli. We're all heartbroken, but he ain't ever gonna be the same." He sniffled and swiped at his eyes. "I don't know what we're gonna do without her. Momma was the heart of our family. Daddy ain't comin' back here. You know that right? He said there's no sense in it because he was only doin' it to give momma the extras he wanted her to have. He said I'm in charge now if I want to stay."

"Of course, you have to stay. We could never get along without you." She drew back and grasped him by the shoulders, looking him in the eye. "Sam, I could never get along without you," she gulped. "I love you," and with that declaration she burst into tears burying her face in his chest.

Samuel stared down at the top of her head first in amazement and joy, and then in horror as the potential repercussions of the situation hit him. As he wrapped his arms around her he worried that she didn't realize the danger this put them in.

"Loreli, you can't...we can't...oh Lord, what are we gonna do?"

"Do? What are we going to do?" she snapped, pulling away from him with sparks practically shooting out of her bright blue eyes. "We're going to love each other and take care of each other. That's what we're going to do. I love everything about you Sam. You're smart, you're kind, and you're handsome. Shoot, you're my best friend in the whole world. You have the best touch with horses I've ever seen, and that is no small feat. It says a lot about your heart and who you are as a person. I wish… I wish…oh dang it, you know what I wish. You do love me too, don't you?" she asked, momentarily frightened that his answer might be no.

Samuel's face softened as he reached out to touch her cheek. Cupping her small freckled face in his large palms, he ran his thumb across her cheek and lips. Tears trailed down his face as he whispered, "Of course I love you. I have always loved you, from that very first day when you gave this show-off boy a curtsey. You are so beautiful, but we can't… it's too dangerous. Your father and your brother would never allow it. In fact, nobody would tolerate a colored man and a white woman together. You know that."

"Love is about the color of a person's heart, not the color of their eyes or their hair or their skin." Her eyes flashed and her face was set in that stubborn expression he knew all too well. "I see your heart," she said placing her hand on his chest. "I know you. I know who you are inside where it counts and I will never love anyone the way I love you."

Samuel stroked her long, red hair and tried to rein in his emotions, but when she placed her lips on his, all reasonable thought left his head. All he could think about was how soft her lips felt and how she tasted like the blue berries she must have eaten at breakfast. The kiss deepened and he wound one hand tightly in her hair; with the other he pulled her against his body where she seemed to melt and become part of his own flesh. He slowly lay down on the bank pulling her with him and reveled in the feeling of her curves as they nestled against him. All thoughts of faceless, hooded men who carried torches, and crosses burning in door-yards were pushed to the back of his mind. He was determined to hold on to this perfect moment in time for as long as possible, even if it cost him everything he had.

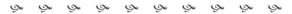

THE WAYSTATION

"Oh, poor you," Rachel exclaims. "I'm sorry about your mom. It's not fair that you had to lose her when you were that young. That must have hurt so much. I'm glad that you had Loreli though to help you get through it. It sounds like she loved you very much."

Samuel sighs, "Yes it did help to take my mind off my broken heart, and despite what people were gonna think, we fell in love; deeply in love. We became as close as two people can get. I knew folks would think it was wrong and I tried to stop it, but I couldn't. Then we did our best to hide it, but…well, when you're young and in love, you can barely keep your hands offa each other. We were always hidin' out in one of the stalls stealin' kisses and Loreli wasn't shy about holding my hand or huggin' my neck any time she felt like it. Like I said, she was a strong-willed girl."

SAMUEL
HILLSBORO, NC 1925

Months of stolen kisses and fervent declarations of love passed quickly. Samuel found that those secret moments helped him to work through the pain of his mother's death. He didn't miss her any less, but the sadness was eased whenever he found himself in Loreli's arms, and they made sure that happened as often as possible.

"You and I are going on a picnic," Loreli declared one early autumn morning. "We only have a couple of months before it gets too cold for picnicking and I am determined that we're going to make the most of what's left of the nice weather."

"Aw now Loreli, I've got a lot of work to do. Brutus here threw a shoe and after I take care of that I've got to repair that stall Twister kicked the tar out of. Your daddy's expecting me to get all of that done today and I can't let him down."

Loreli, who was never willing to take no for an answer, took a running start and leapt into the air pinning him up against the side of the stall. She threw her arms around his neck, wrapped her legs around his waist and proceeded to kiss him with a great deal of enthusiasm, determined to change his mind.

"Come on Sam," she pleaded between kisses. "Please. You know you want to come and have a picnic with me. We can cuddle under that big willow tree down by the creek. Those branches are so thick no one will even know we're in there. It's the perfect hiding place." As she was speaking she unbuttoned his shirt and ran her hands lightly over his chest and neck and followed it up with gentle butterfly kisses guaranteed to break down his resistance.

THE WAYSTATION

Samuel's head spun and his heart pounded. He felt like all the blood had left his brain and traveled to another part of his body, one that Loreli was making a point of rubbing up against. He began to kiss her back with equal intensity convincing himself that he could take the afternoon off and work until well after dark if that's what it took to get everything on his list done. Being distracted was a mistake; dropping his guard was a bigger one. He never heard them coming.

"Shit. I knew something was going on. See, I told y'all, and I was right. Loreli, you are a nigger loving whore. Boy, you take your hands off of her right now before I kill you where you stand!"

Samuel froze. He stared at the five hooded men, two of whom were holding guns that were pointed directly at him. He gently placed Loreli on the ground and held out his hands to show that he was cooperating. He wasn't positive, but he had a fairly good idea who these men were. There had been stories going around about the terror they'd been spreading among the colored families in the area. There had even been rumors of hangings in a few of the outlying areas, but up until now he had never truly believed it. He thought it likely that the one doing all the yelling was Loreli's brother, John. It sounded like him anyway, and it looked like he was in charge.

"Yes sir. I don't want any trouble."

"Holy shit, you were right. What are we going to do with him John?" one of the hooded men asked unable to contain his excitement.

"Shut up. I said no names dumb ass. Jesus." He threw a flour sack at one of the men. "Put this over the nigger's head," he ordered.

Samuel stood perfectly still, trying to appear as passive as possible, his mind racing while he tried to figure out how he was going to get out of this mess alive. He managed to stay relatively calm until they began to tie his hands behind his back. That's when Loreli started screaming and he panicked, thinking they'd hurt her. He was furious at the thought of them touching her and, determined to protect her, he ripped his arms away from the man behind him and pulled the sack off his head all in one motion. Once he could see again he began to take swings at anyone he could reach, guns or no guns.

"Take your damn hands off of me John," Loreli yelled. "And y'all let Sam go now. He didn't do anything wrong. Let him go!"

Once Samuel realized she was not being hurt, he concentrated on trying to fight his way out, figuring his only chance was to run as far and as fast as he could. He managed to connect solidly with one of the men's faces, and judging from the screaming and the blood soaking through his hood, he must have broken his nose.

All the yelling and banging into the stalls had put the horses in a terrible panic and the sound of their cries and kicking hooves were added to the chaos. Twister, aptly named because of his ability to remain unbroken despite repeated attempts, was especially agitated. He continuously kicked the wall of his stall that was adjacent to the one containing the fight. One of the men got too close to him and Twister bit him on the shoulder drawing blood and adding one more voice to the screams filling the barn.

Samuel took advantage of the man's concern with his punctured shoulder and put all he had into lifting him off his feet and sending him flying over the edge of the stall where he landed at the horse's feet. Twister, now not only panicked but angry as well, reared up and came down repeatedly on the man's head with both feet, crushing his skull and putting an abrupt end to his screams.

For a moment, the fighting came to a complete stop. Samuel could hardly believe what he had done and looked at Loreli in horrified silence, knowing he had just signed his own death warrant. A black man could not kill a white man and live; they would never allow it. That's when the shovel connected with the back of his skull and he knew no more.

He came to when they were tying the rope around his neck. They hoisted him up on his feet and forced him to stand on a small barrel. His head swam and ached something fierce as he teetered precariously on wobbly legs. He knew he only had a moment left and sought her out with his eyes. He gave her what he hoped was a look of courage and called out to her, "I love you Loreli and I always will. Don't you ever doubt that."

"No, no!" Loreli screamed. "Please don't do this John. Think about what you're doing. Oh God, please don't. Sam! Sam!"

THE WAYSTATION

The last thing he saw was her tear-streaked face and running nose as she cried hysterically and fought the iron grip her brother had on her arms. Then they kicked the barrel out from under him and he fell, jerking the rope tight. His body swung in circles as he fought and the life was slowly squeezed from him. The fall was not enough to break his neck, and his death was not quick. When it was finally over, his swollen tongue protruded from his mouth and his eyes bulged from their sockets. Urine soaked the front of his pants and ran off the tips of his shoes pattering in large drops in the dirt only inches below his feet.

Once John was certain Sam was dead, he released Loreli. She ran to Sam's body and in desperation, even though in her heart she knew he was already dead, wrapped her arms around his legs and tried to lift him to take the pressure off his neck. Her father found her there more than an hour later, lying in the dirt at Sam's feet, too exhausted to cry anymore. He cut the rope and Sam's body fell to the ground in a crumpled heap.

SAMUEL & RACHEL

Samuel shakes his head, "I never meant to get him killed, I truly didn't. I'd never hurt a fly before. I was scared and tryin' to protect Loreli, that's all. But those boys didn't care. I just gave 'em one more excuse to do evil. The last thing I can remember is chokin' and tryin' so hard to breathe. It hurt and burned somethin' awful." He rubs his neck as if he can still feel the pressure of the rope.

"I locked my eyes on Loreli right before I blacked out. I'll never forget how she looked with those tears pourin' down her sweet face and her nose runnin' 'cause she'd been cryin' for so long. She was reachin' her hands out to me and screamin' my name, but she couldn't get to me 'cause John was holdin' her. And then I was gone."

Rachel was sobbing. "Oh God, Sam. Oh, God, that's awful. What horrible people. I can't understand how they could do that just because you two loved each other. I feel so sorry for you and for Loreli."

"Thank you, Miss Rachel. That's mighty kind of you to say, but please don't cry. I'm okay now."

Rachel wipes her tears away, struggling to get her emotions under control. "Okay, yeah, I know you are. I'm sorry for getting so emotional. That was a tough story to listen to and I feel terrible for both of you. I can only imagine how terrified she must have felt and how worried she was about you. It makes me sick to my stomach."

"Yeah, well, it took me a long time to quit worryin' about her. I had to learn to trust that the good Lord would watch over her. It's been my constant prayer that He brought a good man into her life, one who took good care of her and loved her with all his heart just like I would have done."

"You're a sweet man, Sam. I apologize for interrupting; please finish your story."

"Well, there ain't much more to tell. When I woke up, I was here. I didn't have any idea of how I got here, but at least Sarah was here and she was real kind, and explained things to me and helped me settle in. I have been here ever since and I've been content. I've got Sarah and Wren to love, and good, honest work to do. God is good."

The sun is beginning its descent behind the hills and the shadows are stretching out long and deep. The birds have long since returned to their nests, and the crickets and frogs are taking up their nightly chorus. Rachel and Sam walk slowly side-by-side back to the house. The smell of supper is in the air and Sarah is calling their names.

Rachel reaches out and takes his hand, "Sam?"

"Yes, Miss Rachel."

"You know God doesn't blame you for that man's death, don't you? You didn't do anything wrong. You were only trying to protect yourself and Loreli. There's no fault in that."

"Well, maybe the Lord God Almighty don't blame me, but I blame myself. I had a hand in takin' another man's life whether I meant to or not, and I can't forgive myself for that."

"You are such a good man. I've never met anyone as kind as you. You've got to forgive yourself so you can move on. You have to, so you can finish your journey to heaven and see Loreli again."

"I want to, more than anything, Miss Rachel, more than anything."

LORELI
HILLSBORO, NC 1925

Her father never considered allowing her to attend Samuel's funeral, and in fact had insisted that Doctor Monroe keep her sedated for most of that first week, declaring that she was extremely traumatized from witnessing the hanging. That decision had been the kindest thing he could do for her. She was wounded and broken in a way that could never be completely mended. Seeing Samuel's body lying in that plain wooden coffin would have pushed her over the edge of the abyss from which she might never return.

Time crawled and at times seemed almost to stop entirely, yet day by miserable day she continued to wake up in a fog of grief and go through the motions of life. Three months had gone by and while she was no longer being drugged into passive complicity, that brilliant spark that lit up her personality had died. The fire was gone. She no longer cared about bathing or gave any consideration to her appearance whatsoever. Her once vibrant hair hung in oily tangles around her face and she carried an odor of neglect which permeated every corner of her bedroom. She hadn't left her room, let alone set foot in the stables, since that day, and there was a distinct possibility that she might never do so again; it was simply too painful.

On the day of Samuel's funeral, Richard Shannon ordered that the hanging tree be cut down and the wood disposed of. He had no intention of using it as firewood in his home. He didn't want to chance Loreli thinking that the fire in her room was fueled by the traitorous tree. He could imagine her staring at the flames and wondering if this was the branch from which Samuel had hung. He couldn't mend her broken heart, but he could do everything in his power to smooth the way for her in hopes that one day she would heal.

Richard had, of course, known of Loreli's affection for Samuel; he wasn't blind. She glowed like a candle any time he was around. Loving a colored boy was not an acceptable choice for her, but he'd written it off as puppy love and felt confident that it would burn itself out before it had a chance to flower. But John had taken matters into his own hands, and disaster followed. Now Loreli was nothing but a pale imitation of the girl she once was, and he had no idea how to fix her. He desperately hoped that one day she would find her way out of the darkness where she existed these days. He wanted his daughter back.

She shuffled aimlessly around her room, as she did most days, and finally came to rest in a chair near the window where she sat endlessly pleating the folds of her nightdress. Her gaze wandered from her lap to the window where she could see the yard in the front of the house. As she stared, she heard a door close below and John walked into view leaving tracks in the light dusting of snow left behind from the night before. He was headed in the direction of the stables which could be seen in the distance. She immediately leapt to her feet and began pounding on the window, screaming obscenities. Tears streamed down her face though she was completely unaware of them. This was the first time she had seen John since he'd murdered Sam and the surge of anger surprised her. She thought she was long past feeling anything ever again.

Feet pounded on the stairs and in the hallway. Her father and Mrs. Hamilton, the housekeeper, burst through her bedroom door in a panic. She continued to scream and beat her fists against the window until suddenly the glass gave way and broke beneath her hands cutting her fingers and wrists, and leaving one particularly nasty gash on her forearm. She seemed oblivious to the pain and clung to the sides of the window frame continuing to cry and curse her brother, while blood ran down her arms and dripped from her elbows leaving a pattern of large drops on the floor around her bare feet. John continued on his way in the yard below, resolutely ignoring her cries, though his shoulders tightened noticeably and his step faltered at the crash of the breaking glass.

Her father and Mrs. Hamilton spoke calmly and softly to her as they led her away from the window and sat her on the edge of the bed. Mrs. Hamilton hurriedly removed her apron and used it to wrap the deep cut on Loreli's forearm. Her father sat on the bed and wrapped his arms around her, cradling her carefully to keep from touching her injuries.

He spoke quietly to the housekeeper, "Mrs. Hamilton, please fetch the doctor if you would, and quickly."

"Of course, Mr. Shannon," she answered, hurrying away, fearful for Loreli's sanity and seeing this as yet another step towards what in her heart she saw as an inevitable ending.

"Shush, shush sweetheart. It will all be fine," he cooed rocking her gently and speaking nonsense words as if she were a skittish horse. Though Richard was more accustomed to comforting a frightened horse than his daughter, he did his best. Up until recently, she'd always been such a strong and independent little thing. This was new territory for him. He wasn't entirely sure what would work, but he continued to sit and gently rock her until she finally calmed down and fell into a type of trance. He wasn't sure which was worse, the cursing or the detached state, but at least the screaming and the tears had stopped.

Eventually, the rattling of a carriage could be heard through the broken window, followed by the thud of the doctor's heavy footsteps on the stairs. Relieved that help had finally arrived, Richard handed Loreli's care over to Dr. Monroe. Richard gently laid her down then stood near the door as the doctor examined her injuries.

"Most of these aren't too bad," Dr. Monroe muttered as he worked. "Loreli, these are going to be a bit sore for a few days. This one on your arm is a mite deep. It's going to need a few stitches. Now dear, I'm going to give you something to take away the pain and help you relax." He held her hand to keep her calm and, without taking his eyes from her face, addressed Richard. "Richard, can you come over here and keep her comfortable while I prepare the syringe?"

Richard took the doctor's place on the bed, practically wringing his hands as he watched him drawing liquid into the syringe. "Will she feel anything when you sew her up? I don't want her in any more pain, she's gone through enough."

"She won't feel a thing; the opium takes effect very quickly." He made quick work of the injection and the stitching up of her arm. After wrapping it in a clean bandage and cleaning up the rest of her cuts, he packed up his bag and indicated that Mrs. Hamilton could finish cleaning up the rest.

"Now, she's going to sleep for quite a while, which is the best thing for her. I'm leaving you this bottle of laudanum. Mrs. Hamilton, please make sure you give her a spoonful every 2 to 3 hours as needed for the pain. You'll also need to keep fresh water handy as it will make her thirsty."

"Yes sir. I'll make sure she has everything she needs," Mrs. Hamilton answered.

"Thank you," Richard said shaking the doctor's hand. "I appreciate you coming so quickly. I don't know what we would do without you."

The doctor gave him a grim look. "You be sure to send for me if she develops a fever or has any vomiting. Otherwise I'll be back tomorrow to check on her. Don't worry, she'll be fine. She's a strong young lady. It's her emotional state that has me more concerned than her physical injuries. Have you considered that a change of scenery might do her good? Would it be possible to send her somewhere to stay with family for a while? I think it's best to get her away from all the bad memories here. Maybe a place with a little more social life and people her own age."

"Well no, I hadn't, but perhaps you're right; that seems like a good idea. My sister, Beatrice, is a widow and lives alone in Boston. I'm sure she'd love to have the company and would be happy to have her come and stay for as long as she needs. Beatrice is quite the social butterfly and should be able to introduce Loreli to lots of new people. It would be a nice change for her and maybe it will help her snap out of this terrible melancholy."

"Excellent idea. I suggest you contact her as soon as possible. Well, if you'll excuse me I've got other patients to see. Don't be discouraged Richard. Young people are resilient. Loreli will come around, just give her time." He reached out and shook Richard's hand and gave him a nod of encouragement before closing the bedroom door quietly behind him as he left.

Richard sat on the edge of the bed stroking Loreli's limp hand as he absently watched Mrs. Hamilton fussing around the room gathering bandages and cleaning up the glass and blood from the floor and windowsill. He hoped Dr. Monroe was right.

Two weeks later, Loreli sat impassively on a velvet bench across from her father and stared at the passing countryside. The cuts on her arms and hands were healing well, but were still visible. Thankfully it was quite cold, so there was no need to explain her gloves to anyone. They had a private cabin on the train to ensure that she had peace and quiet. Her father did not want her to have to field questions from curious travelers about their plans for the upcoming Christmas holiday. It was December the nineteenth and Christmas was right around the corner, though she couldn't care less about it. She was on her way to Boston to be safely deposited at the home of her widowed aunt and given a new chance at life; at least that was the way her father had explained it. Not that it mattered. As far as she was concerned, her life had ended on August 27, 1925 and how she lived from this point forward was of little consequence to her. If her heart stopped beating at this very moment she would rejoice knowing that she would soon be with Sam.

TONY – LOCATION & DATE UNKNOWN

Tony opens his eyes to find he's sitting on the driver's bench of an old wagon and holding a set of reins in his hands. Startled, he immediately looks down at his chest to see if he is covered in blood. He should be, considering his last memory is of the cops opening fire on his ass. His shirt looks perfectly normal, but his chest aches terribly, and there is a persistent burning in his gut. He runs one hand down his chest to his stomach and can't feel anything wrong, but he does notice that his hand is shaking.

What the hell is going on?

"Are we going to hit the road bub or what?" a male voice with a distinctive east coast accent asks from behind him. "We're all getting a little antsy back here."

He immediately swings around and is amazed to find the bed of this wagon is full of people, and not just ordinary people. This group looks like they recently stepped out of a gangster movie set in the 1920's. The man who spoke to him is dressed in a black pinstripe suit and vest, with a colorful bowtie and he's wearing a bowler. He is holding an unlit cigar in one hand and is enthusiastically waving the other hand around as if to indicate which direction they should travel. The other male passengers wear various suits and working clothes. The women are mostly dressed in straight skirts with rolled stockings and bobbed haircuts. One young lady looks like she is wearing a wedding dress and one masculine-looking gal is wearing what can only be described as an aviator outfit, complete with goggles and a funny cap that comes down over her ears.

Tony is inclined to tell the man to go fuck himself and then demand to know where he is, but finds that he can't speak. It isn't as if he can't open his mouth, he is simply unable to form words. He licks his lips and tries again, only to find that he is completely mute.

The horses choose this moment to begin the trip. The sudden lurch forward causes Tony to almost fall backward, and he is forced to grab the edge of the bench to keep his balance. He turns back around and faces forward with no idea of where they're heading, but the horses seem to know where they're going. He figures he might as well go along for the ride until he has a better idea of what's happening.

Jesus, he could sure use a beer.

LORELI & BEATRICE
BOSTON, MA
JANUARY, 1926

She'd been here a month and, to her credit, Aunt Bea had not questioned her once about Sam. She was certain her father had discussed their relationship and his murder with her, but Aunt Bea was kind enough not to mention it. Instead, she tried to pretend that Loreli was on an extended holiday. Bea did her best to be cheerful and enthusiastic despite the aura of melancholy Loreli wore like a heavy winter coat. Christmas had been a dismal affair, despite her father and aunt's obvious attempts to brighten her spirits. The Christmas tree was beautifully decorated and evergreen boughs were scattered throughout the house bringing with them the heavenly scent of pine, which normally would have reminded her of fond childhood memories. But when her father prayed over their Christmas luncheon and gave thanks for the Lord's blessings, she burst into tears and ran from the table. She hid in her bedroom until the following morning, the thought of going through all the Christmas rituals more than she could bear.

In truth, she was angry with God for allowing Sam to be murdered. She tried and tried to reconcile the reality of his death with God's promises, but always came up short. In her heart, she couldn't believe that a loving God would allow him to be taken from her in such a brutal manner. If He supposedly loved her and wanted only the best for her (and Sam), how could He possibly think this was right? It was an argument that up until this moment had circled around in her mind like a squirrel in an endless search for a nut.

But that was over now. This was the day everything changed and she had hope. For the first time in five months, she felt happy and was looking forward to her future. She stood before a full-length mirror in her nightgown and studied her reflection, and then turned sideways cupping her hands around her rounded tummy. It seemed to have appeared overnight, as if heaven had given her a gift in answer to her prayers. She could hardly believe it. Because her depression had been so crippling, she hadn't noticed her missed cycles for the previous four months and doubted that anyone else had either; it wasn't a topic that was likely to come up in polite conversation.

She smiled a secret smile and traced the arc of her tummy. Raising her nightgown, she closely examined the pronounced bump where up until recently she was nothing but skin and bones. Pulling the nightgown up over her head, she dropped it to the floor and stood completely naked, taking a long look at her changing body. Her breasts were larger than before and much more sensitive to the touch. She held one in each hand marveling at the weight of them and fingered her nipples imagining the feel of a baby suckling. She almost laughed aloud in delight at the thought. Moving down her rib cage, she caressed the growing mound of her belly and ran a finger down the shadowy line that traveled from her belly button to disappear into the patch of red hair below.

This was God's way of easing her pain; she was sure of it. She was amazed by His mercy and love. How could she ever have doubted Him? This child sleeping within would give her a living, breathing memory of Sam. This son or daughter would be her way of holding on to him and loving him forever, and she was grateful beyond words. Her heart and soul finally felt at peace.

Downstairs, Beatrice excitedly opened the invitation which had just arrived.

Grace and Morton Foster cordially invite you to join in celebrating the birth of their first grandchild, Evangeline Marie Winters.

Festivities will commence at 4:00 pm on Saturday, January 27th.

Refreshments will be served.

Please RSVP no later than January 20th.

THE WAYSTATION

This was the opportunity Beatrice had been waiting for. It was the perfect chance for Loreli to finally meet some of the young men and women from the finer families in the area without the added pressure of a formal dance. Best of all, the Fosters had a handsome son by the name of Franklin who would be perfect for her, and he would certainly be in attendance. Excited to share the news, she flew up the stairs as fast as her age and bulk would allow and, forgetting to knock, burst through Loreli's door waving the invitation.

"Sweetheart, I have wonderful news...," the words died on her lips as she took in the sight of Loreli standing naked in front of the mirror, her undisguised pregnancy on full display. "Oh, dear Lord," she gasped, crumpling the invitation against her chest and collapsing onto the nearest chair. She could feel the flush rising in her cheeks and fanned her face, fearful she might faint. This was not a situation she'd planned for and had no idea what to say.

Loreli, not the least bit embarrassed, picked up her nightgown from the floor and slowly turned to face her aunt. Pulling it over her head and letting it drop to cover her nakedness, she approached Beatrice. She knelt at her feet and took hold of her hand. "Aunt Bea, I know it's a shock, and honestly I'm just as surprised as you, but please try to understand how happy this makes me. I never thought I would be able to say those words again, but I am genuinely happy. I feel like I've been given my life back. I loved Sam with all my heart and he loved me. I won't ever believe that was wrong; love is never wrong. Why else are we here but to love and be loved?"

Beatrice gulped and fanned herself before trying to speak, but gave up after a couple of failed attempts and waved her on. Loreli waited patiently until she was sure her aunt wasn't on the verge of an apoplexy before continuing, "That bastard of a brother of mine stole Sam's love away from me, but now I get a second chance. Don't you see? This is a miracle, a gift from God. He gave me this child to mend my broken heart and I am so thankful."

"But honey what will people think? My goodness, what will they say? This will ruin any chance of entering good society or making an appropriate match. What kind of future can you or this child have? Please consider your situation."

"Oh, Aunt Bea, none of that matters to me. It's never mattered to me. All I want or need in this world is right here." She looked down and caressed her stomach. With tears swimming in her eyes, she declared, "This is all the future I need. This child, our son or daughter, will have all the love I can give; I promise you that. I will live out the rest of my days perfectly content. I even know what I want to name the baby. Would you like to hear the names?"

Beatrice nodded, still feeling as if she couldn't catch her breath. She struggled to pull in air while hoping that the little sparkles she could see in her peripheral vision didn't portend an impending swoon. She couldn't imagine how she was going to break this news to Richard and that thought alone froze her tongue to the roof of her mouth.

Loreli happily continued, and seemed intentionally oblivious to her aunt's discomfort. "If it's a girl I'll name her Mary Elizabeth after momma and Sam's mother. I think he would like that. If it's a boy, I'll name him Samuel Richard after Sam and daddy. I do hope it's a boy; Sam would be so proud."

Beatrice continued to nod weakly and patted Loreli's hand, "Yes dear, those are lovely names. I'm sure they will do quite nicely." Loreli sat on the floor and rested her head on her aunt's knee. Beatrice absently stroked her niece's hair and worried over the letter she would have to pen to Richard later that day. She had no idea how she was going to break the news to him and hoped he would find Loreli's improved frame of mind a joyous enough turn of events to compensate for the shock of her unexpected pregnancy.

RICHARD
HILLSBOROUGH, NC
APRIL 22, 1926

A lone rider could be seen approaching at a full gallop, the dust billowing behind him. Richard watched him drawing near and felt uneasy. A rider coming in at that speed generally meant bad news. When the rider was finally close enough to make out his face, Richard realized it was Tom Bowden who worked at the post office. That meant a telegram. "This must be it," he mumbled. "Reckon I better get my bag together." In fact, his bag had been packed and ready to go for the last three weeks, his train ticket purchased and sitting on top. He hadn't been able to concentrate for more than a month worrying about Loreli and the baby. He supposed he should have gotten on a train last week, but he didn't want to be underfoot and of no use to anyone. Instead he'd chosen to wait until he was summoned. In hindsight, perhaps that wasn't the best decision.

"Mr. Shannon," Tom said as he reined in his horse and held out the envelope. "Telegram for you, sir."

"Thank you, Tom, I appreciate you getting it out here to me so quickly." After handing him two bits and waving goodbye, Richard turned and walked into the house opening the envelope as he went. As expected, it was from Beatrice.

RICHARD PLEASE COME IMMEDIATELY STOP
DO NOT DELAY STOP
LORELI AND I WILL BE WAITING ANXIOUSLY FOR YOUR ARRIVAL STOP
BEATRICE

He and Beatrice had decided between the two of them that no mention of the baby should be made in the telegram. Secrets were impossible to keep in a town this small, and he was certain he wouldn't have even arrived in Boston before the news would have spread from one end of town to the other.

Grabbing his bag and throwing it in the back of his truck, he hollered at one of the hands to get in and wait for him. Then he went to track down John and make his excuses. He was uncomfortable with the idea of leaving him in charge in his absence, but he had little choice in the matter. Besides, John did fine as far as ranching and horses went, it was only his inability to deal with people appropriately that worried him. Even at the age of almost twenty-five John still had a lot of maturing to do, and for reasons he couldn't begin to fathom, was an angry young man. Nevertheless, Richard was leaving and John would be running things. He'd have to deal with any consequences later.

He found John in the round pen attempting to work with Twister. Since that disastrous August day, they had abandoned all attempts at breaking him. Apparently, John had decided it was time to start again. Richard stepped up on the rail and waving to get his attention called out, "John, I need to speak with you, son."

Giving up on his effort to saddle Twister, he jogged over to his father while keeping a wary eye on the unpredictable horse. Being bitten or trampled was not high on his list of things to do today. Setting the saddle atop the railing, he quickly pulled himself up and over so he could stand in safety outside of the pen and out of the horse's reach. Not one to pass up an opportunity to create havoc, Twister trotted up to the rail and shoving his nose up under the saddle, flipped it off and over, barely missing the back of John's head but still managing to clip his shoulder with one of the stirrups. Twister tossed his head and showed his teeth in a way that might be interpreted as an evil grin.

John jumped out of the way and shouted, "Dammit, you vicious piece of horseflesh. You keep this up and I'm going to cut you up and feed you to the hogs!" Twister didn't appear to be the least bit intimidated by John's threat and simply turned tail and trotted away, giving him no more notice than he would a fly.

THE WAYSTATION

Richard felt the urge to snicker until he remembered that the last time Twister raised hell it had resulted in the death of two people. Sobered, he returned to the task at hand. "John, I need you to run things here for a few days. I just received a telegram from your Aunt Beatrice. She tells me Loreli has taken ill and is asking for me. I'm not sure how long I'll be gone, but I know I can trust you to handle anything that comes up."

"Of course, Daddy. You know I'll take care of everything. You get on out of here and don't worry about a thing." He paused considering his words, "I hope she's going to be okay." He started to speak again, but then realized the futility of it. Her current emotional state was a direct result of his actions, and though he still believed he was justified in hanging the nigger, he did feel some regret that she was continuing to suffer because of it. However, he was convinced that it was for the best and she would eventually forget all about Sam.

Richard clapped him on the shoulder and said, "Take care son. I'll be back as soon as I can."

As Richard and the ranch hand drove away, John heaved a great sigh and turned back to face Twister. Picking up the saddle he said, "Come on you big bastard, let's try this again."

Richard was fortunate in that he only had to wait a couple of hours for the train to arrive. It was a lucky coincidence that Beatrice's telegram had arrived early in the morning, or he would have missed this train and had to wait until the next day before he could leave. As he got situated in his sleeper car, he once again second-guessed his decision to delay traveling until Beatrice summoned him. It was going to take three days to reach Boston and by then the baby would already be born. Since there was nothing he could do about it, he opened his newspaper and tried to read, refusing to dwell on something he couldn't change. Worrying about it now was a waste of time and he had bigger problems than missing the baby's birth. He had to figure out where they went from here.

LORELI & BEATRICE
BOSTON, MA
APRIL 22, 1926

Beatrice grabbed Coral by the arm, "Go and fetch Mrs. Mason as quickly as possible. Tell her it's urgent."

Beatrice anxiously fluttered around the entryway until Coral, her housekeeper, left to find the midwife. Mrs. Mason, an elderly black woman who had helped deliver more babies over the years than she could count, had come highly recommended by Coral and several other domestics in the neighborhood. Beatrice and Richard were determined to do all they could to protect Loreli's reputation, and each felt that it was best to use a colored midwife rather than Beatrice's personal physician. They feared it was going to be obvious that the baby was of mixed race, and to make matters worse, she was an unmarried woman. According to Coral, Mrs. Mason had delivered more than a few babies who were born on the wrong side of the blanket, so they felt confident in her ability to be discrete.

Loreli's moans could be heard drifting down from the bedroom and Beatrice rushed up the stairs to comfort her until Mrs. Mason arrived. She was pacing around her room trying to hold her hair off her neck and rubbing her lower back at the same time. "Oh, Aunt Bea," she exclaimed, "Please see if you can find some ribbon. I need to tie my hair up. I'm so hot and miserable and the feel of it on my neck is more than I can bear right now."

"Of course, dear," Beatrice answered and rummaged through Loreli's dressing table until she found a length of ribbon. Directing Loreli to sit on the stool, she pulled up her red hair, now a dark amber color from the collected sweat, and secured it with a knot to keep it in place during the long hours to come.

Kissing her aunt's hand in gratitude, she resumed pacing until another contraction started. Grabbing the bedpost, she begged, "Please rub my lower back Aunt Bea, it hurts so much." Loreli lowered her head and clung to the wooden spindle while her aunt did her best to try and rub away the pain through the thin fabric of her nightgown.

They continued this cycle of pacing and rubbing until Mrs. Mason finally arrived 45 minutes later. Beatrice felt a flood relief at the sight of Coral and the midwife. She never would have admitted it to Loreli, but she had begun to fear the midwife wasn't coming and she would have to be the one who delivered this baby. The idea terrified her.

Mrs. Mason handed her hat and coat to Coral before rolling up her sleeves and getting down to business. Pulling a roll of newspapers from her carry bag, she spread them out over Loreli's bed. Then she pulled out a thick linen sheet and shook it out spreading it over the top of the newspapers. Beatrice had already removed the pretty bed covers and covered the mattress with a heavy cotton blanket in anticipation of the midwife's arrival. Once Mrs. Mason was satisfied with the level of protection this afforded the bed, she motioned to Loreli saying, "Come on now young woman, lay down for a minute and let me take a look-see so we know what we're dealing with here. Loreli waddled her way towards the bed only to be struck by another strong contraction. She stopped stock still and bent over placing both hands on her knees and puffed away like a steam engine until the pain subsided, then finished her trek across the room to the bed.

After getting Loreli settled to her liking, the midwife pushed both of Loreli's knees up and anchored her heels against her bottom. "Now honey, try to leave your feet there if you can. I know it might be a bit uncomfortable at first, but this is the easiest way for me to see what's going on and it's the best position for getting this baby out." Then she grasped the hem of Loreli's nightgown and flipped it up and over her knees and belly exposing her completely from below her breasts, leaving her naked as a new born babe.

Embarrassed, Beatrice immediately averted her eyes and developed a sudden interest in making sure there was ample light in the room, opening the curtains wide and turning on all the lamps. After running out of things to do she asked, "Is there anything you need or anything I can bring you? Hot water or clean cloths perhaps?"

"Well Missus Gregson, some hot water will be handy when it comes time to tidy up the baby and momma here, but for now just a few clean cloths and maybe a little fresh drinking water. She's liable to get a bit thirsty with all this panting she's doing. Now dear," she said patting Loreli's knee, "don't you worry, I'm not saying you're doing anything wrong. You keep right on doing what you're doing and we'll let nature take its course."

Eager to have something useful to do, Beatrice immediately snatched up the water pitcher and rushed out of the room to find the clean cloths and get fresh water. If she was lucky, maybe Loreli would be covered up when she returned. How she wished Richard were here, not that a labor room was any place for a man, but it would be a comfort to know he was safely ensconced downstairs in the parlor with a nice brandy and cigar while he waited. The moral support would be a fine thing to have if she needed it. Who was she kidding? She needed it right now.

By the time she'd gathered the cloths and water and made her way back to the bedroom, Mrs. Mason had finished her examination and Loreli was quietly resting between contractions. Mrs. Mason was standing by the window and motioned her over. Beatrice hurried across the room, dreading what she was certain would be bad news.

Taking Beatrice by the arm and pulling her close to keep Loreli from hearing, the midwife whispered in her ear, "Missus Gregson, I think you need to reconsider having your doctor present for this delivery."

Beatrice felt her stomach drop and whispered back, "What do you mean? What's wrong? Is it the baby? Is my niece in danger?"

The midwife gave her a look filled with pity. "The placenta is not where it should be; it's too low. I've seen this before. It's very dangerous for both the mother and the baby."

Beatrice looked confused. "I don't understand what that means."

With great patience, she explained, "The baby needs to pass through the cervix, the opening, during the birth, and because the placenta is not where it's supposed to be, he has to force his way past it and it can tear away. Loreli could bleed to death. Please, Missus Gregson, please call the doctor. I won't be able to save her if that happens. We don't have much time. This baby is coming soon."

Shooting a panicked look at Loreli, Beatrice bolted from the room. Twenty minutes later she burst through the door practically dragging Dr. Carmichael behind her. Taking only a moment to assess the situation, he turned to Beatrice and said, "Thank you Mrs. Gregson. I think perhaps you should wait downstairs for now. We're going to have our hands full here and we want to do our best for your niece and her child. Please, go on down and try to relax. We'll talk when it's all over."

Beatrice gave Loreli one final kiss and squeezed her hand as if to say you can do this, then stood at the door feeling guilty because she felt relieved to be handing over the responsibility for Loreli to the doctor. She was reluctant to abandon her, however, she didn't want to be a distraction either, so with one last desperate look at her niece, she said, "I'll be praying for you all," and closed the door with a quiet click.

Twenty minutes later Beatrice heard a baby's cry and heaved a great sigh of relief. It was her hope that soon the doctor or Mrs. Mason would come down and announce all was well, but almost forty minutes passed before the doctor finally descended, his tread heavy on the stairs. He looked exhausted with deep lines etched into his face. Beatrice was afraid to leave the safety of her chair convinced that her shaking legs wouldn't support her.

"May I sit?" he asked, indicating the chair next to hers. Feeling completely numb, she nodded. Taking both of her hands in his he spoke with great tenderness, "I'm very sorry Mrs. Gregson. I did everything I could, but in cases like this there is little that can be done unless the mother is in a hospital, and even then, there are no guarantees."

Beatrice felt as if she were speaking from deep within a dark well. "Loreli? Oh no, not my sweet Loreli. Please doctor..." She couldn't bring herself to continue and began to sob burying her face in his shoulder.

He allowed her to cry for a bit, and when she finally pulled away, he handed her his handkerchief before continuing, "She delivered a healthy baby boy, but there was too much bleeding. I was unable to stop it. Don't blame yourself Mrs. Gregson. Even if I had arrived sooner, there was nothing I could have done. Sometimes these things…just happen," he trailed off knowing it was a weak excuse at best, but at a loss to offer a better explanation.

"Her father… Oh dear God, poor Richard. He's on his way here now and doesn't know. This will devastate him. He lost her mother in childbirth too." She paused to gather her courage, "May I…may I see her?"

"Of course, but are you sure you're up to it?"

She lifted her chin and with great determination answered, "I have to be; she is my niece and my responsibility. I owe it to her father to be there for her and her son."

Together they ascended the stairs with the doctor holding Beatrice by the elbow, prepared to catch her if she should stumble. As they approached the door, she hesitated, certain there was every possibility she might faint or at least make a spectacle of herself. But when she gazed upon Loreli's beautiful face, to her relief all she saw was peace. She was whiter than the sheet upon which she lay, and her freckles stood out in sharp contrast against her pale cheeks, but there was no sign of the pain or suffering she had endured. Instead she appeared to be sleeping with one small hand lying curled on her breast. Someone, probably Mrs. Mason, had brushed her long red hair and carefully arranged it around her face and across her shoulders restoring as much of her natural beauty as possible, a small kindness which Beatrice appreciated. Laying a hand on each side of her face, she placed a gentle kiss on her forehead and wished her a silent good bye.

Mrs. Mason watched from a chair across the room where she was holding the baby in a cocooned bundle. She was softly patting him on the bottom and murmuring nonsense words. As Beatrice approached, she stood and gave her seat to the grieving woman and then placed the precious cargo in her arms. Pulling back the blanket, Beatrice stared at the face of Loreli's son, transfixed, as most people are, by the undeniable beauty of a newborn child. He had his mother's fair skin, freckles and chin, and what she assumed was his father's nose and full red lips. Those lips were pursed as if he were trying to suckle the air. His curly hair was a deep auburn and his eyes appeared to be a muddy green, but because the eyes of many newborns tended to be a muddy color, it would take time before they would reveal their true color. She hoped they would be green.

"My goodness, you are a beautiful little boy, aren't you? You precious, precious child. One day I'm going to tell you the story of the wonderful girl who was your mother. She was so in love with you. Do you know what she named you? She named you Samuel Richard for your daddy and your granddaddy; the two men she loved most in this world. You can be proud of that name." Finally tearing her eyes away from the baby, she spoke to the midwife, "We need to hire a good wet nurse immediately. Do you know of anyone Mrs. Mason, or can you recommend someone doctor? This child needs to be fed immediately."

RICHARD
BOSTON, MA
APRIL 25, 1926

Richard had his baggage in hand and jumped to his feet the minute the train pulled to a stop. Impatient to exit, he pushed his way past several slower moving passengers, apologizing as he went. Manners be dammed, he needed to see his daughter. The second his feet hit the platform, he began scanning the crowd for a cab. Flagging down the first one he could find, he threw his belongings in the back and climbed in offering the driver double his normal fare to get him to Beatrice's home as quickly as possible. The cabby was more than happy to comply.

The moment the cab pulled up to the house he knew something was wrong. The curtains were drawn and there was a black ribbon decorating the door. No. Oh God, no! He threw a handful of bills at the cabby without even bothering to count them, grabbed his bags and bolted to the door. His heart raced in his chest as he waited for an answer to the ringing doorbell. Coral's mournful face peered through a side window briefly before she finally admitted him. She was dressed all in black, her face and downcast eyes said it all. An anguished cry broke from his lips as he dropped his bags and rushed from the entryway into the parlor.

Beatrice sat before the fire in her mourning clothes rocking the baby. Tears filled her eyes and spilled down her cheeks as she stood to greet him. "Richard, my dear, I cannot tell you how sorry I am. I had no way to reach you." She reached out with one hand to caress his arm and leaned in to kiss his cheek.

"Where is she?" he managed to choke out, his own tears soaking the front of his coat. "Where is my baby girl?"

Beatrice took a fortifying breath, turned and laid the baby in a bassinet before saying, "Follow me dear," and led him to the other side of the room.

He somehow managed to force one foot in front of the other and followed her, praying for strength. A fringed brocade curtain partially hid a set of double doors that opened into a smaller sitting room. This is where he found his beautiful child. She lay in a cloud of cushioned silver-colored silk that lined the gleaming mahogany coffin. "She looks beautiful; so peaceful. She can't be gone," he managed to croak before falling to his knees. He lay his forehead against the coffin and burst into agonized sobs. To lose a wife and now a daughter was more than any man should be forced to endure.

The next two days passed in a blur of one heart-wrenching task after another. Arrangements were made to transport Loreli's body back to Hillsborough. They didn't bother holding a memorial service since she would be laid to rest at home and didn't have any friends or family in Boston other than Beatrice. This also alleviated the necessity of fabricating another lie to explain the cause of her death. Fortunately, the doctor was bound to silence and the midwife well compensated to do the same. Beatrice would be traveling with him and planned to stay for a few weeks or even months, until he felt strong enough to manage on his own.

He sent a telegram to John the day after his arrival in Boston to break the news of Loreli's passing; they were the most difficult 46 words he'd ever had to compose.

WE HAVE LOST OUR BELOVED LORELI TO SCARLET FEVER STOP
MY HEART IS BROKEN BUT WE MUST CARRY ON STOP
FUNERAL ARRANGEMENTS WILL BE MADE WHEN WE RETURN STOP
BEATRICE WILL BE TRAVELING WITH ME STOP
TELL MRS HAMILTON TO PREPARE A ROOM STOP
PLEASE KEEP US IN YOUR PRAYERS STOP
DADDY

The day of their departure, he sent John one more. This was one more deception in what was beginning to feel like a long line of them, but it would allow them to secretly transport little Samuel and the wet nurse to Hillsborough. He felt it was very important that John never know of Samuel's existence. Richard wouldn't put it past him to kill the boy out of pure hatred and a twisted desire to keep their bloodline pure. No matter what the circumstances, little Samuel was his grandson and the only child Loreli would ever have. He was going to do everything in his power to protect him. He had a plan to keep the child safe, but many things had to come together correctly to make it work. The telegram to John was the first step.

PARK MY TRUCK AT TRAIN DEPOT AND LEAVE KEYS WITH STATION MASTER STOP

ARRIVAL IN 3 DAYS TIME STOP

BRINGING LORELI HOME STOP

DADDY

Then he sent one final message.

MONTROSS FUNERAL HOME

722 POST ROAD HILLSBOROUGH NC

FUNERAL SERVICE NEEDED FOR MY DAUGHTER LORELI STOP

WILL BE ARRIVING BY TRAIN ON MAY FIRST STOP

PLEASE ARRANGE FOR TRANSPORT OF CASKET STOP

RICHARD SHANNON

He watched Loreli's casket as it was loaded into the baggage car, then fetched Beatrice, the wet nurse, and the baby from the cab. The three of them trudged aboard their private sleeper car where they went about the business of making themselves as comfortable as possible in preparation for a long journey with an infant. Despite the work, little Samuel was a much-needed distraction from the misery that constricted their hearts like a steel band.

RICHARD
HILLSBOROUGH, NC
MAY 1, 1926

The trip was uneventful other than the inevitable smell of soiled diapers in the close quarters of a train car. At least it was spring and the weather pleasant, allowing them to keep the windows open and fresh air circulating. Though Richard would gladly have borne the smell for years if it meant Loreli could sit beside him instead of riding in a box in a separate car.

When they arrived at the station, Beatrice went directly to the hotel where she would wait until Richard's return. The wet nurse took the baby and walked away in the opposite direction. Hopefully no one would realize they had arrived together. With a grim expression, Richard watched the men from the funeral home load Loreli's casket into their hearse and stayed frozen in place until they were no longer in sight. Refusing to allow the sadness to overwhelm him, he hired the porter to help him carry and load their baggage into the back of his truck and drove off alone. They were lucky and no one at the train station took note of Beatrice or the black woman with a baby. With any luck, they would be able to pull this off without John, or anyone else for that matter, being any the wiser.

Once he passed the last building in town, Richard pulled over to the side of the road. The wet nurse emerged from a wooded area where he had instructed her to wait. "Did you have any trouble?" he inquired as he held the door open for her.

"No sir. No one spoke to me or saw me go into the woods."

Satisfied, he put the truck in gear and continued down the road. The drive to Sam's home was a quiet one. The baby slept and the wet nurse stared out the window. This left him plenty of time to compose his speech. Richard and Isaiah had not spoken since the day of Sam's funeral. He knew Isaiah would probably just as soon spit on him as have a conversation, but he had to try. Too much was at stake and he owed it to Loreli to protect her son. He wanted her to be proud of him and to find rest in the afterlife. This was the last thing he would be able to do for her as a father and he was damned well going to do his best.

As he pulled into the dirt yard at the front of Isaiah's home, he noted the neglected look of the place. At some point since Elizabeth's death and Samuel's murder, Isaiah had obviously stopped caring about the state of his home. When Elizabeth had been alive, the place had been immaculate and she'd always taken great pride in the beautiful flowers she cultivated in the beds bordering the porch. Now dirt and leaves lay scattered all over the porch and not a single flower bloomed. In fact, all her beloved plants had long since died and been blown away in the wind. Only dirt and a few sticks remained.

He turned off the engine and stepped from the truck, not approaching the steps, and waited to see how Isaiah would greet him. The porch screen banged open and Isaiah emerged to welcome him with a scowl that was only partially hidden behind the barrel of his shotgun. "Get offa my land Mr. Shannon. I got no use for you. You already broke the heart of this family, and we ain't got nothin' else to give. What more do you want from us?"

"Isaiah, please listen to me. It's not what I want from you, it's what I want to give to you."

"There ain't nothin' you have that I want. I've said all I'm gonna say on this matter. Now get the hell offa my land!"

"That's where you're wrong Isaiah. I believe there is something you will want very much." He reached through the window of his truck and the wet nurse handed him a squirming blanket-wrapped bundle. As Richard turned from the truck, he let the blanket fall open revealing little Samuel who yawned and stretched and kicked his feet. He held him out as a peace offering, convinced that Isaiah would not be able to resist the draw of his grandson.

"What'd you bring me a baby for? I ain't got no use for babies."

"You dimwit, stop your barking for a minute and listen to me. This isn't just any baby, this is Sam and Loreli's baby. This is our grandson and I need your help to protect him. We need your help," he emphasized.

Isaiah fell silent and gave careful consideration to the child Richard held. He laid the shotgun down on a bench with a trembling hand and walked towards Richard and the baby, one tentative step at a time as if he were in a daze. "Sam's baby? My Samuel's baby?" he whispered in disbelief. When he was close enough, he held out his arms and said, "It wasn't loaded. You know that, right?"

"Of course I know that," Richard answered and placed little Samuel in his arms. "Meet your grandson, you old fool. His name is Samuel Richard."

"My grandson, Samuel." Isaiah seemed to like the sound of that and smiled for the first time in more than a year. He took his time examining little Samuel's ten fingers and ten toes, kissing each hand and foot with great tenderness, then kissed the freckles scattered across his cheeks. He brushed his curly auburn hair with his fingertips and said, "My sweet little redbone. God has truly blessed me today." He raised his eyes to the heavens and gave heart-felt praise, "Thank you Lord God for this unexpected blessing. You are a God of great love and I thank You for such a generous gift. Please forgive me for the anger that has plagued my heart for so many months. Your mercy knows no bounds." After finishing his prayer, he clasped Samuel tight against his chest and said, "I'll do anything you need me to. You got a plan?"

Relief flooded through Richard's body as he grasped Isaiah by the arm. "Thank you. I knew I could count on you. Between you and me, we're going to keep this boy safe. I don't have much time today. I need to get back to town, pick up my sister, Beatrice, and take her out to the house. Then I have to make the arrangements for Loreli's…" he choked on the words and had to stop and compose himself, knuckling the tears from his eyes before he was finally able to finish. "I have to make the arrangements for Loreli's funeral."

Isaiah looked up from his inventory of little Samuel's ears. "I heard about Loreli, Mr. Shannon. I am very sorry for your loss. There ain't nothing worse than losin' a child. I know your heart must be broke into a million pieces just like mine. No one should have to outlive their children; it ain't right. Did she pass...I mean, was it truly scarlet fever or...?" He let the question trail away.

"No, it wasn't scarlet fever. I made that story up to protect her and little Samuel. I didn't want John or anyone else to know the truth." He had the grace to look mildly embarrassed by that concern, but Isaiah nodded his head as if to say he understood, so Richard continued. "We lost her when..." he cleared his throat a couple of times and forced himself to go on. "There were complications when little Samuel was born. The doctor couldn't save her. He said they might not have been able to save her even if she had been in hospital. She was gone shortly after I boarded the train for Boston. I never even got to say goodbye." Too late Richard realized that John had robbed Isaiah of the same thing.

He heaved a heavy sigh. "I'll stop by tomorrow and you and I can have a long talk. I think I have an idea, but you and your family need to agree. For now, please keep Samuel with you so John doesn't find out about him. Mrs. Tibbins," he indicated the woman still sitting in the truck staring at the two of them, "is a wet nurse. She's been keeping him fed on our trip. Emma's still nursing her littlest one, isn't she?"

"Yeah, she is."

"Do you think she could take on little Samuel as well or would it be too much for her?"

"Course she can. She'd be pleased to."

"I'm glad to hear it. That helps. I'll get this lady back on a train to Boston then. I'm sure she's anxious to go home." He pulled one of the smaller bags from the back of the truck and placed it on the porch. "Here's his things, including plenty of diapers. Are you sure you're going to be okay dealing with a newborn, Isaiah?"

"Oh yes," he answered. "Little Samuel and me are gonna be just fine. Aren't we, you precious boy?" Samuel responded by immediately spitting up. Taking it in stride, Isaiah wiped it away and cleaned his fingers on his pants before continuing. "You head on outta here and get your sister. I'll take him straight over to Emma's place. We'll see you tomorrow. Don't you worry about a thing."

As Richard drove down the road heading back to town, he watched Isaiah in his rear-view mirror getting smaller and smaller, but still waving, until he was completely gone from sight. He felt as if a huge weight had been lifted from his shoulders and was confident his plan would work, providing he could convince Isaiah and his family that a move north was in all their best interests. But he'd cross that bridge tomorrow. For now, he had to concentrate on taking care of his daughter and his sister. He also needed to keep all his stories straight to prevent John from getting suspicious.

One month later, they put Richard's plan into action. Isaiah sold his farm and he and his family moved north to Philadelphia taking little Samuel with them. They had no friends or family there, so no one would question the idea that the baby was Emma's son. Richard managed to find both Isaiah and his son-in-law work in a steel mill manufacturing rails for the Pennsylvania railroad. It was good, long-term work because the railroad business was booming. They did well there and adjusted easily to city life. They made enough from the sale of their farm to buy a nice house on three acres. They planted a new garden and built a chicken coop and a barn that they eventually filled with a milk cow and a couple of horses. No one gave them or the baby a second glance and eventually they stopped worrying for his safety and built a comfortable life.

Richard managed to hold out for three long months after their departure before he couldn't bear the separation any longer and began investigating the possibility of investing in the mill where Isaiah worked. This gave him an excuse to travel to Philadelphia on several occasions, supposedly for meetings, but also to allow him to spend time with his grandson. After striking a deal with his new partner, he returned to Hillsborough and immediately sold his ranch and all his land for a tidy profit.

By way of explanation, he told John, "I won't be back any time in the foreseeable future. I can't bear to stay in this town one day longer. There are too many memories of Loreli and your mother here. I need to start fresh someplace where everything I see doesn't remind me of them."

John, though a bit dazed by his father's sudden desire to move north and leave everyone behind, regained his swagger once his father told him how much he would be receiving from the sale.

"Consider this your inheritance," Richard announced as he handed him a bank book showing a balance large enough for him to buy his own property and still have enough left over to start his new life in comfort. He considered this ample compensation for eliminating John from his life and felt reasonably sure that he would not be traveling north to visit.

Richard was eager to begin his new life, and boarded the train to Philadelphia with a spring in his step and a hopeful expression on his face.

TONY – SOMEWHERE ON THE ROAD TO THE WAYSTATION

Why in the hell am I still here?

He wants a drink of something, anything, preferably cold and alcoholic, and time to lie down and rest. He feels like he's been sitting on this bench and driving these horses for years. For all he knows, it has been years. He doesn't even like horses, never has. He feels as if his eyes are full of sand, his skin itches and his ass is numb. In fact, his entire body feels numb from the base of his spine to his knees. His chest and stomach continue to ache and burn from where those piece-of-shit cops had shot him. His beard is still a constant aggravation and the raw hole he's picked in his cheek hurts. He'd give anything for a line right now. He is in serious need of a pick-me-up.

He can't figure out who the hell these people are he keeps shuttling and why he can't talk to them. He's tried time and time again to speak, but it's like his tongue is stapled to the roof of his mouth. The last group he'd been stuck driving were dressed like a bunch of ragged civil war soldiers and they spent their entire trip yacking about places he'd only read about in school and singing a lot of songs he'd never heard of. Apparently, several of them were related and they talked endlessly about hunting, fishing and some girl named Brenda Mae. Shit, really? Brenda Mae? He wanted to swing around in his seat and tell them all to just shut the fuck up; they were dead. Life was over and this Brenda Mae had long since turned to worm food. Didn't they get it?

Tonight's group is the worst one yet. They mostly appear to be methed-out junkies, but they are awfully damn happy for a bunch of crack heads; he can't understand it. What in the hell do they have to be so happy about? He runs his parched tongue across his chapped lips dreaming about a cold beer and a cigarette.

Up ahead he can see lights glowing in the distance and knows they are approaching one of the stopping points. He can never figure out when one will appear, and the rest stops randomly change from one trip to the next. He hasn't been to the same one more than once or twice and it feels like he's been making these trips forever. Their numbers must be endless. It's always the same. He pulls into a yard in front of a big house, the style and color of each house varies, but the feel of each place is essentially the same. His passengers are greeted with hugs, smiles, and encouraging words, and then taken inside to get something to eat and drink. No one has ever offered him a thing or even acknowledged his presence. He is always thirsty. Would it kill them to offer him a cup of water? After a few hours, they all troop back out laughing and grinning like they are on their way an awesome party, and once again, no one will even glance his way. It sucks.

The back end of each trip is the worst. There is always a heightened sense of anticipation from the people sitting in the back of his wagon and the sensation seems to increase with every turn of the wheels. The air itself seems to gain weight and then when he thinks he can't take it anymore, there will be a blinding flash of light that makes his eyes feel like they are melting right out of their sockets. He'll blank out for a bit and then come back to consciousness with his hands covering his eyes, tears streaming down his face, and his skin hurting like it has a bad sunburn. His passengers will be gone and he'll be left alone feeling rejected and despised. It is the most depressing experience he's ever gone through, and he is caught up in this never-ending loop, doomed to endure it over and over again. He feels like he is going crazy. Once again, he licks his cracked lips and wishes for all this shit to hurry up and be finished. He knows he is being punished, but how long does he have to suffer through this until it's his turn to be whisked away to Heaven?

Being forced to endure these trips is bad enough, but lately he's begun to notice a pervasive feeling of being watched; especially when he is alone. It's as if something is constantly lurking just beyond his field of vision, and it makes him nervous as hell. It reminds him of the demons that had tormented him after Cara died. Is it possible? Can they have followed him into death? He wants to cry out, "What the fuck do you want from me?" but he is denied that luxury. Instead, he has to carry the weight of constant worry, and it is an ever-increasing burden that seems to gain weight minute by minute. He has a feeling it won't be long before they break through whatever is holding them back.

JOHN

The old man finds himself sitting beneath a large mimosa tree. He has no idea how he has come to be here. He turned 83 on his last birthday, and it's not an unusual occurrence for him to become confused or forget things. He hopes he hasn't wandered off again. Delilah will pitch a fit and probably restrict his outdoor time again, and earning that privilege back is always such a pain in the butt.

However, this doesn't feel like one of those times. In fact, he feels amazingly clear headed and focused. He stands up and is brushing the dirt off the seat of his pants when he realizes he doesn't have his walker, but has managed to stand up easily and isn't even feeling weak. Pain has been his constant companion these last few years ever since he took a tumble down the steps at his son Roy's house and broke his leg in two places. Blasted thing has never been the same. But now there is no pain. Curious, he stands on one leg and pretends to play hopscotch. Strong as an ox. Then he tries the same thing with the other leg, his weak one. Fit as a fiddle. *I'll be damned, I'm good as new; better even.* He hasn't felt this good in longer than he can remember.

The thud of a door closing catches his attention and he turns toward the house. A woman is stepping off the porch steps and is walking in his direction. She wears a welcoming smile and John feels his face returning the favor. When she reaches him, she holds out her hand and he takes it without a second thought.

"Welcome," she says, squeezing his hand. "You must be John. My name is Sarah. I've been expecting you."

"You have? Huh, well it's always nice to be wanted, but I have to say I'm a little confused. Where exactly am I?"

THE WAYSTATION

"This is the Waystation, and I know this may come as a bit of a surprise, but you have passed from your earthly life and will be here with us for a bit before moving on."

"Passed? You mean I'm dead? Well, that explains a lot. So, this isn't heaven I take it?"

"No, not quite, but you don't have much further to go."

"Alright, I'm dead. I can accept that. I'm an old man. Death isn't exactly a surprise at my age. But why am I here?"

"I could try and explain it to you, but I think it's better if I just show you. Would you like to take a little walk with me? I think there's someone you should meet. I believe you'll both have a lot to talk about."

"Well, that's terrific. Sure, let's go for a little walk. I'm feeling pretty spry today."

As they make their way towards the barn, John admires how neatly the place is kept and how nice everything smells. "It's been a long time since I smelled air this clean. I've missed the country life. I can smell horses too. Next to my wife's peach cobbler, that's the best smell in the world."

Sarah has faith that everything will ultimately unfold according to God's plan, though she is a little concerned with how it will play out. She's about to get her answer.

"Sam," Sarah calls as they enter the barn. "Sam, are you in here? I've got someone with me I think you should see."

"Yes, Miss Sarah. Give me a second to finish feeding my girls and I'll be right there."

John freezes. That voice. He knows that voice. *Sam. Samuel? No, it can't possibly be him. That was almost 60 years ago. Oh, dear Lord, why?*

He looks at Sarah wide-eyed and almost panicked. Her face is serene. She gives his hand a squeeze of encouragement.

Sam comes out of the stall brushing his hands on his pants and gives them a big smile. "Welcome sir." He holds out his hand. "I'm Samuel, it's good to meet ya."

John nervously extends his own liver-spotted hand and places it in Sam's much larger young-man's hand. "Nice to meet you. My name's

John." He stares up at Sam's smiling face, waiting for that moment of recognition, but it doesn't come.

He doesn't know me. Well, why should he? I'm an old man now and I don't look anything like the big-headed boy he'd remember. But he looks exactly the same.

"Welcome to the Waystation. We're mighty pleased to have you here. I expect you'll want to get settled and maybe get yourself somethin' to eat. Then maybe after that I can show you around a bit. We've got a real nice place here."

"Ah, hell son. We may as well get this out of the way. I couldn't eat or drink anything anyway, my stomach's too tied in knots."

"Sir? Is somethin' wrong? Is there anythin' I can help you with?" He looks to Sarah for a hint about what's going on, but she remains silent. Sam is a patient man by nature, so he is content to wait.

"Stop being so damn nice to me. After you hear what I have to say, you might not feel the same way."

Sam doesn't want to rush the old man, knowing he'll spit it out eventually. John shuffles his feet around before he finally manages to work up the courage to continue. "You knew me once, a long time ago. My name is John Shannon." He stops, unsure if he is about to receive a blow from the hand which has just shaken his in welcome.

When the blow doesn't come, he hurriedly adds, "I need to ask you for your forgiveness. What I did to you…well…it was horrible. I was wrong and had no right to pass judgement on you. I was young and arrogant; full of myself. I thought I had all of life's answers and knew better than everyone else. If I could go back and slap some sense into the young man I was then, I would gladly do it. I sinned Sam. I sinned against God and I sinned against you. Can you ever forgive me?"

"John Shannon?" Sam repeats, wearing a dazed expression.

"If you need to punch me in the nose, you go right ahead and do it. I deserve it and so much more. You just let 'er rip son, I'm ready."

"John!" Sam grabs him by both arms and lightly shakes him. John squeezes his eyes shut and waits for the pain. After a moment, he cracks one eye open and takes a peek. Sam is staring intently at his face, but doesn't seem inclined to start beating him any time soon.

"What happened to Loreli? Was she alright? Was she happy? Tell me. I have to know."

John blanches at this, convinced that this revelation will be the thing to push Sam over the edge. He steels his nerves before answering, "She died Sam. I'm sorry, but she passed on less than a year after you."

Sam looks crushed. "She took ill?"

"She...well, she was so heartbroken when you...she loved you very much. She was very depressed and never left her room. Daddy decided to take her to Boston to stay with his sister. He was hoping a change of scenery would do her good. You know, get her away from the memories. When she was there, she passed away. It was very sudden."

"What happened?"

"Daddy led everyone to believe that she died of scarlet fever. He did it to protect her honor and to keep me from knowing the truth. I didn't find out that he lied until after he passed. She died in childbirth Sam. She died bringing your son into this world."

"My son?" Sam seems to like the way the word rolls off his tongue. "I have a son. Sarah, did you hear that? I have a son!" He throws his arms around Sarah giving her a huge bear hug, and spins her around the room, grinning and proclaiming, "I have a son. I have a son." He sets Sarah back on her feet and takes hold of John again. "Is he happy? Is he healthy? Tell me about him."

John feels more at ease now that it appears Sam has no intention of beating him to a bloody pulp. He even manages to smile.

"His name is Samuel Richard, after you and daddy. Loreli told Aunt Bea that was going to be his name if he was a boy. He was raised by your family. They moved to Philadelphia right after daddy brought him back to Hillsborough. He still lives there. I've kept tabs on him over the years. He's doing real good Sam. He graduated from the University of Pennsylvania with a degree in business. When he was a baby, my daddy bought in as a partner in a steel mill in Philadelphia so he could be close to him. Your daddy and your sister's husband worked in that mill. When daddy passed, he left it all to your son. It's called Wellman Steel now. He's married and has two grown sons and a daughter. You're a grandpa three times over."

Sam looks stunned at the news that his son is so successful. "Thank you, John. Thank you for letting me know. I'm grateful."

"The good Lord knows I can never repay all that I took from you and Loreli. One day I hope you can find it in your heart to forgive me, even though I know I don't deserve it."

Sarah interrupts, "Why don't you come on up to the house with me, John. I've got a couple of pies in the oven I need to check on and I'm sure you could use a bite as well. Sam, would you like to join us?"

"No, thank you Miss Sarah. I've got a lot to think on right now. If y'all don't mind, I think I'll take a walk down by the creek for a bit."

Sarah stands on tiptoe and gives him a kiss on the cheek. "I understand. Take your time." She and John leave Sam alone to ponder the miracle of a son and grandchildren.

SAMUEL

Sam paces along the creek bank for an hour before he finally calms down enough to sit and think, and more importantly, to pray. Seeing John again has been a complete shock and something he hadn't been prepared for. But on reflection, it makes sense that God would send John here so Sam would have to find a way to forgive him. Forgiveness is high up on God's list. After all, He sent His own son down to earth to die so every man, woman, and child could be forgiven for their sins. Even Jesus understood that, and when he was dying asked his Father to forgive the very people who put him up on that cross. The way Sam saw it, if Jesus could do that, then he could too.

Sam kneels in the grass and bows his head. "Dear Lord, I never expected to say this, but please help me to find it in my heart to forgive John. I realize now that he was a headstrong young man with a lot of wrong ideas in his head, and for reasons I don't understand, a lot of anger in his heart. I truly believe that he feels real bad for what he did. He has humbly asked me for my forgiveness and I know that until I can willingly give it, I can't come and dwell with You in Your kingdom."

"I have so much to be thankful for. I have a son who is living a good life. I have grandchildren, and while I didn't get to hold any of them in my arms, I know that one day we'll all be together. And I have Loreli, and I know she loved me until the day she died, just as I have loved her. Thank you for these blessings, Lord. Help me to make You proud. Help me to show love and kindness, even when it's difficult. Thank you, Father. In the name of Your son, Jesus, amen."

When he's done, he sits back and watches the water flow by imagining the conversations he and his son will have, and about the day when he will hold Loreli in his arms again.

RACHEL

Rachel lays on the warm rock enjoying the feel of the sun baking her skin and drying her hair. She sits up and fluffs her mane trying to speed up the process; it's grown out so much since she's been here. She checks on Wren to make sure she's okay. Wren is happily paddling around in the shallows attempting to catch one of the baby fish who like to hide in the water weeds. What she plans to do with it, if she ever catches one, Rachel has no idea. But knowing Wren, she probably has ideas of raising it herself and becoming its mommy. Poor little thing, she is obsessed with being a mommy. It's cute but kind of sad at the same time.

Rachel has been lying with her eyes closed mulling over Sarah and Sam's stories, grieving for their pain and loss, reliving the tales which are so vivid in her mind. She feels an immense wave of sadness every time she thinks about what they endured and how the memories still hurt them. It's hard to understand how two such loving, caring people can blame themselves for the circumstances surrounding their own deaths. Some people have awful things happen to them simply because they are bad people and they bring it on themselves. But that isn't the case for Sarah or Sam; they are remarkable people who obviously love God and do everything they can to fulfill what they believe is His purpose in their lives. It's a little confusing.

Even with everything they endured, both Sarah and Sam have such a sense of peace about them. Rachel is finally beginning to understand that peace and how remarkable they are. The moment it began to make sense to her was when she'd questioned Sarah about her ability to accept all that had happened without allowing it to make her resentful. Sarah's response made sense and has opened Rachel's eyes.

THE WAYSTATION

She said, "God loves us enough that He doesn't control our actions. He gives us free will to make our own choices, and that's what determines our fate. Of course, Satan does his best to manipulate us. He became king of the earth when the Lord cast him down from heaven, and he takes great joy in doing everything he can to help us destroy ourselves. I believe each of us are responsible for how our lives turn out. We can't blame God because we make bad choices, and we can't be bitter about it either. Life is a gift. What we do with it is up to us."

And now John is here. She's amazed that Sam has been able to accept his arrival so calmly. She doesn't know what's going on under the surface, but she supposes it helps to get news of a son he never knew existed. Still, this is the man who is responsible for Sam being hanged. Learning that Loreli died so soon after his own death was also tough for him. When she talked with him about it, he told her it simply meant they would be together shortly, and he was admittedly looking forward to that day. He said it hurt his heart to learn she died in childbirth, but knowing her the way he does, he has no doubt she would have gladly given up her life for their son.

Wren is also a mystery. Why in the heck is she here? It makes no sense at all. Sarah told her Wren has been waiting for her to arrive so she can complete her own journey. But what does that mean? How does her own arrival affect Wren? She should have moved on long ago. Rachel wrinkles her nose in frustration. Is there something she's supposed to do or say so Wren will be free to go? She doesn't get it.

Now that she's certain Cara is Wren's mother, she feels it's her responsibility to get Wren back to Cara where she belongs. That is the very least she can do for Cara after failing her so horribly in life.

In the meantime, they are expecting another group of travelers tonight and Sarah has told her it's possible it might be one of their bad nights. She'd asked her to take Wren down to the river and try to tire her out as much as possible so she would sleep soundly. From the look of things, she feels like her mission has been accomplished. She's sure Wren is going to go out like a light tonight and it will take more than the appearance of a wagon full of the dead to get her up and moving again.

Thinking about the possibility of it being one of their "bad" nights makes her stomach clench and for the first time since her arrival, she feels anxious. "Come on Rachel, relax," she chides herself. "It's not like anything really awful can happen to you, you're already dead, right?"

That makes her chuckle and she decides it might be a good idea to offer up a prayer and get a little bit of help. She clears her throat before beginning, "Okay God, I'm trusting You not to let me freak out or do anything to embarrass myself. Please help me not to be scared or do something stupid. Amen." She doesn't know if it was an appropriate prayer or if He has gotten the message, but she feels better already, so it certainly hasn't hurt. Just the simple act of handing off the responsibility has made all the difference.

Screw the hair, she decides, and stands up. She won't be entering any beauty contests today and nobody is going to criticize her anyway. She leaps into the air and grabbing her knees, cannon-balls into the deep end of the water making a huge splash and scaring away all of Wren's little fish. She surfaces, spitting water and laughing, and begins to splash Wren who immediately starts splashing back, giggling madly. There aren't a whole lot of things better than a warm summer day and a water fight with someone you love. Yeah, she can let her worries go; God has her back.

TONY & RACHEL

Night has fallen and the crickets are heartily singing with their usual level of deafening enthusiasm. Rachel can also hear the squeaking of bats as they swoop through the night sky eating their fill of the bugs flitting about. That's a good thing because it will keep the mosquitos down and make the evening more pleasant for everyone.

She sweeps the last of the dirt from the porch steps then stops to gaze at the full moon. Resting her butt on the railing, she studies it. It shines in a particularly lovely way tonight as it peeks out between the branches of one of the mimosa trees. She can see a large glowing ring surrounding it. A brief flash of childhood memory strikes her as she recalls her grandpa telling her that means there is a lot of moisture in the air. With a happy heart, she suddenly realizes she'll get to see him again soon. He died two years ago of a heart attack and she still misses him constantly.

Beaming at the thought of her grandfather, she lights the lanterns, one after another, their glow filling the porch and flowing down the steps in a warm spill of light. Moths begin to flutter eagerly around their flickering flames beating their wings against the glass. "Give it up guys," she says. "It won't end well for you anyway."

"Rachel" Sarah calls from within the house. "Are you about done out there?"

"Yep, I'm coming in right now."

She picks up her broom and hurries inside to help set out the food. It's going to be a busy night.

Tony's wagon rolls along in the same tedious fashion as every trip that has come before. He is bored to tears and sick to death of sitting

233

on this damn seat. At this point, he'd even welcome a conversation with one of the crack heads riding in the back. The girls are currently reliving their lame childhoods by singing old New Kids on the Block songs at the top of their lungs and the guys are beating out an accompanying tempo on the bench seats. It's aggravating as hell and he fervently wishes they would stop, but it isn't like he can turn around and yell at them, so he's forced to listen to their incessant celebration.

Up ahead he can see the beginnings of a glow appearing far down the road, this means another of those stopping points is coming up. They'll all bail on him there, but tonight that is fine with him, at least the singing will stop. Occasionally there is something to be said for the blessing of silence.

Rachel has just put out the last of the pies and is fanning the napkins in her usual pattern when she begins to hear the faint sound of wagon wheels. "Sarah, they're coming down the road."

"Thank you, dear," Sarah answers bumping the kitchen door open with her hip and setting the last two pitchers of tea on the tables. "Are we ready?"

"Yep, I think that's everything."

"Well then, let's go on out and see what God's got in store for us tonight, shall we?"

Rachel swallows nervously, "Okay."

"Don't worry, dear, you'll be fine," Sarah reassures her. "Remember, nothing can or will happen to you. The Lord has His hand on you." Sarah gives her an encouraging smile, and taking Rachel's hand, leads her out the door to greet their visitors.

Tony shifts in his seat for what feels like the ten billionth time and tries to find a comfortable position, but it doesn't exist. The wagon's wheels creak and groan and his back and buttocks protest in time to the bumps. The singing has finally trailed off as his passengers focus on the approaching lights.

About damn time.

They pass slowly under two huge trees and through their moon-dappled shadows before coming to a stop near the porch. He's seen this house a couple of times before and recognizes the woman hurrying toward them with a big grin on her face. The girl following her is new though. She's holding up a lantern and is calling out, "Hi everyone. We're so happy to see you."

Her face comes into focus as she raises the light higher. To his horror, he recognizes her.

Holy shit, it's Rachel! She's dead too?

His stomach feels like it has fallen out and landed somewhere near his feet as wave after wave of anxiety washes over him. The intensity of the sensation makes him feel sick. He can't stop staring at her though; she looks amazing. Her face glows in the lantern's light and her eyes are bright and excited. He doesn't remember ever seeing her look this good. His first instinct is to reach out to her, but then he hardens his heart and stares at his feet instead. She won't respond anyway, so what's the point.

Rachel's smile falters when she realizes who's sitting in the driver's seat. Her heart seems to have lodged in her throat and she can't catch her breath. Her feet have taken root in the dirt.

Tony? Oh, my God, it's Tony.

Fear and anger grip her heart and tears threaten to spill from her eyes. She quickly averts her gaze and tries to calm down. She cautiously peeks at him again. He looks like shit and has aged at least ten years. There is a nasty hole in his cheek and he looks miserable. He slowly raises his head and meets her eye.

"Rachel, honey, are you going to join us?" Sarah asks.

She finally shakes free of her paralysis, noticing that everyone has already disembarked and gone inside while she's been standing frozen in place. Sarah stands on the porch holding out her hand.

"Come on inside, dear."

She dutifully lowers the lantern and takes one last agonizing look at Tony before she turns and follows, closing the door behind her.

Tony's heart pounds out a frantic rhythm in his chest, feeling as if it might burst free at any second. He tries to swallow but can't get past the lump in his dry throat.

Rachel is here. She's dead. How did that happen?

His hands itch to slap the reins against the horses' backs and get the hell out of here, but he is unable to move.

LAURIE JAMESON

What am I supposed to do now?

He sits in torment for several minutes before he realizes the air has grown very still and oppressively heavy. All the nighttime noises have disappeared as if every cricket and frog has simply vanished. He has trouble drawing breath and his ears feel as if they are stuffed full of cotton. The night lays weightily on his shoulders like a wet wool blanket.

A dark, nasty smelling mist begins to flow in and circles around the trees and flowers. It slowly creeps up the legs of the horses until it is finally close enough to stretch its clammy fingers out to him. The temperature begins to rise and he starts to sweat, yet his bones feel chilled to their very core and his teeth ache with the cold. His fingers have gone numb and feel as useless as blocks of ice wrapped around the reins. Terror seizes his heart and he starts to panic. Desperate, his eyes probe the warm safety of the house hoping for help.

Rachel stands transfixed, gripping the porch post tightly, her eyes never leaving Tony. How she wound up back on the porch, she has no idea, but here she stands, frozen in place and unable to turn away. Her nostrils flare at the foul smell flowing through the dooryard. Watching the dirty mist flow past the steps, she flashes on every horror movie she's ever seen, so she isn't all that surprised when those imagined horrors come to life. As the shadowy, demonic shapes began to emerge from the miasma, she is enveloped by a hot wind that smells of rot and decay and of the putrid things which dwell in that dark fog.

She closes her eyes and repeats Sarah's words, "Nothing can harm you, Rachel. God has His hand on you. You're safe." She opens her eyes and steels herself for what she imagines is coming. She is here to witness this, so watch it she will. The night song, which had been so loud earlier, is gone now. The air is hushed...waiting.

Tony stares into Rachel's eyes, terror flooding every cell of his being. As a loud pounding fills the air, he tears his panicked gaze from Rachel's face to scan the darkness surrounding him. Shapes too terrifying to be borne emerge from the mist on huge, bowed, claw-tipped legs. Glowing misshapen eyes shine redly from monstrous grinning teeth-filled visages. The demons call and whisper his name in overlapping chilling hisses, spittle flying from their weeping mouths. This is his meth-fueled nightmare come to life. This is what he has always known was out there waiting for him. These are the things he feared were living behind his bedroom door. They have finally found him.

Tony's bladder lets go, spilling a flood of warm urine down his legs. The reins fall from his numb fingers and he finally finds his voice as he begins to scream; great gut-wrenching, terror-filled screams. His eyes bulge from their sockets as the demons reach out to him with their long filth-encrusted nails. Their skeletal fingers wrap around his arms and drag him from his seat.

The demons drape the arms of a rotting corpse around his shoulders, the head lying against his chest. Chains are wound around him securing the decaying flesh to his body. His screams cease to make a sound, and instead have become a continuous stream of wheezing noises. The smell of putrefied flesh fills his nose and he imagines he can feel pieces of the rotting skin sloughing off and sliding down his body.

Once the chains are locked in place, the beasts spirit him away into the darkness, emitting shrieks of victory and celebration, pulling the mist behind them like a shroud as they disappear. Within seconds the horrors vanish through a dark tunnel. The night resumes its peaceful chorus, as if someone has turned the volume back on. Once again the air smells sweetly of wet grass and mimosa blossoms.

RACHEL

The feeling returns to her fingers in sharp little stabs as she gradually releases her death grip on the post. With a shaking hand, she carefully wipes sweat from her forehead and temples, relishing the return of the cool evening breeze and breathing in the sweet fragrance of the night air. Poor Tony, he was clearly terrified and had every right to be. Watching the demons chain a rotting corpse to him brought back everything she'd read about the body of death.

So, it's true.

She's surprised to find that she has sympathy for him. Leaning against the railing, she waits for her heart to resume its normal rhythm and her panic to subside. What he did to Cara was horrible, but this is beyond what she had previously hoped his punishment would be. She can't even begin to imagine what lies in store for him. If the Bible is correct, it is an eternity of dwelling among monsters like these and possibly things that are even worse.

"The Lord shall reward the doer of evil according to his wickedness," she whispers. "Wow, You really meant it, didn't You?" She gazes one last time at the darkness and says, "I forgive you, Tony."

The chatter of many happy voices floats through the doorway as she turns from the night and the sight of the empty wagon with patiently waiting horses, to the light which pulls at her heart and spirit. As she closes the door behind her, Samuel and John emerge from the shadows and unharness the horses, leading them to the barn while Sam murmurs encouraging words to them.

"Come on now with me you sweet gals, let's get you somethin' to eat and drink. Y'all have had a long night already and deserve to get yourselves a little rest before you have'ta continue on your journey."

238

THE WAYSTATION

Sam, John, and the horses disappear into the barn and the bats return once again to feast on the night bugs, filling the air with their squeaking, while the crickets and frogs take up their raucous song.

After several hours, the travelers happily pile back into the wagon to finish their journey. Rachel notices that a new man sits in the driver's seat holding the reins.

Where did this guy come from?

None of the passengers even realize that Tony is gone and has been replaced. Rachel shudders. Ignorance is bliss.

WREN

She wakes all at once to the sight of sunshine streaming through her windows and a feeling of excitement in her heart. Rachel always has fun stories to tell of the people who pass through and she can't wait to hear her newest one about last night's group of travelers.

Jumping from her bed, she runs for the bathroom to brush her teeth so she can hurry up and get downstairs as fast as possible. She smells coffee and bacon; the others must be up already and she doesn't want to miss anything.

RACHEL

She sips her coffee and relishes the taste of her hot, buttery biscuit as she delightedly watches Wren giggling and acting like the sweet little girl she is. Fortunately, one of the travelers last night had been the proud owner of a pet monkey and shared several hilarious stories of the antics and chaos of life with their pet. She is having a lot of fun entertaining Wren with tales of Dexter the monkey.

When she finally went to bed last night, she was afraid she would be haunted by what she'd witnessed, but instead fell right to sleep and woke this morning feeling well rested and refreshed. She doesn't think she even has to worry about having bad dreams tonight or any other night. In fact, her heart feels lighter after finding the ability to have compassion for Tony and giving him her forgiveness. It feels like the last chain tying her to her life (and death) has been severed and she is finally free. It is an amazingly liberating feeling. It gives her a better understanding of how and why Samuel is finding it in his heart to forgive John.

She wonders why she doesn't feel any hate in her heart for Marco. She suspects he was complicit in her death, although she isn't entirely sure. All she has is that brief hint of a memory and truthfully, it isn't of much consequence anyway. She'd been so deep in her depression, and with the way she was abusing alcohol and drugs, it had probably been simply a matter of time until she either overdosed or had some kind of accident. It seems like it was inevitable. No, she can't find it in herself to despise him. Besides, after what she witnessed last night, he will probably have to pay for his actions and be punished in ways she doesn't want to think about.

She lets go of that dark thought and makes a conscious effort to be cheerful. "Do you want to hear another one?" she asks once Wren finally quits giggling.

"Yay, another one, another one," Wren crows with her mouth full of bacon.

"You got it," she says, and launches into another tale of Dexter's adventures which involved an ice cream cone and a grumpy old lady who wound up wearing it like a hat. She grins at Sarah and Sarah winks back with a twinkle in her eye.

SARAH

The breakfast dishes are done and the mess from the previous night is stacked carefully on the counters in the kitchen until she can get to it a little later in the day. She is gathering her things to join the others in the garden when she pauses, closing her eyes, listening to an inner voice. In her prayer time when she speaks with God, His words don't come to her with the blare of heralding trumpets or great peals of thunder, but instead as a quiet whisper, like a breeze kissing her skin, bringing with it a feeling of peaceful surety.

She opens her eyes and nods. "Yes, soon. I believe it will be soon. Thank you, Lord." She leaves the kitchen and makes her way to the garden with a contented smile on her face.

English peas tonight. I have a taste for peas and maybe some honeyed carrots.

Wren and Rachel can help her shell them quickly and then they can get on those dishes from last night's guests. Hanging her basket over her arm, she places her sun hat carefully on her head and wonders what things will be like with all the changes coming.

RACHEL

The next morning, she walks out to the clothesline with her basket of linens, and decides the cleanup the day before wasn't all that bad. Maybe they're getting more efficient working together as a team. The peas and carrots were fabulous (of course), and she found out she liked shelling peas. It was fun racing with Wren to see who could shell the most in the shortest amount of time. She had the advantage of longer, stronger fingers, but Wren had the advantage of experience.

For the main dish, Sarah made amazing fried chicken that tasted better than any she had ever eaten before (sorry Mom). She didn't want to think about the killing or plucking of the poor bird though. Sam was kind enough not to make her participate in that part, so instead she chose to contemplate the perfectly crispy, brown and seasoned skin.

Dang, I'm turning in to a total chow hound.

Setting the laundry basket down, she pulls out a wet bed sheet and begins the job of hanging the linens on the line to dry. After hanging all the sheets and pillow cases, she stands in the middle of them surrounded by their cool fragrance. It's like standing in the center of a sweet-smelling maze. She holds one and buries her face in its dampness, inhaling the scent of soap. "I think dryers should be outlawed, this is a much better way to dry them," she announces to no one in particular.

I can't believe I never did this before. Grandma had a clothesline at her house; I should have offered to help. I didn't know what I was missing.

She picks up her now empty basket and glances around at the trees and flowering bushes, noticing all the variations of green, from a pale yellowish green all the way to a deep forest green and everything in between. There are little flickers of movement everywhere as the birds flit from tree to tree and call cheerfully to each other.

THE WAYSTATION

It's so beautiful here. I'm really going to miss it.

That thought stops her in her tracks. "Whoa," she exclaims. "Where the heck did that come from?" And suddenly she knows; it's time. She runs to the house to tell Sarah.

The clock is ticking down.

GOODBYES

Rachel is nervously pleating the hem of her shirt over and over again until Sarah reaches out and holds her hand.

"There's nothing to be nervous about. Remember what you told Lisa. It all gets really good from here."

Startled, she asks, "You heard that?"

"Of course, I hear everything. I'm a mother," she jokes and waggles her eyebrows, causing Rachel to let out a burst of relieved laughter.

Sarah hands her the last platter of sandwiches to carry from the kitchen. "Go ahead and take this out for me, then could you please find out what Wren is up to? She's been buzzing around here all day like a bumble bee in a bottle. Maybe you can get her to settle down long enough to get a brush through her hair so she looks nice when everyone gets here."

"That's for sure. I'll see what I can do." After placing the platter on the bar, she calls out "Wren, come on, honey, let's brush your hair."

"I'm coming," she answers, and flies down the stairs at a pace that would have caused Rachel to tumble to the bottom and probably break a couple of bones in the process. Watching her, Rachel reflects that children of her age seem to have a special sense of balance that allows them to do things which would kill most adults. It must be a gift God gives them so they can survive long enough to grow up.

Wren struggles to sit still on the bar stool while Rachel brushes through her curls and remove the odd piece of leaf or grass tucked inside. "There you go. I think we're all ready now and just in time too."

The clop of horses' hooves and the squeak of wagon wheels drift through the windows. Wren shoots off the stool in a flash. She wants to be the first to greet the visitors. Sarah and Rachel follow at a more

246

leisurely pace and find her jumping up and down on the porch in excitement, calling out, "Hi. Hi everyone. Welcome to the Waystation. I'm Wren. Come on in and get something to eat. We've got pies and cakes and sandwiches and all kinds of good stuff. Oh, and ice tea too if you want some."

The evening unfolds as many have before with conversation and laughter, good food and drink, and the anticipation of a great adventure. It's been nice having John around, because he's older, and the elderly travelers feel comfortable talking with him. They seem to have a lot in common. It's amazing how well he's found his place in their little family. Eventually everyone files out the door and takes their seats in the wagon where they wait patiently for their departure.

Wren, who has temporarily disappeared, comes running from the barn with a box in her hands. She solemnly hands it to Samuel and with great seriousness explains, "Now you need to be Snowball's momma, Sam. I won't be here and he needs to know he's loved. Will you take good care of him for me?"

With equal solemnity, Sam bends down and carefully takes the box from her. "Of course, I will Miss Wren. I'll take the best care of him just like you would. But you know that he don't really need to be cared for any more, right? He's ready to fly off now and find himself some new friends."

"I know he's all grown up now, but he has to know you'll be here for him if he needs you. It's important that he knows he has a family."

He nods his head. "You're right, family is very important. Don't you worry, he'll always have a home here." Then he carefully sets the box down and lifts her up, wrapping her in his arms and giving her a fierce hug. He whispers in her ear, "I love you, little Missy. You be good and I'll see you real soon." Then he kisses her cheek and places her gently back on the ground.

Wren hurries to Sarah, throwing her arms around her waist and burying her head in her stomach. "I love you, Sarah."

Hugging her back with equal enthusiasm she replies, "I love you too, sweetheart. You have a good trip now." Caressing her face one final time, Sarah shoos her off to the wagon where she eagerly climbs aboard to wait.

Feeling like a cloud of butterflies are trapped in her stomach, Rachel puts her arms around Sam and rests her head on his massive chest with a sigh, "Goodbye, Sam. I'll miss you so much. Thank you for everything, like teaching me to ride and fish, and well, for everything. You are a kind, kind man. You were here for me when I needed you. I love you."

He gently pulls away and holds her gaze, "You'll be just fine, Miss Rachel. You are a fine woman and I am very proud of you. You take care of yourself and know this ain't really goodbye. We'll all be meetin' up very shortly, you can count on that."

She reluctantly lets him go and puts her arms around Sarah's neck. With tears in her eyes she declares, "I'll never forget you and everything you've taught me. You showed me what a good woman looks like and you're the strongest person I've ever met. I'm proud to have known you. Thank you for being so nice to me. I love you very much."

Sarah hugs her back and kisses her on the cheek, "I love you too. I'll see you again, dear, I promise. Now get in that wagon and let's get this show on the road."

With a feeling of great anticipation, Rachel climbs on board and sits next to Wren who grabs her hand and says, "This is it, huh Rachel?"

"Yep. Are you ready?"

"Ready? Of course, I am," she declares. "I'm on my way to meet my momma. I've been waiting my whole life for this day." As the wagon pulls away, Wren can be heard announcing to everyone, "This is my sister, Rachel, and we're going to meet my momma. This is my best day ever."

Sarah and Samuel stand side by side and wave until they can no longer see even the dust that's kicked up by the wagon's wheels. Then reaching out and taking his hand in hers, she asks, "I think it's time. Are you ready Sam?"

He checks something within his heart, and after only a slight hesitation he nods, "Yes, I believe I am, but I have one last thing to do. John, I need to tell you something."

THE WAYSTATION

"If it's about the horses, don't worry. You know I've been enjoying taking care of them. Tallulah and Belle are in good hands. I've missed it for a lot of years and it's nice to feel useful again. I haven't forgotten how to feed and care for chickens either."

"I know all that," Sam says and reaches out and embraces him.

John looks thoroughly startled then hugs him back.

Sam whispers in his ear, "I forgive you." Then he lets him go and claps him on the shoulder. "We'll see you later John. Take good care of our place."

John's mouth hangs slightly open for a moment, and then he breaks into a huge grin. "Thank you, Sam. Thank you." He wipes away tears of gratitude which are rolling down his cheeks.

Squeezing Sarah's hand, Sam lifts his face to the night sky and with great joy shouts, "Lord, if it be Your will, we are ready to come and dwell with You in Your kingdom."

As the sound of his shout fades away, a gentle hush descends over the yard and then a breeze picks up, ruffling their hair and building in strength until it sends leaves flying. A light begins to glow in front of Sarah and Sam. As it grows in intensity and spreads to envelope them, they both close their eyes against the glare and with smiles on their faces, wait eagerly for their own exodus to begin.

The radiance expands to encompass the entire yard and in a brilliant flash, they are gone.

AFTER

The light shines with such brilliance, that all living things shutter their eyes against it lest they be blinded. John has his eyes squeezed tightly shut, and Lazy Boy crouches behind one of the pillars on the porch until the light fades and the normal noises of the night resume. The cat slowly emerges, yawning and stretching first one back leg then the other, and then lays himself out comfortably on the top step. Licking a paw, he begins to methodically wash his face and ears.

At this moment, it's quiet, but that will change. It always does. Sooner or later new people will come, but for now he has the old man for company, and he is content to wait. Maybe a tasty cricket will hop by and he can have a little midnight snack.

John sighs and turns to Lazy Boy, "Well, it's just you and me now cat. Guess we better get on those dishes."

Lazy Boy bats at John's leg as he steps over him on his way into the house. He has no intention of going inside unless the old man plans on sharing some of the leftovers.

As the door begins to swing shut, John calls out, "There's some cream left if you want it."

The cat is up in a flash, and squeezes through the door just before it closes.

SOMETIME LATER

The man shuffles dispiritedly down the road leaving small puffs of dust to float in his wake. He feels like he's been walking for days and perhaps he has. It's hard to tell because he's lost all sense of time. His blistered feet ache and sting and remind him yet again that he needs rest. Licking his lips, he tries not to think about the drink of water he desperately wants. Up ahead he can see large trees and a building, and his spirits soar. There should be water there; he can practically feel it sliding down his throat already. Thinking about his throat, he is immediately reminded of the pain which plagues him non-stop. He rubs his hand against his neck, trying to erase the memory.

Finally reaching the porch of the house, he calls out a greeting in a strained and scratchy voice. "Hello? Hey, is anyone home?" There is no answer other than the sighing of the wind through the trees and the hiss of a large, orange tabby cat who is curled up on a bench and eyeing him with mistrust.

Warily watching the cat, the man says, "Well, it looks like it's just you and me dude. Do you think it's cool if I go inside and get a drink?" Lazy Boy doesn't bother to answer, but at least stops hissing. The man takes that as permission and enters the building, gratefully anticipating the chance to sit down and rest.

As the door closes behind him, Lazy Boy stretches and hops off the bench only to resettle on his favorite spot on the top step. Apparently, this guy is going to be here a while. This must be one of his new humans. He sighs in displeasure and hopes there is a girl coming too. He likes girls. They're sweet to him. He can hear the man banging around inside

251

and closes his eyes as Marco exclaims, "Pie! Hell yeah, I'm starving. Thanks God; you rock dude."

John rounds the corner of the barn holding the four fat catfish he caught down at the creek. It hadn't even taken him that long; not too bad for an old guy. Sarah's pies and cookies aren't going to last forever, and he figures this new fella might appreciate a good fish fry. He knows there's cornmeal and onions in the kitchen and can still remember how to make hushpuppies. It seems to him like this might be a good way to get acquainted.

It will be interesting to see how the two of them get on. God has extended enough grace to forgive him of the horrible thing he did and give him a chance to one day go on to heaven. This young man is being given the same chance. The boy has a long road ahead of him and a lot of things to work through. Maybe they can help each other. It should be easier if they do it together.

SAMUEL

S am finds himself standing all alone on the shore of a large lake. The sun sparkles off the water, and he can hear the quacking of ducks. It has the feel of a warm day, but the sun is heading towards the horizon and the breeze is pleasantly cool. He has no idea where Sarah has gone, but figures she is with her beloved Chester and Abigail, and that is how it should be.

He bends down and picking up a handful of small flat stones, begins to skip them over the water, enjoying the sound they make. Waiting…

The sky is just beginning to turn glorious shades of red and orange, decorated with streaks of thin purple clouds, when he sees her. She is walking towards him, wearing a light blue summer dress, the breeze causing it to dance around her slender legs. Her long, red hair hangs loose, reflecting the last of the dying sun's rays.

The stones fall from his hand, but he isn't there to hear them hit the ground. He is where he has always belonged, in her arms.

AUTHOR'S NOTES

I thought it might be nice if I gave you the definitions of the Mexican slang I used in the shower scene where Marco is stabbed to death. You can thank me later.

Chavo: Street slang for a boy or boyfriend.

Pocho: An Americanized Mexican, or Mexican who has lost their culture (which largely refers to losing the Spanish). It's a derogatory term which refers to someone who's trying to "act white." I struggled for days trying to find out what the proper term would be and asked my Spanish speaking friends for help, but they were all too Americanized. (Thanks a lot guys.) Fortunately, an elderly Mexican gentleman on my commuter train overheard me discussing my problem and volunteered the information. Thank goodness for the helpfulness of strangers.

Pinche: In Mexico, it's an all-purpose insult enhancer, which would be roughly equivalent to the use of fucking in English. In Mexico, it's also used as an adjective to describe something as insignificant, lousy, miserable or worthless.

Wedo: A derogatory term in Spanish for a white person, or a Mexican who behaves like a rich, white person. It's used a lot in Southern CA.

Hijo de La Chingada: A fucking bastard or a motherfucker; about the worst thing you can call someone in Spanish, especially in Mexico.

I suspect some of you may be wondering where I came up with the idea of locusts pretty much devouring an entire town. The truth is, I can't take credit for inventing it; it really happened. Google the grasshopper plague of 1874 in Harmony, Kansas. It's interesting stuff.

Thanks for making the time to take this journey with me. I hope you enjoyed the ride as much as I. One last thing…could I ask a favor of you? Would you please take a moment and leave an honest review of The Waystation on Amazon and perhaps Goodreads, if you're a member? Indy authors live and die by our reviews, and we count on you, our readers, to get the word out there for us. Thanks!

Laurie

AUTHOR BIO

Laurie Jameson had a completely unremarkable childhood as the only child of Mississippi born and raised parents. Though she grew up in southern California, she spent every summer of her childhood and part of her high school years in Mississippi, and is no stranger to the odd ins and outs of southern life. If you haven't experienced a sea of roaches crawling across your front porch on a muggy summer night, then you haven't grown up in the south and probably can't relate to the entire "southern thing."

Her love of reading started before she even had a complete grasp on the alphabet. As a toddler, she could often be found under her parents' dining room table with her blanket and her story books, looking at the pictures and telling herself the tales contained within their pages. As she grew, she often found reading more interesting than the world around her. She spent many family vacations with her nose in a book, completely oblivious to whatever sights her parents were vainly trying to point out to her, often responding with, "If you've seen one tree, you've seen them all." Yes, she was that kid at school who spent recess comfortably situated in a patch of shade reading while everyone else ran around playing.

She never had any intention of becoming a writer. She stumbled on it quite by accident after having a rather intense dream and telling her husband it would make a great book. He talked her into writing it by presenting her with a new laptop and telling her to get on with it. Five years, lots of tears, many glasses of wine, way too many toffee peanuts and too many chicken enchiladas later, success. No one said it would be easy, and that's probably a good thing, because they would have been lying. But it's certainly been interesting.

Made in the USA
Columbia, SC
25 July 2024

39307984R00159